# BORN OF FIRE

## THE CLOUD WARRIOR SAGA

### D.K. HOLMBERG

ASH PUBLISHING

# CONTENTS

# RETURN TO PAR-SHON

The massive tower of black stone dwarfed Tannen Minden. Shadows streaked from the stone's base, stretching out like some wispy finger that strained to touch all of the lands. The shadows might not reach him, but the effect the tower had, the soft chill in his heart, managed to reach him.

"I've avoided this long enough," he said softly.

Amia squeezed his hand. She didn't need for him to say anything more. The shaped bond between them, at once stronger and deeper than any bond he shared with the elementals, allowed her to know exactly what he felt.

"It does not have to be now," she said.

He glanced over at her. Sunlight reflected off the band of gold at her neck, and her blond hair shimmered. He resisted the urge to run his hand through it.

"That's not what you've implied before," he said, and she smiled. "With everything that I've done, I've put it off more than I should. And besides, you said the wedding couldn't take place until—"

"After," Amia said with a smile.

After. The bond between them was more than any ceremony could create but was a formality expected of her as First Mother. Not to mention Tan's own mother's expectation.

Amia touched his nose with the tip of her finger. "Not only your mother wants this wedding."

Tan touched the sword at his waist as he straightened. They both wanted the wedding as well. After everything that they'd been through, they deserved it. Now there was peace, but both knew they had to do this before they celebrated.

His sword had a reassuring weight, even more so over these last few months, as he had finally taken to learning how to wield it properly. There was only so much that shaping could do to keep him safe. If needed, he wanted to be capable of fighting in other ways.

A Chenir swordsman had taught him the most. He had a graceful way of moving that Tan still hadn't managed to master, and one that likely came from the emphasis on movement and rhythm that began in the cribs of Chenir. That was how they spoke to the elementals.

Tan sighed. Thinking of Chenir only reminded him of how much had changed—and how much hadn't. With the threat of Par-shon gone, old animosities had returned. None with the same fervor as before, but how would they ever learn to serve the same purpose if they couldn't remain united after defeating a common enemy?

Amia studied him and took his hands in hers, trailing her

fingers over the back of it. "You need to stop thinking about what you can't control."

"Control would be nice," Tan said with a laugh. "What I'd like is consideration. None of them would still be there if not for the others."

Amia smiled and rose onto her toes to kiss his cheek. "You act as if they have always been able to see beyond their borders."

"You can."

She tipped her head in a shrug. "I'm Aeta. We have wandered so long that the borders no longer are meaningful."

"Those who have taken to traveling again, what have *they* found?"

Amia laughed. "Better than before, if that's your concern."

"Even knowing…"

She nodded. "Even knowing."

The Aeta were spirit sensers, and some could even shape it, manipulate the element of spirit to force connections. The connections weren't what people feared: it was the possibility that the Aeta might force something against their will, push them to act in ways that they otherwise would not. Control them.

Too many had survived such control already.

And that was why they had come here. "These people deserve…" Tan still didn't know *what* the people of Par-shon deserved. Those who had crossed the ocean, using bonds forced upon the elementals, were gone. Many had died, and those who had survived had lost their bonds, leaving them without the same strength.

But that wasn't the reason he had avoided making the crossing.

"I know," Amia said.

Par-shon was a city-state. A place unlike any other that he had visited, and isolated for so long that they were different than other nations, strange and unfamiliar in ways that Tan still didn't understand.

And he was to rule them.

"They will know that I've come," he said, nodding to the peak of the tower.

The draasin Asgar had come ahead of him at Tan's request, and the black and scarlet-scaled elemental now perched atop the tower, sending streamers of flame down along the sides as a warning to Par-shon. He had not asked the draasin to refrain, wanting the people of Par-shon to know that he had returned. And, if he were honest with himself, to fear that he had come. He still didn't know whether to trust their submission, even though Amia sensed no animosity from them, only fear. After defeating the Utu Tonah, Tan should not have expected anything else.

"I think you've announced that as well as you could," she agreed.

He smiled. "I could have announced it *better*. Think of what if I had asked Sashari and Enya to come as well."

Amia's eyes narrowed as they watched Asgar. "I think one draasin is enough, don't you?"

It wasn't only one draasin, but she knew that as well. Tan had other bonded elementals and never really traveled alone. Asgar had transported Kota across the ocean, bringing the great hound with him. Tan could sense her distantly, prowling across the Par-shon countryside, waiting for him. When this was over, they had other tasks ahead of them. That, more than anything, was the reason that he'd come.

"Maybe for now," he said.

He took her hand and lifted them on a shaping of wind and fire, stabilizing it with earth as they soared down the valley toward the city and landing at the base of the tower. Months had passed since he last came to Par-shon, and in that time, much had changed. Not as much as he would have wanted, but the world was different. In some ways, he thought it better, but without Asboel flying with him, hunting with him, he didn't know that he could truly say that.

Amia squeezed his hand.

Tan made his way into the black stone Par-shon tower. When he had come the last time, they had named him Utu Tonah for defeating the previous Utu Tonah, a man who had forcibly bonded the elementals and nearly destroyed all the lands across the sea. It was a title Tan did not want, one that he did not deserve, but he could no longer hide from the responsibilities placed on him, responsibilities that he had claimed by working with the other nations to unite them against Par-shon. And now, if he *was* the leader of Par-shon, he ruled over a defeated people who no longer had the same identity or ability to defend themselves, much less so now that he had forbidden forced bonding.

"That is why we're here," Amia reminded him.

"And then we'll celebrate."

She smiled. "Then we will. After."

Could he really have come to claim his title?

Tan didn't think he could avoid it any longer.

Walls that once held runes designed to impede shaping had long since been repaired. Surprisingly, the panels that replaced the damaged runes depicted the elementals, almost as if it were intended to honor them, something that he would never have expected from Par-shon. The halls were otherwise empty, and the one person that they encountered as they reached the wide stair leading to the upper levels of the tower scurried away as soon as Tan and Amia were seen.

Each step echoed hollowly on the tile, giving the entire place an empty sort of feel. "Where is everyone?" he asked aloud. Even his voice seemed to echo strangely along the walls before falling mute.

"You set a draasin on the top of the tower. Where do you think they have gone?" Amia answered.

They reached the landing leading toward the wide hall where he had first met the former Utu Tonah. Tan remembered that visit well; it was scarred into his mind as a time when he had not known if he would escape alive. He remembered all too well the fear he had known as he worried about Amia, uncertain whether Par-shon would do anything to her.

When he'd returned, he had done so as conqueror.

And now he came as ruler.

If he didn't, he risked someone else coming to claim the title and ruling in his stead. He would not accept another attempting to become the next Utu Tonah, especially not if they intended to rule in the same way as the last and force bonds onto the elementals. In some ways, he *had* to lead.

Tan could almost imagine Asboel laughing at him, the draasin's voice faint in the back of his mind. He knew it wasn't real, that the only way to reach Asboel—or at least the *memory* of Asboel—was to reach through the fire bond, and he had not done that.

At the end of the hall, he stopped. A wide woman stood in a doorway, her hand pausing on the door handle. When she saw him, she froze. Tan half expected her to run, much like the last person they had seen, as she had the last time Tan had been in Par-shon. This woman knew him, though, and had met him before he had defeated the Utu Tonah. She had been a part of his torture.

Water swirled around her, shaped by her without the need for a bond. It had not surprised him that others still possessed the ability to shape without the bonds forced on them, especially given what he'd learned of some of the bonded shapers that he'd encountered while fighting Par-shon.

"Garza," he said.

She bowed deeply to him, her forehead dropping below her waist as she genuflected. "Utu Tonah," she said in a hushed whisper.

Tan tensed, resisting the urge to snap at her, knowing that would not do anything, not even make him feel better. Garza had been a part of what had happened to him here, but she was not to blame for what the Utu Tonah had required.

Amia sent a relaxing wave of spirit sweeping over him.

He squeezed her hand and cleared his throat. "You may stand," he said to Garza, who straightened and kept her eyes fixed on the ground.

"Where can I find Tolman?" he asked.

She pointed without saying a word.

Tan waited for her to say something—anything—but she didn't. He guided Amia toward the end of the hall and then up the stairs, into a wide, open space. It was the room where he'd first met the Utu Tonah. Now it was empty, a space where there once had been dozens of people. Now there was no one.

"I sense him," Amia started.

Tan did as well but couldn't see him until he found a doorway at the end of the room that he hadn't seen before. The door didn't require him to shape it or do anything more than simply twist the handle.

The other side led out the top of the tower.

Asgar craned his neck to look at him, his wide golden eyes reminding Tan of Asboel, as did the massive spikes protruding from his long neck and back. Leathery wings were furled in, making him even more imposing in some ways. *Maelen*, he started. *These fools think to bow before me. Shall I eat them?*

Six people lay prostrate in front of Asgar. A soft murmuring came from them, something like a chant. He watched, curious what they might do, but they didn't seem to notice him.

He was surprised to note that one of the draasin worshipers was Tolman. The older man bent his neck to the ground, leaving his back exposed.

*I think you would find others more satisfying.*

Asgar snorted. *You might be right, Maelen. No sport in this.*

Tan smiled. *No sport, and you wouldn't want to kill your worshippers.*

Asgar regarded the Par-shon lying in front of him with amusement burning in his eyes. *Yes. It is only right that the draasin be honored like this.*

Tan laughed again.

"What is it?" Amia asked.

Tan leaned and whispered what Asgar had said. She started to smile as he did.

"I imagine Asboel would have thought differently about having worshippers," she said.

Tan could imagine Asboel's reaction. His friend would have snapped and might *have* eaten them, but then, Asboel was one of the ancient draasin, so old that he had a different perspective on the world. Asgar had been born into a world where Tan lived, where he could guide the interactions with the elementals, and where the draasin had never been attacked the same way, hunted as they had been centuries ago. He never had to fear shapers seeking the draasin simply because they were creatures of fire, or hunting them because they could. In many ways, the world Asgar knew was a better world than the one Asboel had known. And if Tan had anything to say about it, Asgar would never know the torment that Asboel had experienced, the thousand years frozen in a lake, all for the benefit of protecting something the kingdoms had created.

"I think Asboel would have made it clear that he had no interest in such worship," Tan said. He stepped forward and used a shaping of wind to lift Tolman to his feet, drawing him up.

The thin man gasped, and then realized that it had been Tan who shaped him. His bow was nearly as deep as the one that Garza had demonstrated.

"You can stand," Tan said.

"Utu Tonah. You have returned."

Tan suppressed a sigh. "Will you attempt to worship each of the elementals that I show you?" he asked.

"We do not worship—"

"You're lucky he has a sense of humor. He wanted to eat you."

Tolman's eyes widened.

"I suggested that he might find another meal more appetizing," Tan went on.

Tolman took a step back before catching himself. "You are generous, Utu Tonah, and your compassion is unrivaled."

Tan shook his head. "We won't be able to work together if you bow like this."

"You would... work with me, Utu Tonah?"

"Tan," he said. "Please call me by name."

*You should have them call you Maelen. That is a more suitable title than the one that they have chosen for you.*

*I don't think they would appreciate the name the same way the draasin do.*

*The Great One named you well.*

*And Maelen named you well.*

Asgar chuckled within his mind, although it sounded

something like a snort aloud. The Par-shon bowing in front of Asgar all took a step back, away from the draasin.

"You have to be direct," Amia said softly. "They will expect you to lead, so you will need to lead."

Tan nodded. It wasn't comfortable for him to lead, but it was the reason they'd come. He needed to pull Par-shon back in line with the other nations, to work with them rather than against them. And he couldn't have Par-shon become a threat.

"Have them stand and return inside," Tan said to Tolman.

Tolman bowed and turned to the other five. He barked a quick word in Par-shon, and they scrambled to their feet and hurried back inside the tower, leaving Tolman the only other person of Par-shon with Tan and Amia.

He glanced from Tan to Asgar, as if uncertain which he should fear more.

Tan smiled tightly. Asgar might eat Tolman, but Tan could shape him, and Tolman knew that Tan had been the reason the Utu Tonah had been defeated, not the draasin. Still, there was something terrifying and majestic about the draasin, and he didn't blame Tolman for staring at him.

"How does Par-shon fare?" Tan asked.

Tolman pulled his eyes up and met Tan's. "You ask about the fate of Par-shon?"

"I would know what has changed in the time since the Utu Tonah was defeated. Tell me, Tolman, how do your people fare?"

"They are your people now, Utu Tonah. You rule as you see fit."

If he intended to rule, Tan needed to have Tolman and the others understand that he wouldn't rule the same way the previous Utu Tonah had. He had no intent of remaining in Par-shon for long. Long enough to see that those who remained ruled as he would choose. He would be as benevolent as possible, but he would have them fall into line. There would be consequences for what had happened before.

"As I see fit," Tan repeated. "Have the runes all been destroyed?"

When he had come through the last time, carrying the body of the former Utu Tonah, he had destroyed as many of the runes pressed into the tower as he could. He would not be surprised that others remained, probably more than he could detect. Given the purpose of the runes—to prevent shaping and sever the connection to the elementals—he *wouldn't* be able to detect them.

All except spirit. The Utu Tonah had not understood spirit.

"The runes are gone as you required, Utu Tonah," Tolman answered.

Tan watched him, searching for some sign that he might be hiding something from him, but saw nothing. With spirit, he layered a light touch on Tolman, searching for additional evidence of what might be concealed. There was a time when Tan would have felt a twinge of guilt at using spirit in this way, but that time disappeared when Par-shon attacked.

"That is good. And what of the other request I made?"

"Utu Tonah?"

Pulling through his connection to Amia, Tan could access

a greater connection to spirit than he could otherwise. Using this connection, and drawing through his warrior sword, he sent a shaping of spirit that washed over all of Par-shon. As he did, he listened for the response.

He detected nothing.

"Your shapers," he said. "I would know your shapers."

"But Utu Tonah, you have instructed that we have no shapers."

Tan took a deep breath, pushing back the surge of irritation that he felt. That hadn't been his instruction, but he would give Tolman the benefit of the doubt, knowing that the man must have been under some fair amount of strain trying to monitor Par-shon in Tan's absence.

"When I left the last time, I asked you to come up with a list of the shapers who were able to use the power of the elements without the forced bonds. I know that there are shapers within Par-shon who do not require forced bonds for their ability," Tan said. "There might even be shapers capable of bonding to the elemental the right way." He didn't want to think about whether his way even *was* the right way. Forced bonds certainly weren't the way the elementals were meant to bond. Most would never choose a bond, but for those that did, there was great power in that connection. "I would have you bring the list to me. Those who have potential but still have not learned will go to the university to learn. The others will be given an opportunity to be useful and prove themselves."

He had debated what to do with those who demonstrated real potential. There would be shapers, and some with potential. With as few shapers as existed in the world these days, Tan thought it best to find some way to pull them all together. They would need training, and the university could offer that education. Having them learn there, from shapers with an increasing ability to connect to the elementals and speak to them, to know the benefits of the bond the same way that Tan did, would be another opportunity to bring their people together.

"Utu Tonah," Tolman said. His face had gone white, and Tan wondered what he'd said that bothered him. "It will be as you ask. If you don't mind a question."

"You never have to fear asking questions, Tolman," Tan said.

"Might you share how you intend for them to reach the university?"

Tan smiled and nodded to Asgar. The draasin had agreed, mostly because he thought it amusing and figured that he would have the opportunity to scare some of the Par-shon shapers. But Tan had wanted to use the draasin for a different reason. Using the draasin, sharing the fact that the elementals were not something to be feared, would hopefully keep the future shapers of Par-shon from wanting to attack the draasin when they leaned to control their abilities.

Tolman's agitation faded as he gained control of himself, and he nodded. "When we present them to you, how long will you remain here?"

Tan hadn't considered how long he and Amia would stay in Par-shon. He had intended to come and find the shapers, and then use the time while in the country to learn what he could about the hybrid elementals that had been created, elementals that he had managed to heal while wrapped in the power of the combined shaping from each nation, but he had not intended to remain much longer than that. But when he left, what would he do? Returning to the kingdoms meant that he would be subject to Roine's moods. He had spent time in Incendin, learning more about the people there, as well as working with Cora in the Fire Fortress. Even Doma and Chenir had offered him lessons.

When he returned, he and Amia would marry. But not before.

It was Amia who reminded him that he had been away from Par-shon for long enough. He owed it to the people to make an appearance; either that or to assign someone to rule —truly rule—in his stead. He was not willing to abandon Par-shon to someone who might not have the same goal that he did.

"I will remain as long as I'm needed," Tan said. "Now. I would like to know where I will sleep."

## 2

## THE UTU TONAH MEETS THE COUNCIL

The Utu Tonah occupied an entire separate estate nearly the size of the palace in the kingdoms. Servants bustled into action prior to their arrival, likely having been warned that they would soon be coming. Tan had been tempted to take something smaller, but Amia reminded him that they needed to maintain appearances while they were in Par-shon.

An ornate hearth took up a large portion of the main room, and before doing anything else, Tan shaped flames onto the logs. Saa was powerful in Par-shon and leaped into the fire, swirling with much more strength than in any place else Tan had been. He stared at the flames, reaching through the fire bond to connect to saa, and enjoyed the brief presence in his mind. He found himself doing that more and more these days, a reminder of when Asboel had been alive.

"You could find another to bond," Amia said.

She wrapped her arms around his waist, resting her chin on his back. She no longer carried with her the scent of the Aeta; she had been within the kingdoms too long. Instead, the clean soap and lilac perfume reflected the kingdoms, where she had chosen to make her home.

He touched her hands as he held onto her. "I don't know that I *need* to bond to another." Now that he could reach the fire bond, his connection to fire—and not just to fire, but to Fire—was different and stronger than it ever had been. Asboel had given that gift to him.

"Don't you think that you'd be stronger with the elements if you did? What of Asgar? Or the other draasin?" Amia asked.

It was a familiar conversation, and one they had too many times before. "I can't bond to another draasin," he said softly. "I don't know if I could even bond to another fire elemental. Doing so feels…" He couldn't put an easy label on how it felt, only that he didn't think that he could do that. At least not yet. It felt too much like a betrayal of a friend he still hadn't properly mourned.

"You wish to honor his memory," Amia said. Tan nodded. That was all that he wanted. "Then do it through your actions and the way you honor the elementals. Think of all that you've already accomplished and know that he would be proud."

*The Daughter is wise, Maelen.*

The sudden intrusion of Asgar made him jump. In some ways, it reminded him of Asboel. The draasin had listened to everything that Tan did in the weeks before his death, and had offered comments and wisdom. Having Asgar there was both familiar... and jarring.

*You shouldn't be listening,* Tan said to the draasin.

*You are connected to the fire bond. I assumed you wanted me to listen.*

Tan smiled at the comment. Asgar hurt, too. Losing Asboel had been hard on them all, but Asgar had expected to know his father longer and have the opportunity to learn from him. Without Asboel, the younger draasin would have Sashari and Enya, but neither would be able to teach him as Asboel could. In that way, Tan suspected, he *needed* to remain connected to Asgar. Without him, the elemental would never learn some of the lessons that Asboel would have taught.

*You have grown strong, Asgar. That is all he ever wanted.*

*As have you, Maelen. Remember that he chose the bond. He chose you, Maelen.*

Tan smiled at the thought. What had once been terrifying, the idea of having the draasin alive and aware in his mind, had become a comfort. He longed for it at times and missed the connection more than he could ever truly admit.

"You treated Par-shon well," Amia said. "But they will expect you to lead. They will *need* you to lead." She released him and faced him, brushing a hand along his cheek. "You are compassionate, which Par-shon needs, but you have a connection to the elementals that they have lost. That is what they really need from you. Somehow, you have to bring that connection back to their people."

"That's why we're here," Tan said. "But what of the Aeta? Without you there—"

"You know that we are connected, even now. I am not the only one blessed by the Great Mother," she said. "And you know I did not want the title to begin with."

Tan smiled. "Much as you know that I don't want *this* title."

She pulled him close and kissed him. "The title suits you, though. And this way, I can say that my beloved is not only the greatest warrior shaper, and bonded to the elementals, but he is also the Utu Tonah of Par-shon. I think Mother would have been proud. She would have welcomed you to the People."

Tan laughed, letting the comfort of the connection between them linger and wishing they didn't have to do *this* before they could marry, but in that, Amia was right. "Do you think she knew what would happen?"

"I think she recognized that you had much potential, Tannen. It does not take a great spirit senser to know that, though."

The door to the room opened, and a servant entered. She had long, dark hair and heavy earrings in the shape of the runes Tan had forbidden. She bowed deeply when she saw who was in the hall, and looked away. "Utu Tonah," she said, "there is something for you in the great hall."

Tan sighed and took Amia's hands. "It begins," he said.

The servant led them down the hall and into a wide, high-ceilinged room. Artwork adorned the walls: faces of people that seemed surprisingly familiar, and scenes of battles and attacks that appeared to be little more than a way to demonstrate prowess over the elementals. Those would have to go.

A line of men and women, all of similar age to Roine and his mother, stood waiting for him. They whispered silently to themselves until he entered, and then all conversation ceased. As one, they looked at him.

Tan frowned, waiting for someone to step forward and explain why they had come. None did.

*I think they wait for you,* Amia sent to him. The shaped connection between them allowed for the ability to speak without words, much like he did with the elementals. And in some ways, Amia served as his connection to spirit.

*Careful, Maelen, the Daughter will grow angry if you don't appreciate her for more than her connection to the Mother.*

Tan pushed away the sense of Asgar within his mind, attempting to suppress the amusement he felt. Unlike his father, Asgar had a playfulness about him that was... refreshing in a way. *If you've been watching, then you know that I appreciate her for much more than her connection to the Mother.*

He sensed Amia's blush and she covered her face with her hand.

*What do they expect me to do?* Tan sent the question to Amia, wanting to bypass Asgar, but given the way the draasin had inserted himself into Tan's mind, or maybe it was the connection through the fire bond, he wasn't sure that he could truly exclude Asgar.

*They expect you to lead,* she told him.

Tan looked at the faces of the people in front of him. One of the men, an older man with thinning hair and ears a size too large for his head, watched Tan with disapproving lips pressed together. Much like many of the others, he wore a long robe embroidered with runes in white all along the hemline. The time Tan had spent with the First Mother, and in the archives in Ethea, had taught him the meaning of most of the runes, but not all.

A woman next to that man had a black necklace with a different pattern of runes set into stones. A smaller piece of jewelry held her dark hair back and away from her face. She watched Tan with uncertainty.

As his gaze stopped on each of the people arrayed in front of him, he shook his head slowly. With a sudden certainty, he realized that he might have had the runes in the tower destroyed, but there with countless others remaining. Not only runes placed on tiles that were designed to weaken and separate shapers from their abilities, but in other places, like the earrings the servant wore, or the embroidery of the man standing across from him. How many others had similar clothing?

Tan could eliminate the clothing and forbid earrings or other jewelry, but he couldn't exclude everything, could he?

This was the culture of Par-shon, one where the elementals were subjugated rather than celebrated. Somehow, he would have to change that culture, though Tan wasn't certain that he could.

"Who leads here?" Tan asked, stepping forward. He

placed one hand on the hilt of his sword for effect but had no intentions of unsheathing it.

A woman—younger than the rest—stepped forward, her hands clasped in front of her stomach. Both wrists bore wide bands of leather, and he didn't miss the brandings pressed into them.

He tipped his head to the side, quickly sensing the patterns on the jewelry and the clothing. Were these somehow for bonded elementals as well?

"You lead here, Utu Tonah," the woman said. She might be younger than the rest, but she had a voice like steel, and she spoke without fear as she stared at him.

Tan forced a smile as he tried to determine whether the jewelry contained bonded elementals. The bonded that he'd encountered from Par-shon had always used brands placed on their bodies. That had been the way that the Utu Tonah had bonded. But what if there was another way to share a bond?

"Why are you here?" he asked.

The woman regarded him with a measured gaze for long moments. "We are here to serve as needed."

Serve. What would their service entail? Would it be like Tolman, a man Tan had seen fit to allow to rule in his stead, or would there be something else?

He knew so little about Par-shon. Maybe this had been a mistake coming here. Maybe he should have left it under the rule of another.

*It is right that you are here,* Amia reminded him.

He took a deep breath and straightened his back, taking

the time to pace around the people so that he had time to think about what he needed to do and what he might say. He had to exude confidence but not arrogance. He needed to demonstrate his ability, but not reveal too much of his ignorance. But he *had* defeated the previous Utu Tonah. That was the reason that he was here.

Maybe he should have asked Roine for his advice, perhaps even brought the old warrior. He might know a better way to handle this. But had he brought Roine, the emphasis of his visit would have changed. Tan hadn't decided whether Par-shon should remain independent. It was part of the reason he hadn't shared with Roine that he was now Utu Tonah.

"What are your roles in Par-shon?" he asked.

No one spoke.

Tan stopped in front of the first man he had seen, the one with the sour expression on his face. He looked as if he didn't want to be here. Not that Tan could blame him; he didn't want to be here either.

"Who are you and what do you do?" Tan asked.

The man's hard mask cracked slightly. "I am Leon Szety, Master of Coin, my Utu Tonah."

Tan took in the man's dress and his tight posture. "What does that mean in Par-shon?"

The man started to sputter. "What does it mean?" he repeated, then seemed to catch himself. Incredulity faded, and he bowed slightly. "My Utu Tonah, I am responsible for collecting your taxes and ensuring the wealth of Par-shon."

Tan studied him a moment before moving on. The next

person he stopped in front of was an older woman. She wore a simple dress, but the ornate belt looped around her waist had many of the same runes that the others wore. Tan recognized most of them and noted a pattern. His mind began piecing it together, but he couldn't *quite* make out what it represented. There was something to it, almost a phrase.

"Who are you and what do you do?" he asked her.

She didn't look up or bother meeting his eyes. "I am Marin Leftas, my Utu Tonah." She spoke so softly that her voice didn't carry very far. "I am the Mistress of Souls."

"The Mistress of Souls?" Tan frowned. "What does that mean?"

She still didn't look up at him. "It means that I am responsible for the well-being of your people."

Tan studied her again, thinking that he understood. She was a priestess of some sort. Cora had suggested once that the people of Incendin were devout, but he hadn't spent enough time there to really understand. Within the kingdoms, the university was almost a religion.

"I would like to understand more. We will speak again later," Tan said to her.

She looked up at last and met his eyes. There was a strength there, and with a quick sensing of spirit, he detected compassion. She nodded.

Tan moved on, deciding to speak to the younger woman who had stepped forward when he first spoke. "Who are you and what do you do?"

She stared at him confidently. "I am Elanne Asan. I am the Mistress of Bonds."

Tan frowned, taking in the bands of leather at her wrists and the loops of silver hanging from her ears—noting the runes upon them as well before noticing what had been worked along the hem of her dress. These were subtly embroidered, almost as if intending to be hidden.

"Bonds. You mean of the elementals."

Elanne stared at him defiantly.

Anger surged up in Tan, and it took a moment for him to realize that he was feeling some of Asgar's irritation. The draasin still sat atop the tower, but he focused on what Tan experienced, listening to the conversations. He had the sense that were he attacked, Asgar would find a way to reach him even within the Utu Tonah's palace.

"As you know, I have forbidden the bonds."

"Utu Tonah," she began, "you are not of Par-shon. You do not understand the importance—"

Tan lowered his voice as he addressed her. "I do not have to be of Par-shon to know that the bonds that you forced on the elementals are unnatural."

She blinked.

"As I have said, the bonds—all bonds—are forbidden, unless they are freely given." He looked around at the people collected around him. As he did, he pulled on spirit, drawing strength from Amia and through the warrior sword sheathed at his side. Power surged through him.

He focused on the runes the people in front of him possessed. He had thought that he had severed all the bonds, that his connection to the massive shaping used against the

Utu Tonah had freed all of the bonded elementals, but perhaps he was wrong.

These people, all of them leaders of some sort within Par-shon, had not fought against the kingdoms. They had remained within Par-shon, hidden and protected. Was it possible that he had missed some bonds? It was a mistake he would correct now.

Tan sent spirit slamming into each of the runes, sweeping his focus around the room. A loud *crack* sounded within his mind.

Elanne gasped. The leather bands on her wrists snapped open. Her dress flared with a flash of white light, and then the runes disappeared.

All around him, the same happened. Jewelry cracked and broke. The embroidery on Leon's robe, as well as the others with similar embroidery, surged with light and then disappeared. Even the servant, the woman who had brought him before these leaders of Par-shon, lost her earrings to his shaping.

He felt something like a release of elementals, but not the same as when he had fought the Utu Tonah. Then it had been clear what he did when he released the bonds.

*Careful, Tan,* Amia sent. *These people are respected within Par-shon. They form a ruling council. They are the reason that the country has run so smoothly the last few months.*

*That's the reason they still live.*

The mood from the people standing before him changed immediately. Everyone other than Elanne cowered from him, taking steps back as if they hoped to recede from him.

"I defeated your Utu Tonah, a man more bonded to the elementals than anyone I have ever seen, and you think you can come before me, hiding bonds from me?" Tan struggled to keep his voice under control, but the anger coursing through him made it difficult. "There will be no negotiation in this. Elementals may bond, but at their choosing. A bond will not be forced." He made a point of meeting the eyes of each person around him. Elanne continued to stare defiantly. If nothing else, he realized that he would have to watch her more closely than the others. "Any bonds I discover will be stripped from you."

*Not far enough, Tan.*

He glanced at Amia before going on. He needed to lead but didn't want to do so in a way that was too harsh—but maybe the people of Par-shon didn't understand anything but an authoritarian approach.

"If this happens again, titles will be stripped from you as well." He breathed out and waved a hand. "Now go."

Some hurried to leave. Others lingered a moment before scurrying off after the others.

The woman Marin hesitated. "How long will you be in Par-shon?" she asked softly.

Tan swallowed. Roine had the kingdoms running as smoothly as they could, working on improving the university and training the children of Althem. Cora promised him that Incendin continued to thrive, especially now that the lisincend had been brought back to fire. Elle helped within Doma, guiding the people, and had become something of their leader, though she didn't want to admit it.

Even in Chenir, the Supreme Leader guided the rebuilding effort.

He had ignored Par-shon too long.

"As long as it takes," he said.

Marin nodded and left, moving quickly.

Elanne remained behind. "You have stripped me of my title."

"I did nothing of the sort."

"No? How can I be Mistress of Bonds if there are no bonds to oversee?"

*You need to work with those who offend almost more than you work with those you agree with,* Amia suggested. *The Mother always warned me that they could cause the most trouble.*

Tan resisted the urge to send Elanne away. Amia spoke sense, and he was thankful that he could have her silent guidance as he fumbled through what he needed to do as Utu Tonah. As frustrated as Elanne made him, he had to find a way to work with the people of Par-shon, even ones that he didn't agree with. Even with those he didn't particularly like. Maybe especially them.

Hadn't he done the same with Incendin? Hadn't he managed to look past the disagreement he had with them and find a way to work *with* them, even after what they had done to his family, and to Amia's?

"You may hold the title, but you will need to find a different interpretation."

Elanne stared at him for a moment. "The others see me as too young for my duties."

Tan had noted that she *had* seemed younger than the others. "They probably see me the same."

Her lips pinched in a frown. "When you... defeated... the Utu Tonah, Par-shon lost the Master of Bonds. As well as his second. And third. And forth." She counted them off on her fingers, bending them back to show nine fingers curled into her palm. "I was the tenth. I *am* too young, but am all that Par-shon had."

"You seem to have filled into your role."

"What choice did I have?" Elanne asked.

"What were your responsibilities as Mistress of Bonds?" Amia moved to stand next to him, and Elanne shifted her attention to the other woman.

"My responsibilities were to maintain the bonds. The Utu Tonah asked for new ways to bond and to maintain the supply, but that hasn't been the role of the Master of Bonds."

She spoke so matter-of-factly about what had been done to the elementals that it disarmed him. "Then perhaps it is good that you are not the first, or second, or third..." Tan leaned slightly toward her so that he could make his point clear. "The elementals do not choose the bond. Some will come willingly, and maybe that can be your focus, but if they do not, you will not force the runes upon them."

"You do not understand, Utu Tonah—"

Tan suppressed the surge of anger, not knowing whether it came from him or Asgar. "They are *not* crops to be used." He tried finding a different approach. Perhaps one that would reach her better, but couldn't come up with anything. Amia didn't seem to have any other suggestions.

"Tell me what you would have me do, Utu Tonah."

Tan suppressed a sigh. Elanne might already be beyond his ability to change. How many more would there be like her in Par-shon? How many more saw the elementals as nothing more than wheat to be harvested for their use?

*This will be harder than I realized,* he sent to Amia.

*That is why you must be the one to do it.*

"If you would understand what I ask, then you will need to understand the elementals. That is your task. Listen to them."

"Not all are like your draasin, Utu Tonah. Some *need* the bond, or they become wild."

Asgar bristled at the comment.

Elanne watched Tan for a moment, focusing on his sword for longer than he felt comfortable. "If you will allow me a question, Utu Tonah?" Tan nodded. "You could have killed us all, couldn't you? Even with all the bonds that we wore."

"I would rather not kill."

"That is not the question, Utu Tonah."

Tan thought of the ease he had now with the elements, an ease that he shared with the elementals, even more so with fire through the fire bond. He could draw more power than any other warrior. Cora had grown stronger since bonding to Enya, and Roine had more strength than he realized, but Tan had come to understand that his unique connection to the elementals granted him incredible strength. But he had to use it wisely. That was why he had come to Par-shon.

"Had I wanted to, yes. I could have killed you all."

Elanne nodded. "You are like him in that," she said,

though it was mostly to herself. Then quickly, she added, "Utu Tonah. Different, though. He would have killed to demonstrate that he could."

"I have no need of such a demonstration."

That wasn't quite true, he decided. Had he no need, he wouldn't have used his shaping on their runes, but anger had gotten the best of him and he had done what he thought needed at the time.

She tipped her head, almost a bow, and then turned and left him.

Tan waited until she was gone and let out a long sigh.

Amia still stared at the door. "She remains uncertain."

"As am I with her."

"Hers is different, I think."

Amia's ability to sense spirit was much more sensitive than his, and she could use it to detect much more delicate and subtle things than he could. Because of that, Tan reined in his frustration and told himself to listen to what she had to say.

"Different how?"

"She hasn't decided whether to help you or not." A smile spread across her face.

"I don't see why you're smiling. If she doesn't know if she wants to help me, I might have to replace her." Or eliminate the position entirely. There was no need to have a bond master now that he had forbidden such bonds, but he would take the time to evaluate everything before making those decisions.

"Because someone like her could be your most vocal

opposition," she started. Tan's stomach sank. That was what he feared. "Or your most vocal support. I think you will need to work closely with her."

Tan sighed again. He hadn't expected it to be easy returning to Par-shon, but he hadn't thought through what he had done by coming here.

Somehow, he felt that this was harder than anything that he'd ever before faced.

3

_____

A NEW SCHOOL

The grounds outside the tower were green with hints of colorful flowers. The flowers were a new addition since the last time Tan had come to Parshon. A gardener walked through the grounds, tending to the flowers, pulling some and weeding around others. Garza trailed after him, surprising Tan by shaping to keep the plants watered.

"That… was unexpected," he commented to Amia.

She stood next to him, scanning the grounds, but her focus was on the line of children in front of them. Most were no older than ten or twelve, but a few were older, and one was nearly Tan's age.

"There are so many," she whispered to Tan.

He looked over at the gathering that Tolman had collected. Each of them was reported to have the potential to shape. Some might never be anything more than sensers, but there was value in adding to the strength in sensing as well.

Others among them supposedly had the potential to shape, with many already beginning to show signs. From what Tan had learned, those with natural shaping ability had been prized by the Utu Tonah and chosen to bond first.

How many of these had once been bonded?

Maybe it was a mistake bringing them to the university to learn. If they *had* been bonded and had the same interest in regaining the bonds as some of the others that he'd already encountered, did he risk bringing them someplace to learn where they would potentially be exposed to elementals not found in Par-shon? Ethea sat on a place of convergence, where the elementals all came together. How hard would it be for someone who had known bonds to want to replicate that and maybe force another bond?

But as he looked at them, he reminded himself these were children. They were not the hardened bonded shapers that Tan had faced in his time dealing with Par-shon.

Tolman waited for him and stepped forward as they approached. "My Utu Tonah," he started, bowing deeply. Tan noted that he wore nothing with runes, and he didn't think that Tolman had worn anything with runes on them the last time he'd seen the man. "These are the candidates you requested."

Tan stopped in front of them. *How many harbor hatred?* he asked Amia.

*They are frightened. They fear that you will attack them as you did the Utu Tonah. They think you intend to kill them.*

Tan hated that he had to prove his unwillingness to hurt the people of Par-shon. Had the previous Utu Tonah treated people so poorly that they would all feel that he could do the same? What kind of ruler does that?

But, he realized, he had experienced a ruler as bad, or worse. Althem had used spirit shaping to control his people. How was that not worse than what the Utu Tonah had done?

Using spirit, Tan laid a gentle shaping onto the children in front of him, calming them. As he did, he realized that he had been mistaken. Several were older than he had been when he first went to the kingdoms after he had first bonded. How frightened would he have been to stand in front of a warrior shaper—and one who had killed their ruler—without any ability to do anything?

He would have been terrified.

"Par-shon had more potential than I realized," Tan said. He had to say something, not wanting to let the silence stretch on too long.

"Utu Tonah?" Tolman asked.

"Tell me, Tolman, how many were bonded?"

"Many were bonded, my Utu Tonah. That was how we introduced their ability to them."

Tan tried suppressing his annoyance but knew that he failed. "There are other ways to discover abilities," he said to Tolman.

His face went ashen, and he nodded. "Of course, my Utu Tonah."

Tan studied him, wondering why Tolman would be so deferential to him but look at him with such fear in his eyes. Tan had never treated him with the same casual aggression he had been shown when he first came to Par-shon. He hadn't demonstrated the same disregard for the people, had he?

Staring at Tolman would provide no answers.

Tan stepped past him. "How many of you were bonded to elementals before?"

Most shifted their feet nervously until one stepped forward. She was young—possibly only twelve—and barely came up to his chin. Lanky brown hair dropped to her shoulders, but her eyes had a bright light. "I was bonded, Utu Tonah."

"What elemental were you bonded to?" he asked.

"Saa, Utu Tonah."

Saa. Was there a reason a bonded of fire stepped forward more willingly than the others? Fire could inflame passions and lead to increased impulsiveness, traits that Tan had struggled to suppress, especially when he had nearly been twisted into one of the lisincend.

"What is your name?" he asked the girl.

"Fasha, Utu Tonah."

"Tell me, Fasha, did you learn the name of your bonded elemental?"

Her mouth twisted and she started to smile. When Tan didn't return the smile, hers began to fade. "Saa doesn't have names. It is saa."

*Asgar, will you participate in a demonstration?*

He sensed amusement. Since their arrival, Asgar had remained stationed on top of the tower. Tan hadn't figured out why the draasin found it so entertaining to remain so high, watching down on Par-shon, but he sensed the draasin's humor as he did.

*Of course, Maelen. Which one do I get to eat?*

Tan nearly snorted. *The little ones will not be all that filling, will they?*

*Not filling, but they are less chewy. What would you have me do?*

*Nothing more than come down from on high. Do you think the Mother will mind if you do?*

Asgar chuckled, and fire streamed from his nostrils. He swooped down, coming to land in the middle of the garden on a fluttering of wings and a billowing wind. Tan approached him and placed his hand on one of his heated spikes. Steam rose up from places along his back where the draasin heat mixed with moisture in the air.

The children all scrambled back toward the wall of the tower. Some whimpered softly. Only Fasha remained daring enough to stay out near the draasin.

"Do you think the draasin has a name?" Tan asked, speaking loudly enough for all to hear, but directing his question to Fasha.

"That is a draasin," she said.

Tan nodded. "He is one of the draasin, but do you think that he has a name?"

One of the other children, a skinny boy who couldn't have been more than eight or nine, stepped forward and pointed. "How do you know it's a boy?"

"Because I speak to him."

The boy started to smile. "Like a dog?"

*I think I will eat him,* Asgar said.

*I doubt that he would provide you with even a snack.*

*That's not why I would eat him.*

*Where is the challenge in the hunt?*

*The challenge will be you trying to stop me. You would fail, Maelen.*

Tan smiled. "He doesn't much care for being compared to a dog. And he doesn't like it when I compare him to a horse, even though he can carry about as much as one."

The draasin snorted fire at him, and Tan didn't move. This was a lesson the children needed to see. The draasin fire struck but parted around him, leaving him unharmed. Tan had learned long ago that draasin fire wouldn't harm him. Neither would lisincend shaping, or pretty much any other shaping of fire. That was the benefit of his connection to the fire bond.

Some of the children gasped, and a few laughed. A couple stepped forward, more daring.

"How do you know he has a name?" Fasha asked.

Tan patted Asgar on the side. "Because I gave it to him."

The boy leaned to one of the other children. "See? Like a dog."

Tan stopped in front of him, blocking the boy from Asgar. He didn't *think* the draasin would attempt to eat him, but he didn't want to take the risk. Asgar wasn't nearly as jumpy about things like that as his father, but draasin were proud creatures, and with good reason.

"Most of the elementals have a name of their own. They will not share it with you unless they choose the bond." Tan turned and focused on Fasha. "I will ask you again: did saa tell you its name?"

Fasha stared at Asgar, though the expression in her eyes was different than what he'd seen in so many who looked upon the draasin. Most had a look of longing. That had been the way the Utu Tonah had looked upon them, seeing them as a way to greater power. The lisincend had seen them as a connection to fire. And the kingdoms viewed the draasin as a threat, a view that Tan didn't share.

But Fasha had a different light in her eyes, one that gave Tan a certain sense of hope. She studied Asgar with interest, but not one that burned with intensity of control. Rather, it was a curiosity. Cianna had a similar way of looking at the draasin, which was probably why Sashari had been willing to bond with her.

"There was no name to saa," Fasha said.

Tan turned away from her. "And the others of you that were bonded? Did any of you know the name of your elementals?"

The question was met with silence.

Tan had not expected any to have actually known the name of the elemental they had bonded. That wasn't the way that Par-shon bonded, but such sharing would make the bond stronger, and made it more difficult to sever.

"If an elemental chooses you," Tan went on, "they will share their name. That is how you will know you were meant for the bond. It is respect, but respect must go both ways. You must respect the elemental and they, in turn, must respect you."

He wasn't sure why he bothered telling them this, other than that he didn't want them running off to try and force a bond again. If he could convince most of them that there was another way—a better way—then he would have served the elementals.

"Utu Tonah," a boy near the back started. He was tall and thin and had the beginning scruff of a beard. When Tan nodded, he went on, "You have bonded this draasin?"

"Not this one. My bonded was lost in the fighting."

"But you know this one's name."

Tan smiled at the question. At least they were engaged now. That had to mean something, didn't it? "I know his name, but that doesn't mean I have bonded him. Knowing the elemental's name is only the first part in forming the bond. The connection is deeper than that."

"How do we know you can really talk to it?" one of the older boys asked. He was nearly Tan's height, but more muscular. The others around him moved to the side to give him space.

*Asgar. This is where we must demonstrate.*

*Maelen.*

"What would you have me ask him to do?" Tan asked.

Some of the others shouted out suggestions, from having the draasin raise one leg to bring back a deer it had caught. The older boy rubbed his chin and let them speak. Then he raised his hand. The others fell silent.

"Has to be something that proves you can talk to him," the boy said.

"What would convince *you*?" Tan asked.

A smile spread on the boy's face. "Let me ride him."

*Well?* Tan asked Asgar.

*You may claim it, but I am no horse.*

*This is to make a point, that's all. These children come from a place where they don't believe the elementals have anything to offer. The first step is learning that the elementals are more than mindless creatures.*

*Some would argue that you're the mindless creatures,* Asgar said.

Tan suppressed his smile.

"He will allow it."

The boy frowned. "How do you know? You haven't asked him anything."

Tan noted the distinct lack of formality to his questioning. How would the previous Utu Tonah have reacted had he been questioned like this? Probably with violence and pain, Tan figured. This way was better.

"Are you so certain I haven't asked him anything?"

The boy took a hesitant step forward, then another. He stopped in front of Tan, but his eyes were fixed on Asgar. "It's so… big."

"He is."

*He is right to fear me. I might eat him. This one would provide more than a snack. The others would fear me as they should.*

*But I remember when you were nothing more than a hatchling.*

*That is because you are Maelen.*

*That doesn't make sense.*

Asgar snorted. *It does to me.*

"Go on. You wanted proof that I speak to him."

Up close, the boy trembled slightly. The bravado that he'd been showing, likely for the others, faded. He shook his head.

Fasha stepped forward. "I will."

Tan waved the boy away and turned to Fasha. "You need to sit between the spikes on his back. Then you can ride."

With that, she bowed to Asgar, who regarded her with a hint of amusement in his massive eyes, and then grabbed the spikes on his side as she climbed on, settling onto his back between two. She gripped them tightly, something that would not be possible if she had no ability with fire.

*This one is bold.*

*Perhaps too bold,* Tan agreed.

*We will see.*

"How do I make him fly?" Fasha asked.

"You will not. I will ask for you."

*Asgar? I think a circle around the city is enough.*

With a small snort and flap of wings, Asgar took to the sky. Fasha gasped, and through his connection to the draasin, he noted how she grasped tightly to his spikes.

Tan remembered his first flight, but it had been made out of necessity so that he could help Elle. Tan hadn't even been certain that Asboel *would* help. All he knew was that he could speak to the draasin before he ever learned that he could bond to him, and what it meant that he did.

The others in the garden all took steps back as Asgar lifted from the clearing carrying Fasha. As he had been speaking to them, they had been creeping forward, their initial fears wearing off as they became increasingly comfortable with the idea that Tan had summoned the draasin.

When Asgar had climbed above the tower, he turned his attention back to the children. "The bonds you once had formed will be no more," he said. "The *can* be no more." He made his way around the group, drawing their attention back to him. He wasn't certain that he would be able to pull their eyes back to him after they had seen Asgar, but slowly they did. Most looked at him differently. Tan didn't know whether it was a sense of respect or fear. He would rather have the former. The prior Utu Tonah had ruled through fear, and he would not repeat that if he could help it. "You all have the potential to reach the power of the elements without the elementals. That is why you have been brought here. Some of you already have shown the beginnings of what you might be capable of doing." Like Fasha. Had her connection to saa truly given her that much strength already?

A few of the children murmured. They wanted to know what they would be asked to do, and what it meant for them that the Utu Tonah had come to them.

Using spirit, Tan sensed their mood. Most were nervous, more than he had expected, but there remained a level of fear.

He probed more deeply and realized the source of that fear was him, and what he might ask them to do. Tan shifted the direction of the spirit sensing, reaching Tolman as he stood near the wall of the tower, and realized that fear bubbled within him as well, though a different type of fear.

Tan couldn't force these children to go to the university, he realized.

They would go. He didn't doubt the fact that they would do what he asked, but they would do so out of fear, not out of a desire to learn and understand. For them to learn, and understand, and to *believe*, they needed to learn from a different place.

"Tolman," Tan said.

Tolman came forward, hands gripping the cloth of his robe. "My Utu Tonah?"

"Do you think you can find these children boarding within the tower?"

Tolman blinked. "The tower?"

*What are you doing, Tan?*

*I can't send them to the university like this. It will delay our plans.*

*You do not have to apologize. I see what must be done as well as you.*

Amia might not admit to it, but Tan sensed her disappointment.

"If they will take it, I will offer the opportunity to teach them."

Tolman swallowed. "*You* will teach, my Utu Tonah?"

Tan glanced over at Amia. She watched him with an unreadable expression, one shielded from him through their connection to spirit.

"Only those who would allow me. But I will not be the only instructor. There will be others. And they will need someone to oversee them. I would have that person be you, Tolman."

He nodded slowly. "And the others?"

"Return them to their parents."

Asgar approached and landed behind him, coming down

harder and faster than Tan would have expected, but then he saw the look on Fasha's face, the wide-eyed excitement that she wore openly.

She climbed from Asgar's back and bowed to him before returning to stand with the others, who began asking her questions immediately.

*Thank you, Asgar.*

*She has known fire, Maelen.*

*It was a forced bond to saa.*

Asgar snorted before speaking. *Do you think you can change them?*

Tan turned and looked at the children. Tolman stood near them, like a shepherd watching over them. *I hope I can change their thinking.*

*I cannot fly with each of them.*

*You're not strong enough?* Tan asked.

Asgar growled softly. *There are limits to even my patience, Maelen. And some will not be able to listen to fire long enough.*

Tan thought about the way that Fasha had embraced the opportunity, the quick way that she had jumped onto Asgar, and decided that he needed to help as many as he could convince to come around to seeing the elementals in a way that benefited all.

*I intend to stay longer than I planned,* he told Asgar.

*I see that.*

*What of you?*

*I will remain. This place interests me. And there is something else about it that I do not understand yet.*

*What?*

*Later, Maelen. When I have answers.*

The draasin leapt to the air on a flap of wings and disappeared into the clouds.

Tan nodded to Tolman and took Amia's hand, then shaped himself away from the garden.

## 4

## A TIME BEFORE

"Why have you come to me, my Utu Tonah?" Marin asked him.

Tan stood near the edge of the city. It had taken some time to find Marin, but he was interested in understanding her role as Mistress of Souls. Many of the titles Tolman had explained to him made sense, but this one did not.

"I came to understand."

Marin leaned over a bucket and dropped it into a well. It splashed far below. Tan could offer to be helpful and shape the water out of the well, but doing that would only frighten Marin. From what he had seen of her, she had a timid nature and seemed to scare easily, in spite of the title she carried.

Somehow, he would have to get through to each of the people who led in Par-shon. Tan didn't know how he would be able to do that, or even if he could, but if he didn't, his rule would be defined by control. There was no hope of a lasting change if that was how he served as Utu Tonah.

"What is there to understand, my Utu Tonah?" Marin asked. She pulled the rope, and the bucket began ascending from the well.

"What it is that you do. How you have come to sit among the councilors of Par-shon. These are things I don't understand as an outsider," he said, realizing at once that he should not have reminded her. Her back stiffened and her fingers clenched along the rope. "I want to know how to help Par-shon succeed."

Marin remained quiet as she finished pulling the bucket out of the water. She set it to the side and then dipped three ceramic pots into the water, murmuring something softly. Tan couldn't hear the words, and those that he did hear, he didn't understand.

She stood and gently lifted the bucket and sent it back down into the well. "You want Par-shon to succeed, but you have taken away the ability to do so."

"You mean the elementals."

Marin tipped her head. She still hadn't met his eyes, preferring to keep them focused on the ground. The belt she had worn with the runes on them had been replaced by a length of plain rope. She grasped the fabric of her dress in her hands as she stood in front of him. "I mean the strength of the people. How many do you think have these bonds?"

Tan hadn't thought about how many in Par-shon had bonds but suspected that only those working for the Utu

Tonah, his shapers, had been bonded. "Tell me, Marin, what I don't know."

She lifted the three ceramic bottles and balanced them in her arms. "May I speak freely, Utu Tonah?"

When Tan nodded, she started forward, toward the city. Par-shon had a unique style of construction to its buildings, with flat roofs stretching over the streets, shielding them from the sun. Down one street, Tan saw one of the strange lizards that he'd noticed during his initial visit, with two people sitting atop the creature as it made its way through the streets. Many were dressed in thin wraps, and some had wraps that covered their necks and faces.

"You are an outsider, Utu Tonah, and so there is much that you don't know. The people need guidance, leadership, and mostly security. If you are not willing to provide those things, then perhaps another would be better." She stopped at a gate along a long, low wall and twisted the handle to enter the fenced-in area. "For the people, and for Par-shon."

"Would that be you?"

She lowered her eyes again. "I provide guidance for their souls, Utu Tonah."

"I intended for another to rule," Tan started, "but when I get word that nothing has changed, and that those who sought to lead in my time away from Par-shon revert to patterns and behaviors that led to this war in the first place, I was given no choice but to return and see if there is anything that I can do to influence the people."

"Influence?" Marin asked. "Is that what you think you were doing when you destroyed generations of bindings?"

"You mean your bonds?" When Marin nodded, Tan suppressed an annoyed sigh. Was this going to be the conversation that he would have to have with everyone in the city? Would he be forced to convince each person about why they could not bond the elementals, and what the consequences from him would be if they did? "How many generations of bonds did the previous Utu Tonah possess?"

Her mouth twisted slightly. "Generations? It is unfortunate that you know so little, Utu Tonah."

"Then explain it to me," he said. "Help me understand."

Marin pushed open the door and started through. "If you will excuse me, Utu Tonah, but there are others who need my services."

She paused long enough for him to nod to her, and then disappeared behind the gate, closing the door.

Tan lingered for a moment, wondering what she might have meant by that. How could he know so little? He had seen the effect of the Utu Tonah, and had seen the way that he had forced the bonds, stealing them from other shapers, and foraging—harvesting—elementals. Didn't he know enough?

But maybe there was something more that he hadn't understood. Hadn't he once thought Incendin simply wanted to attack the kingdoms because they enjoyed the destruction? There had been another reason, one that Tan had only learned when he discovered Par-shon. He had never known—and had not been able to appreciate—the fact that Incendin had faced Par-shon far longer than any other nation, and that they struggled with their shapers, using the shaping that kept the Fire Fortress burning, to prevent Par-shon from attacking.

Wasn't that safety worth something? There had been a cost, and Incendin had paid it, with shapers willing to embrace fire and turn into the lisincend so that the rest of Incendin could be safe.

He made his way through the street, walking instead of shaping himself along. Amia should be with him. She would have insight gleaned from her years of travel with the Aeta. As a wandering people, they were accustomed to visiting strange places and integrating into the different cultures. But she had remained back in the home of the Utu Tonah, needing to communicate to her people. Just because she had crossed the sea with him didn't mean her responsibilities as First Mother had changed. They were different, and dele-gated, which he knew Amia appreciated, as she claimed she no longer had the desire to lead, but there were decisions that only she could make, decisions that she didn't trust to be delegated.

At an intersection, he stopped and simply looked around. Nothing that Marin said made him feel comfortable that he understood the people of Par-shon as he would need to. And perhaps that was the point. She *wanted* him to question, but for what reason?

He tried seeing if there was something to the people around him, but could identify nothing unexpected. The people were all dressed differently than they would have been in the kingdoms, or even within Incendin and Chenir, places where they had such a different culture than any that he knew. For the most part, everyone moving past him ignored him.

Tan had made a point of wearing the same clothes that he would have worn in the kingdoms. He didn't necessarily want to blend in. That was not the reason that he'd come to Par-shon. He needed to be here, make the necessary changes that he might find, and then leave.

Only, now he wasn't sure that he would be able to leave easily.

In some ways, it frustrated him that this wasn't a challenge that he could simply shape away. He'd grown so skilled with shaping, and so connected to the elementals, that he couldn't imagine a situation where his ability to shape wouldn't be able to save him. There was nothing to this that he could shape.

Tan considered the homes and the shops around him. The style was different, with less of the arching rooflines and more of a flatter and squat design, almost as if Par-shon strained to sink into the land. There almost seemed a pattern to the way the homes were arranged.

Some of the buildings had a series of markings on them that reminded him of the ancient runes, but these were different. He paused at one of them and traced his fingers through the pattern. As he did, a surge of earth pressed through him.

Tan pulled his hand back and frowned.

That wasn't only a rune, it was a mark for the elementals.

There was something similar in the kingdoms. The one that came to mind was on the archives, a rune for golud that helped seal the elemental into the stone. Tan had always assumed that the elementals had chosen to assist with the archives, but what if they were placed there much like the bonds were forced by Par-shon? He'd already learned that the ancient shapers of the kingdoms were in some ways not so different from Par-shon.

Then there had been what the Utu Tonah had said. He had claimed that the kingdoms were the homeland of his ancestors. It might have been a boast, a claim made in the heat of battle, but there was something about it that made Tan wonder.

He hadn't spent enough time thinking about it, wondering whether there might be more to the former Utu Tonah than he knew. What if the Utu Tonah *had* descended from the same people as the kingdoms? What if there were secrets that he had understood that Tan had yet to learn?

He pushed the thoughts away. He *was* different than the Utu Tonah, regardless of what the man had claimed. He was different than those of the kingdoms, for that matter.

But the pattern on the building, a house that seemed no more unique than any of the others surrounding it, had the power of earth within the stone, supporting it in ways that he would not have thought necessary for a simple home.

Tan listened for the elemental. It was there, a distant rumbling sound coming from deep within the earth. There were many elementals that he had no name for, and this was no different. Earth might exist in the bones of this building, but it had been there a long time.

He made his way down the street, keeping his eyes on the buildings. A few others had similar marks, and Tan found the surge of earth within each as he touched them. This bond was different than the forced bonds, wasn't it? Different than what they used with the runes?

Maybe it was not. Could that be why Marin and Elanne were angry with him? The runes they had possessed were different than the ones that the Utu Tonah had placed on his body. They had been fashioned into jewelry, or clothing, and set in ways that may not have been the same.

He didn't know.

Anger had motivated him, and the memory of what the Utu Tonah had done. The people of Par-shon had used the forced bonds of the elementals, hadn't they? What if there was a different answer than what he understood?

Tan reached a small clearing and noted a tall windmill that pulled water from a well. On the blades of the windmill were marks that he recognized as for wind. He wouldn't be surprised to find a mark for water as well.

And he did. On the long drain leading to a hook for the bucket was a mark for water. Tan traced it, feeling a reverberation within him that signaled a connection to water, but different than anything he had experienced.

Were these the marks of people who had used the elementals?

Yet, they were also unlike the marks the Utu Tonah had used. Not only for the fact that they weren't placed on an individual person, but also because they were a different shape and drew from another sense of power. These were older and, in some ways, more like the runes that he'd found in the kingdoms.

Marin had referred to him as an outsider. Tan didn't deny

the fact that he was, and had thought that being an outsider brought him a greater understanding of the elementals. Maybe it did. Maybe his connection to the elementals was the right one, and everything that he saw here was wrong. It was possible that these elementals were trapped, forced by the runes to serve in ways that they would not have chosen, but it was also possible that these were simply markers of power that drew upon the energy of the elementals. If that were the case, then it meant that at some time, Par-shon knew how to work *with* the elementals.

He could destroy the marks, much like he had destroyed the runes worn by the leaders of Par-shon, but what if he was wrong?

He needed more information before deciding.

There were few people in Par-shon he trusted, but could he reach the elementals themselves?

The fire in the hearth flickered with a vibrant energy. Saa flowed through the flames with more strength than the elemental would have managed in the kingdoms. There, saa was little more than a flicker of energy, the barest spark of life. With enough influence, saa was drawn to the flames and could be used to maintain a fire, but the elemental had none of the same strength that Tan had found here in Par-shon.

Amia sat in a large and ornately carved chair facing the fire. The chairs were much more decorative than any he had ever possessed, and Tan felt a little strange sitting in them, almost as if he claimed the title that he didn't want. Amia, though, appeared much more at ease, lounging with her legs propped onto a pair of pillows and a notebook spread across her lap. The colorful dress she wore spilled out around her, and her deep blue eyes danced around the room.

"Are you sure that you detected the elementals?" she asked.

"I thought so, but it was different. These weren't runes, Amia, not like they used in the branding to seal the elementals to themselves."

"What if there was another purpose?" she asked.

Tan shrugged. "Then I would like to know the purpose. If Asboel were still with me…"

He couldn't finish. Asboel knew things that other elementals did not. Mostly that was because of his age. The draasin had lived so long, and had seen the world in different ways than so many others, that he had a unique perspective. Most of the time, that perspective had helped, but there were times when the past conflicted with the present and Asboel struggled to separate what had happened with what could. Asgar didn't share the same struggles. It was that reason that Asgar had not minded working with Incendin when Asboel struggled against what they had done to him.

But Asboel also had forgotten much over the years. Some of that had to do with the time he'd spent frozen beneath the lake, but some Asboel had blamed on the bond, as if the connection to Tan had changed him in some way. Likely it had. The bond had changed Tan significantly.

Amia looked up from her book and met his eyes. "Asboel

would want you to do what was right. And that means deter-
mining what *you* know is right, Tan. He trusted you. I think
you were the only person he could trust." Her eyes lingered
on him as he approached the fire, placing his hands practically into the flames. "You think to use saa to reach the
elementals of Par-shon?" she asked.

Tan pulled his hands away from the fire and glanced over
his shoulder. "The elementals will know more about Par-shon
than I do. I thought that they had been forced to serve, but
what if I was wrong? What if I was misguided when I first
returned?"

"I don't think you can be misguided if you only want to
help the elementals."

Tan hoped that was true, but Incendin had only wanted to
keep their people safe, and some of their greatest shapers had
embraced fire to do so. Wasn't that misguided? The lisincend
would never admit that they had done anything wrong. Fur
certainly wouldn't. But there had to have been another way. If
the experiences he'd been through had taught him anything,
it was that everyone had a reason for what they did.

He breathed out and focused on Saa, marveling again that
it wasn't as difficult as at home. Amia's idea had been sound,
to try to talk to the fire elemental. It seemed bound to Par-
shon somehow, and that was what he sought to understand.

When he'd been trapped in Par-shon, he had sensed the
strength from saa, a sense of power and control that Tan
didn't have in the kingdoms. Asboel had once explained to
him the elementals all represented aspects of fire, and saa was
no different. The draasin were the powerful and authoritarian

sense of fire, the need for control. Saa was something else, the soft, seductive, simmering part of fire. Within the fire bond, he could tell the difference easily.

*Saa.* Tan sent the request to the elemental, using the connection to the fire bond to build a bridge between them. He had no real bond with saa other than the connection he shared to fire, and to the elementals in general, but Tan had no doubt that saa would answer.

*Maelen.*

The voice was so different from that of the draasin. Within the draasin, there was a strength, a sense of power and pride. With saa, it was a slow-burning longing, like the soft hissing of steam from a teapot boiling.

*I would ask a question of saa.*

*For Maelen, saa will answer.*

Tan focused on the voice connecting to him through the fire bond. It matched the elemental that swirled in the flames of the hearth, a surging power that he knew to expect but still felt surprise when he realized exactly how powerful this elemental would be. When he had worked with the children, he claimed that the elementals would grant a name when they bonded, but that wasn't always the case. With the nymid, they were a community, and Tan had essentially bonded to many.

With the draasin, there was no way that he would have managed to bond to more than Asboel. At times, it took all of his concentration to remain focused when Asboel had shouted in his mind. With Asgar, it was another story. Tan had gained experience over time and Asgar, while strong, had none of the same depth of experience and power as his father. Over time, it was possible that Asgar would grow even stronger, but for now, Tan was able to suppress the shouts in his mind. It created a better balance with Asgar than what Tan had with Asboel. Asgar viewed Tan more as equals, knowing Tan only as Maelen, and knowing him only since Tan had learned strength and power with fire and the other elementals. Asboel had known him before he even realized that he could shape, and in many ways had guided him through the initial steps with shaping.

Amia watched him as if knowing the direction of his thoughts. It was possible that she sensed the way his mind had turned, focusing on his lost draasin friend. Some times were easier than others, but lately, especially since coming to Par-shon, he found it difficult not to think of Asboel. Tan wished he had hunted with him, even if only one more time.

He sighed, pushing the thoughts away and focusing on saa. The elemental swirled in the fire, almost as if giving Tan the time he needed.

*Fire misses the Eldest as well, Maelen.*

Tan smiled. *He has rejoined the Mother. I should not mourn.*

*Even the brightest fires burn out.*

It was something that Asboel might have said. *There had been many forced bonds in these lands,* he started.

*Once there were.*

*Do any remain?*

Saa swirled and flickered, the flames leaping for a moment. *Some bonds remain, but they are older than the one who forced the others.*

*I don't understand.*

*The Bonded One.*

*The Utu Tonah,* Tan said, forming an image of him in his mind.

Saa burned brighter for a moment. *The Bonded One. He required much of Fire and did not give in return.*

*What of these bonds?* Tan asked, changing the image to one of the mark on the stone buildings, or the windmill. *Were these placed by someone like the Bonded One?*

*Those were before.*

A series of images flashed through his mind. All were for fire and flickered so quickly that he began to lose track. None of the images involved bonded shapers, nothing like the men and women that Tan had faced when confronting the Utu Tonah. What he saw were more like the runes on the leaders of Par-shon that he'd destroyed.

*Did these give in return?* Tan asked.

*These lands are unlike the places you know, Maelen. It is more than giving and taking.*

*Explain it to me then.*

Another series of images flashed through his mind, this time in the shape of rock formations and landmarks and other places, none of which he had a way of understanding. They continued one after another, the effect dizzying, before finally easing and then stopping altogether.

*I still don't understand,* Tan said to saa.

*These are for protecting.*

*Protecting what? The people?* That had been what he suspected when he touched the earth elemental and found the way that it had surged through him. The earth contained in the mark supported the building, kept it strong. But he didn't think that was what saa implied.

*Not the people. This.*

More images came through his mind, so many that Tan lost track.

He didn't understand, and he sensed from saa that there was no other way to explain to him, which meant that Tan needed to find another way to get answers. Only, he didn't know where.

## 5

# THE ATHAN RETURNS

The shaping that Tan used pulled him on a bolt of lightning, streaking him across the sky soundlessly, moving as fast as thought. Tan was one of the few who could use this shaping to travel. Most of the warrior shapers hadn't learned to master spirit, not as Tan had, and though they could travel on shapings of earth, wind, fire, and water, they couldn't add spirit into the mix.

As Tan had learned, the difference was dramatic. When he shaped without spirit, the shaping came on a rush of wind and a torrent of noise racing through his ears. There was more of a sense of movement, and he could track where he traveled, something he couldn't do when he added spirit, but the shaping was weakened as well. Without spirit, there was none of the same speed.

Amia clung to him, though she had grown accustomed to the shaping. Once, he would have traveled with Asboel, riding along with the draasin, but even while Asboel had been alive, Tan had taken to shaping his travels. Now that Asboel was gone, he had no other choice.

Asgar remained in Par-shon, keeping watch. As long as Asgar remained, the people of Par-shon would think that Tan remained, and that served his purpose. But there were things that he had to learn that he couldn't discover in Par-shon, at least not easily.

With an explosion of light, the shaping took him to the university in the kingdoms. Rebuilt since the attack on the city—it seemed so long ago—the university was, of course, different. Ferran and the other earth shapers who had restored it had altered the design, so it was both more open and more imposing. Stone flowed from the ground, partly shaped and partly assisted by golud, the earth elemental that Ferran had bonded during the last year. Golud lent strength and exuded a sense of age that the building hadn't earned. Tan wondered if he was the only one who detected that.

The shaper circle let out in a plaza outside the university. The stones had been changed over time, but like the stone of the university, they were infused with the strength of golud. Not trapped and not forced, but strength that had been freely given.

This was the reason that Tan had returned.

"Will you find me before you return?" Amia asked.

Tan squeezed her arm. "I'm not sure you'd let me leave if I didn't."

"Do you think that I'd shape you if you didn't do what I want?"

He smiled. *It wouldn't be the first time.*

Amia laughed. "You keep bringing that up, but I think that you don't mind nearly as much as you claim."

Tan shook his head. "I let you believe that."

Amia gave him a quick hug and departed, making her way toward the Aeta camped outside the city. She intended to use their time in Ethea to connect with her people and to ensure that everything ran as it should. Tan had other needs.

His gaze was drawn to the university. He'd had such little time to learn within the walls of the university, and when he *had* been here, there hadn't been any willing teachers. Only after he had discovered his bond with the elemental had he begun to understand. What was the message in that?

But that was how the ancient shapers once learned, wasn't it? They had bonded to the elementals, and through that bond they were able to leverage even more of the power of the elements than they would otherwise, much like what Tan had been able to do. In that way, he was more like the ancient shapers than today's shapers.

Except, he didn't share the same attitude about the elementals that he'd learned from studying in the archives. Now, he understood that not all the ancient shapers felt like that, and finding the strange hut in the middle of the swamp within Doma had provided him with reassurance, but there had been enough of those shapers who had understood the elementals.

A small door opened into the plaza, and a line of children made their way out from within, with a robed shaper leading the way. Tan smiled as Ferran almost herded them outside.

When he saw Tan, he raised a hand and motioned for the children to wait.

"You have been gone again," Ferran said, looking to the shaper circle.

"It was time for me to take a more active role in Par-shon."

Ferran's eyes narrowed slightly. Like everyone else, Ferran had lost friends to Par-shon. The kingdoms had few enough shapers as it was; losing any was almost too high a price to pay. "Are you certain that is wise, Athan?"

Tan almost smiled at the title. Here in the kingdoms, he served as Athan, the voice of the king, only the kingdoms did not *have* a king, not yet. Roine served as king regent and had agreed to fill that role until they decided which of Althem's heirs could assume the throne, but that might not happen, especially with as many children as Althem had.

Tan studied the children all waiting patiently for Master Ferran. How would they choose which of the children would lead? Would he be able to give up the title of Athan then? Roine still expected him to serve, but outside of the king-doms, across the sea, he was Utu Tonah. Could he serve as both?

Did he truly intend to continue to serve as Utu Tonah?

Maybe it would be the same as Amia serving as First Mother. There were parts of the responsibility that he didn't want, but then the alternative left him with a different set of concerns. If not him, then who? Tan didn't think that he was any *more* capable than someone else, but he had been the one to defeat the Utu Tonah.

Ferran's eyes narrowed. "Athan?" he repeated.

Tan sighed. "I'm not sure that I deserve that title anymore."

Ferran laughed and leaned in. With a whisper, he said, "I feel the same way when the students call me *Master*."

Tan regarded the students again, thinking of all that they had been through. What did they know about their heritage? Hopefully nothing. Learning what Althem had done might be devastating to some, but he could easily image others having a different reaction, one where they felt a desire for power, where they believed they had a right to rule.

"How many have shown shaping potential?" he asked.

"More than I expected," Ferran said. "Though, if I am honest with you, I don't know that I thought any would demonstrate any real potential. Possessing parents with the ability to shape is no guarantee that it will pass on."

Tan smiled. "Seems to help."

Ferran turned back to him and chuckled. "You would be an interesting case, I believe. Most shapers don't have a lineage where they descend from shaper after shaper, let alone two of the strongest shapers the kingdoms have known in years."

Tan glanced over at the university. "Speaking of my mother, is she here?"

"You look in the wrong place to find Zephra. She will teach, though not as often as I would like. But most of her time is spent in the palace."

Knowing that his mother wasn't alone brought him a measure of happiness. They had mourned his father, but

Zephra deserved to know a sense of contentment, as did Roine.

"I would also have you teach, Athan," Ferran went on.

Tan nodded absently, his mind going back to Par-shon and the students that he'd met there. When he returned, he would need to teach them as he promised, to determine which of the students he could use and which would need additional time so that he didn't have to fear them chasing after the elemental bonds again.

"I'll come by later," Tan said.

The comment seemed to placate Ferran, who nodded. He raised a hand toward the children, settling them with little more than a look. "That would be appreciated, Athan."

With that, Ferran left him and hurried back over to the group of children, who he ushered out from the university and onto the street beyond.

Tan stood for a moment, debating what he would do, before drawing on a shaping of wind that brought him to the archives.

There was a time that he would have pulled on the wind elemental, but Honl had changed since he'd rescued him from kaas, and even more in the weeks following. Now, Honl was something else. Tan no longer knew if he was even a wind elemental, or if the rescue, and the need to use spirit in Honl's saving, had changed him.

It had been weeks since he'd seen Honl. That time, the wind elemental had asked him questions, querying him about the connections he shared with the elementals, and then had disappeared again. If he searched for him, reaching through his connection to wind, he could probably find him, but Honl was little more than a vague awareness on his senses.

Landing in front of the archives, Tan found the door closed and locked. He frowned. In his time in Ethea, the archives had never been locked. They had been damaged during one of the attacks on the city but never blocked. Had Roine changed something since he'd been away?

Tan had another way that he could reach the archives but hadn't expected to need it. Doing so would take him through the palace and might force him to answer questions about what he had done, and why. Neither of which he was entirely prepared to answer.

He pushed on the door again, but the lock was stout. He could force it open, but that wasn't the message he wanted to send.

No, he needed to reach the archives another way. And that meant through the palace.

---

At this time of day, the palace was full of activity. Servants hurried in and out of the wide open door, some carrying bundles, others with baskets for items that might be needed inside. Tan stood on the edge of the lawn, watching for a moment. In some ways, the activity was no different than what he'd seen in Par-shon, but there had been an undercurrent of fear mixed in. Here, there was nothing other than a sense of purpose.

A few of the servants saw him and nodded. Tan had become well known around the palace, at least enough where they recognized his face and made a point of addressing him. Partly that was because of the amount of time he spent with Roine, but some of that was because of the ring naming him Athan. It carried the weight of his title and within the palace especially, that title carried the most weight.

But it had been weeks since he'd been here.

Tan sighed and made his way into the palace, pausing again in the entryway. Portraits of past kings lined the hall to his right, and a familiar voice came from a room at the end of the hall.

All he'd wanted to do was to reach the archives and have some time there, but if Roine discovered that he'd come to the palace and *not* stopped, he'd be disappointed. Worse than Roine, if Zephra learned that Tan hadn't stopped, she'd be angry.

Neither appealed to him.

As he made his way along the corridor, Roine's voice grew louder. Tan stopped outside the great hall to wait. The line of portraits hadn't changed since he'd been here last, but there was an addition that surprised him: Althem.

Stopping in front of the portrait, he studied the hardened face and the intense eyes of a man who had nearly destroyed the kingdoms. Tan had only met him a few times. The first time, Althem had seemed warm and friendly. Now, he wondered if Althem had been shaping him, though it was possible that Amia's shaping had protected him. The second time had been when he and Asboel had confronted Althem as he tried to use the artifact. It was a dangerous creation, and one that Tan still didn't understand. Had Tan not had full command of his abilities, he would have failed. As it was, he had nearly lost Asboel and had used the trapped power of the artifact to save his friend that time. If he only still had it…

But he couldn't think like that. Doing so didn't help him today, and it didn't honor the memory Asboel would have wanted him to maintain.

"Tannen."

Tan turned to Roine, who now stood in the doorway to the great hall. He hadn't sensed him approaching. "You've added another portrait."

Roine glanced at the portrait. "It seemed fitting that he be added."

"Even after everything that he did?"

"Do you think that all these kings and queens ruled as you would have?" Roine asked, pulling his eyes away from the portraits. He motioned down the hall, to the dozens and dozens of portraits, some faded by time, leaving little more than a blur of what the image should be. "They are a reminder—good and bad—of the kind of rule the kingdoms have known. Some… some have been better than others."

"And some thought to shape the kingdoms and force an image of what they wanted."

Roine chuckled. "That might have been the worst. Better to have the reminder of his rule than to remove it and forget. After everything that he did, the hidden atrocities," he said, shaking his head as he touched his temples, "some we may never fully understand, we need to maintain the reminder. Without it, it might be too easy to forget."

Tan studied the portrait of Althem. At least the artist had cast him in a dark light, leaving his eyes with an awful intensity. "When will yours hang alongside his?"

Roine smiled, and deep wrinkles formed at the corners of his eyes, showing his age. They had been through so much over the last year, and it had aged him prematurely. "Mine should never hang next to Althem's. I am nothing more than a placeholder."

"Are you so sure? I think most would argue that you've handled the transition from warrior to ruler well. There would not be any argument were you to remain king."

"Regent, Tan. King Regent. And I will not be party to a silent coup."

"Why must it be silent?" When Roine started to protest, Tan pushed on. "There is no one else fit to rule. You were Athan at the time of Althem's death. The line of succession would be satisfied."

Roine considered Tan for a moment, a slow smile spreading across his face. "Either you have been speaking with your mother, or you have come to the same conclusion. I'm not sure which worries me more," he said with a laugh.

"I'm not trying to worry you. I only want what's best for the kingdoms."

"Only the kingdoms now?" Roine asked. He cocked his head and stared at him. "Not Incendin, and Doma, and Chenir…"

"And Par-shon," his mother said, coming up behind

Roine. She fixed Tan with an expression she likely meant to be withering, and to many others it likely would have been, but Tan had grown up around her and knew her moods. "Ara tells me that you journeyed across the sea, bringing one of the draasin with you. I thought that we'd talked about that foolishness and the claim that you were Utu Tonah—"

"Foolish to you," Tan said. "But the elementals speak to *me*, Mother, and have made it clear that Par-shon had not changed. That was why I returned."

Roine motioned them into the hall and out of the corridor where servants moved past, trying and failing to give them a wide berth. Once in the hall, Roine shaped the doors closed and crossed his arms over his chest.

"You're the Utu Tonah?" he asked.

Tan glanced at his mother and realized that she hadn't said anything to Roine. "When we brought the body back to Par-shon…"

"They named you ruler?" Roine asked. "And you didn't feel it appropriate to share this with me? Tan, you're my *Athan*. You speak with the voice of the throne."

Heat rose in his cheeks no differently than when his father had chastised him as a child when he'd forgotten to cover the firewood, or when he hadn't paid enough attention while tracking. As he had then, he struggled to find the right words. There wasn't anything that he could say. Certainly nothing that would make it better. He *should* have shared with Roine.

When Tan didn't answer, Roine turned to Zephra. "And you. I would think that *you* would tell me about Tan. It's bad enough that he keeps getting it in his head that he has to serve the elementals over the kingdoms, but at least you've usually backed me up when it came to him."

Zephra took the chastising without saying a word. Some might think that meant she was appropriately chagrined, but Tan knew better. With his mother, silence often meant that she was biding her time, waiting for the right moment—usually when he was alone—to share her irritation. This time, he didn't worry about what she would say to him. It was Roine who had to fear.

The King Regent turned back to Tan. "Why you didn't let me know that we essentially *rule* in Par-shon—"

"You would have him rule?" Zephra asked.

"We're the victors, Zephra. We get to decide what we do with Par-shon."

"Are you certain that's wise? We've got enough trouble in the kingdoms, especially with the unrest in the west."

Roine cut her off with a shake of his head.

Zephra glanced over at Tan and nodded. "Regardless, we have enough going on trying to understand the new political dynamics. Incendin still claims that we should reunite Rens, Doma wants help with rebuilding following the Par-shon attack, and Chenir…"

"I know what we face," Roine said.

"Not if you intend for us to provide rule over another nation. And I know that Tannen might think he's doing what's best, but he should not be the one—"

"*I* am the one who defeated the Utu Tonah." Tan stepped forward as he spoke, placing himself between his mother and

Roine. "You may think *we* are the victors, but in Par-shon, *I* am the victor."

"You can't think—" his mother started.

"I can," Tan interrupted. "You would have shut down the borders, you would have barricaded the kingdoms and abandoned Incendin and Doma, thinking that Chenir had already been lost. So please do not presume to tell *me* what to do."

He took a deep breath, already regretting the way that he'd spoken to them and fearing the way that his mother would react. Since the destruction of their home village to the lisincend, she had been an angrier person, fueled by a drive to defeat Incendin, but also one who wanted to protect Tan as much as she could. The problem was that there wasn't anything that she could do to protect him, not as she wanted to. There were things that he had to do, and learn, on his own. They were the things that had brought him the knowledge and skills needed to defeat Par-shon. Without his connection to the elements and the elementals, everything and everyone would have been lost.

Roine started laughing.

His mother shot him a hard glare, but Roine shook his head and nodded to Tan.

"Whenever I think I know what I'm doing, Tan comes along and shows me how little I've figured out," Roine said. "The boy is right, Zephra. We would have lost had it not been for him. Maybe not yet. We would have secured ourselves behind the barriers, but eventually. It would have been slow, and painful, and many others would have suffered before we fell. And now he's no longer my Athan. He's my equal."

74

Zephra studied Tan, her head shaking slightly as she did. "And he's not a boy," she said softly. "So I must stop thinking of him as one."

Roine chuckled. "I think you'll struggle to see him as anything different than the child you raised, but *I* can see him as the man he's become. Much greater than anything I had ever thought to find when I came to Nor. It seems so long ago that I came looking for the artifact. What I found was so much more." he sighed. "So Tannen. You are the Utu Tonah. Is that what you came to share with me?"

Tan struggled to process the sudden change. "I don't want to be Utu Tonah," he answered.

"And I don't want to be King Regent, so I guess we are well matched, then."

"Which means you both are better suited for the job than most," Zephra added. "I would be more concerned if either of you *wanted* the job."

"I don't want to be Utu Tonah," Tan repeated, "but I don't know that I can trust anyone else to rule in Par-shon until I understand their lands."

"You won't find those answers here," Roine said.

"There was something else I discovered. I intended to see if I could find answers in the archives."

Roine nodded slowly. "You didn't intend to come to us at all, did you?"

"I would have eventually. But the archives were locked."

"Until we come up with a plan for all those texts, I thought it best to keep it locked. There are some who have come forward, wanting to resurrect the archivists, but I've been careful with them so far." Roine paused and glanced to Zephra. "Besides, it is good that you've come. We have news to share with you."

Tan readied himself for whatever awful news they might have, but what his mother said next still surprised him.

"Theondar has asked me to marry him. And I've said yes."

Tan looked from Roine and then to his mother, smiling. "Good. Maybe then we can have a joint wedding."

Roine smiled, but his mother's mouth twitched, and whether from irritation or another emotion, he couldn't tell.

## 6

---

## HONL'S SEARCH

The lower level of the archives appeared no different than the last time Tan had come here, but in a way, it was very different. When he'd been here last, the kingdoms had been on the verge of defeat to Par-shon, and he had sought answers, possibly even the kind that would allow him to somehow rebuild the artifact and discover a way to use it that the ancient shapers hadn't considered. Except, he'd damaged the artifact attempting to shape it. Now it would never again be used.

In many ways, Tan knew that was good. The artifact, a long metal cylinder that had been formed using a combined shaping of each of the elements, somehow binding elementals into it, had been a creation of such power that when he held it, he thought he would be able to shape the world, that he would be able to do anything that he wanted. Such power was dangerous, even to him.

Maybe especially to him. Tan had shaping ability, or else

he wouldn't have been able to use the artifact, but it was more than his ability to shape. Althem had had that, or he wouldn't have been able to use the artifact. Rather, it had been Tan's ability to reach the elementals, his connection to powers more ancient than him, that might have proven dangerous. They had given him a connection and grounding, but would he have been able to maintain that grounding while controlling power like the artifact allowed?

Tan liked to think that he could, but what if he were wrong?

He stared at the wall of books. All around him were the ancient volumes brought and kept here by the shapers who had come long before him, knowledge that should be enough to answer any question that he had, but much like the portraits on the wall in the palace, some of the books served only as reminders of what should *not* be. The harnessing of elementals had been done out of ignorance, not out of a place of knowledge.

How much else was there like that?

Then there was the hut within the swamp outside of Doma. He pulled the book that he'd discovered there from his pocket and set it on the table next to him. He'd left it in the home he'd once shared with Amia, setting it aside for a time when he would have the opportunity to study its contents, but there never had seemed to be the right time. And then he'd taken to staying with Amia in the wagon with the Aeta and had forgotten about it entirely. Maybe there was something in it that could help.

Stamped into the cover was a rune for each of the

elements. The thick leather had the sense of age and Tan folded it open carefully, knowing that this book was older than most books within the archive. He remembered the first time he'd read it, translating the *Ishthin* and realizing that he had found not only an ancient book but one that promised to hold secrets that he needed.

All the time that he'd spent becoming disenchanted with what the ancient shapers had done, only to find *this*.

Tan flipped the first few pages, skimming them. A journal, or letters. The writing seemed directed to someone, almost as if whoever had kept the record had intended it for someone else. Had this other person been the one with the hut in the swamp, or was there someone else? Maybe the person who had written this had been the person in the swamp and the book had never reached its target.

Unlike many of the texts that he'd read in the archives, this one interested him on a different level. Not only could he learn from the past, but he thought that he could begin to understand some of the ancient shapers, and maybe he could understand what they knew and why the elementals had been harnessed, or why there had been a desire to attempt the crossings of elementals, the same crossing that had formed creatures like kaas, or the hounds.

Wind swirled quickly, fluttering the page that had caught his attention.

Tan slapped his hand over the cover to protect it. Had his mother come to the archives to find him? The Great Mother knew she rarely had come down before. Roine visited often enough, but his mother preferred to leave him alone. Or maybe she didn't care for the reminder of the archivists. Tan had never learned.

But it wasn't his mother.

A dark shape coalesced in the chair across from him, taking on the shape of a man about his age, with jet black hair and a cloak that hung limp in spite of the wind. Honl looked at Tan with enough clarity to his features that Tan believed him real.

"You are no longer across the sea," Honl said. His voice had deepened but still had something of an airy quality to it. The wind around them settled, and Honl leaned back in the chair, trying to take on a casual stance.

"I came here for answers," Tan said.

"You think you will find answers here that you cannot in that place?"

Tan swept his arms around him. "There is a thousand years of knowledge here, Honl. There is value in learning what I can from here."

"What of the land across the sea? How many years of knowledge are stored there?"

Tan shrugged. Par-shon didn't strike him as older than the kingdoms, and certainly the buildings that he'd seen didn't appear any older than the kingdoms, but those with elemental support might be more ancient than he realized. The connection to the elementals would make them stouter than any others without, perhaps stout enough that they could survive a thousand years or more without falling.

Hadn't the archives lasted that long? Even when everything else within the city fell, the archives remained. With the elemental's influence, the ancient structure had stood tall.

Tan set the book to the side and leaned forward as he considered Honl. The elemental had changed much in the months since he and Tan first met, and since they first bonded. Honl claimed that he had been there when Tan first used wind to defeat Althem, and then had helped when he needed the assistance of wind to reach Asboel. That had been the start of learning about the Utu Tonah. Without Honl, Tan might not have managed to reach the draasin, and he doubted that he would have escaped from Par-shon. In many ways, he owed everything to the wind elemental.

But the connection to him was different than the other elementals. Each was unique, as they should be, but Honl in particular had been hesitant at first, not wanting Tan to pull him into the attack with Par-shon. Once Honl had overcome that resistance, he had become useful in ways that even Asboel had not been able to expect.

And now... now Honl had become something else. The wind elemental regarded Tan with curiosity, and his dark eyes took on a scholarly appraisal as he stared at Tan.

"What do you know, Honl?" Tan asked. "What have you learned in the time since we last saw each other?"

"We have never *truly* been apart, Maelen." Wind still circled him, touching the bottom of his cloak and making it undulate softly. The cloak itself was no more real than the form Honl had taken. He had once demonstrated that he could take any form he chose and, for some reason, preferred this figure. Each time Tan saw him, his features were more distinct, almost as if Honl were *becoming* this figure. "The bond connects us even when we are not physically together. It is much the same with the Daughter."

Tan smiled. "Not truly apart, but distant enough, don't you think, Honl? I haven't seen you since..." He thought about how long it had been, and how much had changed. "It must have been since we defeated the Utu Tonah."

"You have not needed me."

"And I do now?"

Honl sat, studying Tan for long moments. When he spoke, he did it with a smile. "Like me, you are... unique... among your people, are you not, Maelen?"

"I'm the only one I know of who can speak to all of the elementals. Is that what you mean?"

"That, but you do more than simply speak to the elementals. You can borrow strength as well, draw strength and focus it. Without that ability, you would have failed countless times by now."

"I can," Tan agreed. Without that ability, he would not have been able to rescue his mother in Chenir, or stop the Utu Tonah. Tan could pull strength from the elementals, but he could also shape it without that connection, though his strength was severely limited when he did that.

"I have been searching for a reason for my uniqueness."

Tan leaned back in his chair and sighed. "What if there is no reason for your uniqueness? What if it's simply because of what *I* did to save you?"

"There has to be a reason, Maelen, much like you had a reason for your uniqueness. The Mother brought you at a time when such connections were needed. That is why you are here."

"What if the Mother had nothing to do with the fact that I am here?"

Honl reached toward him, as if trying to touch his hand, before sitting back. "I think of everything that you have demonstrated in the time that I've known you. You have a connection that is unusual. There must be a reason for it."

Tan was no longer sure of any reason he might have been given the ability to reach the elementals. And maybe there wasn't one. Stopping the Utu Tonah had been the only explanation that he had come up with, but could the Mother have cared so much about the Utu Tonah? Or had there been another rationale?

The alternative was that there wasn't. As much as Tan wanted to believe that there was something more about him that made him special, maybe the fact that he had the abilities he did was nothing more than chance.

"And your uniqueness?" Tan asked, pulling the focus back to Honl. "Have you discovered a reason for that?"

Honl paced the perimeter of the room. Honl didn't walk, though his feet appeared to touch the ground. He floated, hovering slightly above the stone. Had Tan not had the connection to wind, he wouldn't have recognized it, but then, Honl didn't move his legs as someone who walked, either. As much as he'd learned and attempted to become human, he still had areas where it was clear that he was something other.

Every so often, Honl paused and looked at the shelves filled with ancient texts. He reached for one and Tan was surprised that he managed to pull it from the shelf and flip it open, scanning the pages before sliding it back on the shelf.

"There is much in this archive. Some of what I've discovered raises new questions, while some answers questions."

Tan frowned. "You've read these books?"

Honl didn't turn around to face him as he answered. "That is a gift that I now have. I have only to... touch... these tomes, and I gain the understanding from within their pages."

Tan stood and stopped behind Honl. Had he simply *read* the book that he'd pulled off the shelf? Having that kind of ability would be valuable, especially as he searched for answers.

"How can you do that?" Tan asked.

Honl twisted to face him. "How can I do any of this, Maelen? How can I speak to you, or take on this form, or simply *know* as I touch these texts? These are questions I have not found answers to."

"What answers have you found?"

Honl swept his hands around him, and the wispy form of his arm swirled through the books on the shelf, passing through them. Honl cocked his head to the side at a strange angle, giving him an unnatural appearance, and then he blinked his eyes and breathed out softly.

"Nearly as many answers as I have questions, but new questions arise."

"Can you tell me about Par-shon?" Tan asked.

Honl's features shifted, flowing into something resembling a puzzled expression. "Par-shon? Nothing of Par-shon, but Par... From what I can tell, that is a place much like this."

Tan's heart skipped a beat. What might Honl have learned? If he did have the ability to touch a book and know the contents, it was possible that he knew everything contained in the archives. Having access to that knowledge, to all of that understanding, would be incredibly valuable.

More than that, could he draw on that knowledge using the connection between them?

Tan reached through their bonded connection. The connection had shifted and changed in the time since the bond first formed. Now it was augmented in a certain way but shaded as well. Tan couldn't simply access Honl, as much as he might like to be able to.

"I don't understand," he said.

Honl swept his arm through another shelf. "This place, this archive, is built on a site of much power." Honl turned to him with his head angled strangely. "You have recognized that, Maelen."

"This is a place of convergence."

"Gatherings," Honl agreed. "Places where the Mother can be felt, if only you know to listen. In some ways, this archive was created to mask this Gathering."

Tan studied the walls, thinking about what he knew about places of convergence. When he'd first discovered the lower level of the archives, he had realized that this was such a place, much like the one in the mountains. The elementals drawn here made this place powerful and made his abilities more potent. He could pull on the strength of the elementals and could use that strength—especially when combined with his ability to speak to the elementals—to create amazing shapings.

The ancient shapers might have been the same. That would be the reason for shielding these places, he suspected, unless they had a different goal. Maybe they had created the archive here to better *trap* the elementals.

Couldn't the ancients have used these gatherings, these places of convergence, to harness the elementals drawn here?

Tan knew that they could.

What of a place like Par-shon, where they similarly trapped the elementals?

"Are you saying that Par-shon is a Gathering as well?" he asked.

Honl leaned forward and swept his arm through another shelf of books. He sighed softly as he did, and he blinked. Could he process all of the books that he touched? Was he able to organize everything that he learned—and actually be able to use it?

"There is... or was... a Gathering there," Honl began. "I think that is how that one became as powerful as he did. Without the connection to the elementals, he would not have been able to force the bonds."

Tan glanced at the books arranged on the shelves and wondered if he would find a similar type of archive in Par-shon, or was there nothing like this?

"Are you certain?" he asked.

How would he not have known? At the place of convergence within the mountains, he had sense of the distinction and the way the elementals were drawn to the land. Here in Ethea, he had noted the power of the elementals, but in Par-shon, not only had he not spent much time there, but the elementals had been bonded, forced away from the convergence. If it *was* a gathering, that would be the reason that he hadn't detected the strength of the place.

Honl turned and cast his gaze around the lower level of the archives. "Synthesizing everything that I learn is difficult," Honl said, "but that much is clear."

"What do you mean by masking the Gathering?" Tan asked.

"This place." Honl floated around the room. The heels of his boots seemed to drag across the ground, but they did so soundlessly. "This building is meant to shield the Gathering, much like the tower in Par-shon is meant to shield it."

"Why would it need to be shielded?"

Honl stopped moving and turned back to Tan. "There is something that I discovered while I was gone, and it's the reason that I returned to you, Maelen. I don't know when, but you will be needed again."

"What did you discover?" Tan's thoughts went to others with the ability to bind elementals, and he worried that perhaps Honl had found someone else like the Utu Tonah. He wasn't sure that he was ready to face that again. It had taken a unified effort to stop him, and he saw nothing that made him think that he could convince Roine or the other rulers to come together again. Not without a clear threat.

"There was a darkness before," Honl said. "And then there was light."

"You're not making any sense."

Honl's eyes narrowed. "No more than I can, Maelen. Defeating the darkness required great strength and power, and ultimately, it was not defeated."

"Do you mean shapers like Par-shon?"

Honl shook his head. "Not like Par-shon. Nothing so mundane as that."

"Mundane? The Utu Tonah was a threat to the elementals, not only to these lands."

"And had he succeeded, had the Utu Tonah grasped the power he sought, what do you think he would have accomplished?"

Tan didn't know. Perhaps nothing more than acquiring the elemental power of the land, but he would have destroyed the essence as he did. Tan had witnessed that change, and it made what had happened in Incendin appear small in comparison.

"What is this darkness?"

Honl appeared to take a deep breath. "I do not know."

"Then how was it defeated?"

"As I said, it was *not* defeated. Stopping the darkness required great effort, but even that was not enough. A way to contain it was devised, an item of such power that even the darkness could not escape."

"You mean the artifact. Is that what it was for?"

"Elemental energy was required, but so too was shaped energy. Both man and elemental, coming together to contain a darkness that separately they could not defeat. Even together, they could not defeat the darkness, only slow its spread."

Tan glanced at the shelf bearing the felt-lined box. Inside was the artifact, damaged by Tan's attempt to use it and now nothing more than a broken bar of metal. "Honl?"

"I am sorry, Tan."

"But it's damaged now—"

Honl floated to a stop in front of him. A chill worked up Tan's spine at Honl's next words. "And worse. I suspect that the darkness has been freed."

## 7

# PAR

"What does he mean that darkness was freed?" Amia asked.

They were back in Par-shon. Not only did the air feel different, almost a tingling sort of energy that slid across Tan's skin that mixed with the distant hint of sea salt, but the energy of the land changed. Was it only because he had been back in the archives that he sensed it as he did, or was there another reason?

They made their way through the tower, stopping in each of the rooms along the halls, searching for something like the kingdom's archives. He could ask Tolman but hadn't found him, either.

A few servants scurried past but fewer than he would have expected in the palace within Ethea. Those he did see hurried onward when they saw him, bowing briefly before moving on.

"I don't think Honl even knows," he answered. The wind

elemental had disappeared again, shortly after their talk, claiming a desire to search for answers. Where would he go that he would find better answers than he had access to in the archives?

Tan had refrained sharing with Amia until they returned to Par-shon, not wanting to worry her, but he suspected that she knew anyway. The shared bond gave her access to much of his fears and worries, a loss of privacy that Tan didn't mind. It was much like he once had with Asboel.

"We don't know if there *is* anything to worry about," Amia said. "You've said that the artifact was designed to draw power, not trap it."

Tan pushed open a door. Nothing but a supply closet. "I don't know what the artifact was for. There was power to it, but what if that power was for a different reason than we knew? I always assumed it was because the ancient shapers had created it to access even more shaping power, but..." It was possible that it could have been designed as a way to contain something else.

Tan thought of all the steps that had gone into securing the artifact. Not only had it been created by shapers with such strength and skill to be able to pull elementals into its making, but it also had been secured in a place of convergence, protected by the elementals.

What if his assumptions had been wrong? What if the elementals at the place of convergence had protected and secured the artifact for a different reason, one in which they were needed to ensure containment of the darkness?

"Tan," Amia said, setting her hand on his arm. "You've

been distracted since speaking to Honl. I know that you worry about what he said, but he doesn't know, does he?"

"He can read with a touch," he said. "He absorbs the information in that way."

"Tan—"

He sighed. What Honl said troubled him, but for reasons more than simply the fact that he might have released an ancient darkness into the world, a darkness that had been trapped by ancient shapers with power that rivaled his. "All I want is peace," he said softly.

"And we'll have it," she said.

"What if he's right? What if this is something bigger than even the Utu Tonah?" He lowered his voice as he looked around the empty halls of the Par-shon tower, but he still didn't see anyone else around. "Coming here is hard enough. These people do not *want* me here."

"No more than they wanted the previous Utu Tonah," she said.

"But he was *from* here."

Amia frowned. "That's just it... I don't think he was. When we were here before, I spoke with others, and those willing to share mentioned how he came to Par-shon and changed the way they were ruled. Before the Utu Tonah, there had been—"

A massive shaping exploded down the hall, cutting her off.

Tan grabbed her hand and pulled her down the hall, in the direction of the explosion. Leaving her here might be safer, but he didn't want to risk separating from Amia, not while in Par-shon with people that he didn't trust.

They rounded a corner in the hall and found a young boy standing there, his eyes wide and his hand on the wall. Tan had seen him with the other children in the garden outside the tower when he first spoke to them about learning to shape.

"What happened?" Tan demanded.

The boy spun to face him, his eyes growing even wider, practically swallowing his face. "Utu Tonah. I... I don't know."

"Who was shaping?" Tan asked.

He saw no one else in the hall. The wall across from the boy had a large chunk missing. Tan detected shaped energy from it but saw nothing that would explain what happened.

"Utu Tonah?" the boy said.

"Tan," Amia whispered.

He turned to her and saw her watching the boy.

"I think *he* shaped."

"But the power that I sensed..."

Tan made his way around the boy and reached toward him with a shaping of spirit. As he layered spirit onto the boy, he detected the residual shaping that matched what he sensed on the wall. This had been the boy who shaped, but he'd done so with so much power that Tan hardly could believe it.

*He's young,* he sent to Amia.

*Often the youngest are the most powerful shapers.*

*I didn't learn to shape until after we met.*

*As I said, often.*

"What is your name?" Tan asked, softening his tone. He didn't want to scare the boy. He'd done nothing other than lose control of a shaping. He would need to work with him, to teach him, but wouldn't be able to do that if he terrified him.

"Mathias, my Utu Tonah. My friends call me Mat."

Tan smiled, remembering what it had been like to be Mat's age. Tan hadn't known anything about shaping when he was that young and barely knew how to sense. His father had taught him many of his earliest lessons, but would Mat's father do the same for him?

"Where is your family?" he asked.

Mat shook his head.

"Your mother. Father."

"They are gone, my Utu Tonah."

Tan inhaled quickly. "How are they gone?" A part of him didn't want to know the answer, but he needed to hear it.

"They served the Utu Tonah before you, Utu Tonah. They went with him…"

Tan nodded. Mat's parents would have crossed the sea and been part of the attack. Many had returned, all without bonds, as Tan had made a point of separating those bonds, but not all had made it back. Many had fallen, not only because of Tan, but the hounds or other elementals that had attacked on Tan's behalf. Even other shapers, or the lisincend, could have been responsible for the loss of Mat's parents. But Tan felt responsible. *He* had led the attack.

"I'm sorry, Mat."

Mat swallowed and tried to hide the redness in his eyes as he wiped his sleeve across his eyes. "My Utu Tonah?"

"You shaped earth here, didn't you?" Tan asked gently.

"I… I didn't mean to. There was something in front of me, like a buzzing in my head, and I tried swatting it. When it went away, *that* happened." He pointed to the chunk out of the wall, his eyes still wide.

"Have you ever shaped on your own before?" Tan asked.

Mat bit his lip and glanced to Amia before answering. "Not on my own, Utu Tonah."

Tan nodded. "Bonded?"

He looked at Tan, and then his gaze shifted to Amia. Tan felt her shaping and wondered what she did to the boy.

"I had a bond," Mat answered.

Tan took a deep breath and studied the boy. "What do you remember about your bond?"

He smiled, and his eyes took on a distant expression. "Noln," he whispered.

Tan repeated the elemental name in his head. The word triggered a memory, but not one of his.

*An ancient elemental of earth,* Asgar sent.

The draasin remained on the roof of the tower, sitting and waiting for Tan's return. He had spent Tan's absence observing but hadn't seen anything that would help Tan understand why Par-shon might be a place of convergence. Asgar couldn't even tell that the tower shielded anything, but he seemed to think that might be more about the fact that the elementals of this land had been bonded, forced away from the place of convergence. Too much had been lost, and there were questions.

Would Honl have answers?

Maybe if Tan could convince the wind elemental to join him. It was no longer about asking him to accompany him, it was more about waiting for Honl to be ready. Wherever his studies took him carried him far from the kingdoms, away from even Par-shon. Tan wished that Honl would share where he went, and he promised to do so eventually, but for now, he had to act without the assistance of his wind elemental.

*The warning is enough, Maelen.*

The thought came distantly from Honl, carried on a drifting of wind, barely more than a breath. Had Tan not been focused on the connection to Asgar and trying to connect to the elementals, he might not have heard him. As it was, it came through as little more than a whisper.

*What do you know of Noln?* he asked Asgar.

*I know little of the ancients. The eldest would have known more.*

It was another reason for Tan to miss the connection to Asboel.

"How long were you connected to Noln?" Tan asked, pulling his attention back to Mat.

"Only a few years."

"Years?" The boy looked barely more than eight. For him to have bonded to the elemental for years meant that he would have been five or six when the bond was placed. "How were you bonded for years?"

Footsteps down the hall caused him to look up. Tolman

strode quickly, but when he saw Tan, his steps faltered, and he lowered his eyes. "Mathias, you do not need to be bothering the Utu Tonah. Run along and return to your session."

Mathias glanced to Tan and then Tolman before nodding and hurrying along the hall. Before disappearing around the corner, he paused and glanced back at Tan for a moment, and then hurried onward.

"I am sorry, my Utu Tonah, that you should be bothered by that one. He can be impertinent."

"Not bothered, Tolman." Tan touched a hand to the stone where Mat had shaped it, feeling the surge of power that had gone through it. "Did you know that he can shape?"

Tolman sighed and turned his attention to the wall. Tan couldn't remember which bonds Tolman had possessed prior to the defeat of the Utu Tonah, but the man still possessed some ability with earth. Maybe that was why Mat had demonstrated earth shaping so easily.

"I know that he has potential, my Utu Tonah, as do all the students you asked me to bring to you."

"This is more than potential, don't you think?"

Tolman turned his attention to the wall. "There is potential here, but potential surges at times. He may become a skilled shaper, but he will need guidance."

"That is why the elementals were bonded to him while he was young? He tells me of an elemental, Noln."

Tolman bowed his head, his eyes still fixed on the floor. "Those with innate abilities are often the hardest to foster. We have learned that they can be guided by the bond."

"But a forced bond."

"It was not always—" Tolman cut himself off and lowered his eyes again. "Pardon me, Utu Tonah. I should not speak so freely with you."

Tan glanced over at Amia. There was something that he missed here, but he didn't have the experience to understand what it was. This was about more than what the previous Utu Tonah had done.

*Honl, I could use your counsel.*

He waited, but there was no answer from the wind elemental.

Tan sighed. Anything that he did would have to come from him. "Tell me how you trained shapers," Tan began. He needed to try a different approach.

"As I have said, my Utu Tonah, we have placed a bond to have the elementals guide the shaper. There is much strength in that relationship. And the Utu Tonah valued the strength of those shapers most of all."

Always it came back to the Utu Tonah and how he had used the bonds, but Amia had suggested that the Utu Tonah had not always ruled in Par-shon, which meant that things must have been different at some point.

"What was it like before the Utu Tonah ruled?" Tan asked.

Tolman risked peaking at him before quickly glancing back to the ground. "The Utu Tonah rules in Par-shon. There is no before."

Tan sighed. "Who ruled Par-shon before the Utu Tonah?"

Tolman tensed. From the way he leaned forward, it seemed as if he *wanted* to say something but decided against it.

*I think there was no Par-shon before the Utu Tonah,* Amia said.

*What was there, then?*

*I don't know.*

Tan looked around, his gaze catching on the now-destroyed tiles that had contained the runes that prevented his shaping. They were similar to runes used in the kingdoms and the runes used on the warrior swords, but they were not the same. There were subtle differences to them, changes that prevented a shaper from using their ability rather than augmenting it.

He stopped at the nearest plate and ran his fingers over it. Like so many in the tower here, the plate had cracked, the effect of Tan's shaping destroying it. Beneath it, though, there was something else.

Tan pried the tile off the wall. Doing so required a combination of earth and fire, mixing the shaping to pull it free.

Tan sucked in a surprised breath.

Another mark was underneath the tile he'd removed, but this was different, more like those he'd seen in parts of the city. He traced his hand along the mark and felt a surge of earth power flood into him. He jerked his hand back.

"What was this place before the Utu Tonah appeared?" he asked, not turning to Tolman. He traced his fingers over the shape, trying to understand and piece together what he knew. Par-shon was a place of convergence. The tower somehow shielded it. And the Utu Tonah had used the elementals to force them to bond.

They had to be connected, didn't they?

"Tolman?" he asked, turning to face the man.

Tolman stared at the ground as if trying to burn a hole through it with his eyes. "We are Par-shon, Utu Tonah. You have the right to rule."

"Please, Tolman," he began, softening his tone. "What was it like before the Utu Tonah I have replaced?"

Whatever it was had a different relationship with the elementals. It might explain the peoples' anger from the way he'd forced the bonds to separate. Wouldn't he feel the same if Par-shon had separated his bonds? Hadn't he felt the same sort of anger when they had placed him in the room where they nearly had?

"There was no Par-shon before the Utu Tonah," Tolman said softly.

"What was there? This place is older than him. I can see the effect of what he did, the way that he placed his touch on the tower, but it wasn't always like that, was it?"

Tolman swallowed and finally looked up and met Tan's eyes. "No. Before the Utu Tonah arrived, there was only Par."

Tan looked at Amia, whose eyes went distant. He could sense the way she reached across the seas, trying to connect to the other Aeta Mothers, but couldn't hear the conversation.

"What do you mean there was only Par?" Tan asked.

Tolman stared at Tan for a moment. "Before Par-shon, and before the Utu Tonah—the first Utu Tonah—came to us, there was only Par."

"Tell me about Par."

Tolman paled, becoming whiter than Tan had ever seen him. "My Utu Tonah," he began, "I don't think that it is my place—"

"Your Utu Tonah asked you about what it was like before he ruled," Amia said. "You would do well to answer him."

Tolman looked at her, his eyes wide and in some ways reminding Tan of the way that Mat had looked at him. "Utu Tonah?"

"Tell me about Par," Tan repeated.

Tolman glanced down the hall, almost as if he thought that he could escape from Tan, as if he intended to run off, but there was nothing there, no support that he could gain by reaching for the children or perhaps the other shapers in the tower. Tolman was left to face Tan and Amia himself.

"Par was different," he began, his voice halting as he started. "A place where we used the elementals in a different way than the Utu Tonah would have us use them."

"Different even than I would ask of Par-shon?" Tan asked.

Tolman nodded. "There was a time when few of us understood that the elementals of our land were able to bond. It was a time when the elementals were a part of our life, and our culture, but not the same way that the Utu Tonah had used them."

"And what of the way that I would have you use the elementals?" Tan asked.

"My Utu Tonah," Tolman began, his voice catching as he did. "There are many of us who don't know what you intend from the elementals. We have seen the Utu Tonah, and how he forced us to use the elementals. We expected much of the same from you."

Tan looked over at Amia, but she studied Tolman without saying anything.

"Where did the Utu Tonah come from?" he asked.

Without the connection to Par, and this place, the Utu Tonah must have known about the place of convergences and what that meant for the elementals. Tan had always thought that the Utu Tonah had come from Par-shon and that his beliefs, and the desire to bind and essentially harness the elementals, had come from the same place, but what if he had been wrong? What if the Utu Tonah had not been from Par-shon, and what if he had come to Par, chasing after the power and strength of the elementals, using the place of convergence to bind to the elementals?

What would that have made the Utu Tonah?

For that matter, what did that now make Tan?

Tolman sighed and looked from Tan to Amia. "You don't know, do you Utu Tonah?"

Tan shook his head.

Tolman frowned. "The Utu Tonah came to Par with the ability to bind to the elementals. He claimed a right to rule, one that he said that we should share. At first, few understood what he intended. He claimed a desire to study, to understand the elementals as we knew them within Par, but it became clear that he didn't want to know the elementals the same way that we knew them. He wished to subjugate them. That wasn't the experience that we had with those ancient powers."

"What experience did you have with the ancient powers?" Tan asked.

He had assumed that Par-shon had shared much of the same perspective regarding the elementals as the Utu Tonah, but what if that wasn't the case? Then he would need to find who he could work with.

"We are of Par," Tolman said. "And Par has long recognized the power of the ancients."

"What of the fact that the Utu Tonah required you to bond?" Amia asked.

"Not all wished for that bond. Most wished for nothing more than the ability to refuse what the Utu Tonah requested of us."

"And the children?" Amia asked.

Tan wasn't sure what she was getting at, but there was something about the children, and the fact that they could shape, that bothered her. That much he could sense from her. But what it was, he still didn't know. It was more than about the way that the elementals were treated, and more than about the way that the children were asked to work against the kingdoms, forcing them to forge a bond that might not have been the right one for them.

"There were those of us who tried to protect the children," Tolman said.

Amia nodded. "That's why you wanted to keep them from Tan."

Tolman considered Tan, taking a deep breath before nodding. "The Utu Tonah is different than the one who came before him, but how different remains to be seen. There are some who think that he might wish to force the same bonds as his predecessor, though we haven't seen any sign of that."

"What of those who have the ability to shape?" Amia asked.

Tolman frowned. "There are several with a different ability than those who were bonded. The previous Utu Tonah recognized them and thought that they would be valuable, but didn't tell us why."

"I don't intent to treat them the way that the prior Utu Tonah treated them," Tan said. "They will learn, but they will not be forced. As I have said, forcing the bond is anathema to what the Mother has asked of shapers."

Tolman's eyes flicked to the portion of the wall destroyed by Mat's shaping. "What of him?" he asked carefully.

"You will work with him," Tan said. "Teach him what you can. And when you cannot teach him any longer, then you will send him to me." There might not be anything that Tan could teach, but he would do what he could. The kingdoms would pose too much of a threat to the Par-shon shapers and would make those of this land feel as if they couldn't do what needed to be done. Tan wouldn't make that any worse than it needed to be.

Tolman's gaze drifted past Tan and made it to the panel on the wall where Tan had revealed the connection to the elemental. "And you, Utu Tonah? What will you do now that you know what we were before?"

Tan sighed and wished that he had the answer, but unfortunately, he didn't.

## 8

## REACHING THE COUNCIL

T he tower was much larger than Tan had expected. He had spent the past week searching through the tower for a place of learning that he would equate to what was in the kingdoms, but he found nothing. Each day, he searched, and each day, he ran into the same dilemma. There were servants willing to help, and others within the palace who were willing to assist him, but none knew of an archive much like the one that he could access in the kingdoms. After the last few days, he began to wonder if maybe there wasn't anything that would be the same.

Yet, his connection to Honl told him that there had to be something more than he knew. There had to be some sort of place of understanding, but it was one that he didn't fully grasp. That was the reason that Tan still searched.

Amia spent her days trying to understand the children. She had offered to teach and used the opportunity to demon- strate a different type of focus than the children would otherwise have been exposed to. The Aeta had another way of focusing on the connection to shaping, one that was different even than the kingdoms, and Tan appreciated the fact that Amia had been willing to demonstrate that with the children. There was much they could learn from her. She claimed that they *were* learning, though Tan had not taken the time to meet with them again.

His time was focused on trying to understand what he might be missing.

From what he could tell, he had to be overlooking something. The covered panels throughout the tower pointed to a connection to the elementals that was different than the one that the Utu Tonah had possessed, but each time he attempted to connect to the elementals so that he could understand what purpose they served here in the palace, he failed to reach anything more than the sense of power that surged through them.

Today was no different. Tan had been back in Par-shon for the last week, and each day he spent trying to study the connection to the elementals that he detected in the hidden panels. Whatever the Utu Tonah had done to hide or shield the connection, there was much more to it that Par-shon possessed, almost a connection as deep as that which the kingdoms possessed. If only he could understand.

The elementals were no help to him. Tan tried reaching out to them, but they had few answers when they did respond to his summons. There was the faint and distant sense of saa, and the faded sense of the earth elemental that flowed through the tower—likely noln, from what he had learned from the boy—but he didn't have the same connection to the elementals who were strongest here. A part of Tan considered simply returning to the kingdoms, but that wouldn't help him understand what took place here in Par-shon any better than what he currently knew. Besides that, it was a source of pride to Tan that he was the only person who could understand the elementals, and returning to the kingdoms, basically running away from the challenge, made him feel as if he had failed.

So instead, he searched.

Tan hated that he did it alone. He should have Amia with him, or one of the elementals, but Asgar watched from above the tower and Honl was someplace distant and far removed. The nymid had rarely bothered to remain involved. And Kota? Tan tried not to abuse his relationship with her any more than he needed to, even if she and the rest of the hounds had no problem with it.

When he opened the next door, he let out a long sigh. He had tried finding something, anything, that would help him understand not only the connection that Par-shon once had with the elementals but also the existing connections.

What he needed was to find the Mistress of Bonds, but she wanted nothing to do with him. She might answer his questions, but she had no interest in actually helping. Elanne had made that clear the last time that he had seen her. Tan wished that he could ask the Mistress of Souls, but Marin was much like Elanne.

Tan recognized that it was his fault neither of them wished to work with him. He didn't understand the connection that Par-shon had with the elementals, but had he taken the time to question, to try and understand, he might have had less of an issue, but he had come to Par-shon thinking that he had all the answers. Hadn't that been the same way that he had approached Incendin? And just like in Incendin, Tan didn't know what he was doing.

What he wouldn't give for the elementals to help, but there had been no assistance from them, either. Saa had given the advice that it could, which had guided him back to the fact that he knew nothing about Par-shon.

He needed to know where the previous Utu Tonah had come from. If he could trace him back to his own lands, it was possible that Tan could understand the expectations

Tan turned his attention to the Utu Tonah's home. Everything about the building was ornate. From the incredibly detailed artwork that adorned the path leading to the home to the trim around the doors. The Utu Tonah had appreciated the fancier side of things.

Tan didn't care for that nearly as much. He hadn't done anything to remove it, but he didn't need the decorative trim or the heavy carving like the prior Utu Tonah had. The rooms were all equally ornate, though Tan found one, a smaller room that had nothing more than a desk and a few strange books, that he thought might be from the Utu Tonah prior to the one Tan had unseated

Tan took a seat behind the desk and pulled the books in front of him. He had a distinct sense of the fact that the previous Utu Tonah had once sat here and had once had these same books in front of him. The man might have been

many things, but Tan hadn't had the sense that he was ignorant. Rather, he suspected that he was intelligent and driven
by power and the might of his office.

He flipped through the pages. All were written in *Ishthin*,
but in a longhand and difficult-to-read form. He wished for a
moment that he had Honl's ability to simply absorb the
knowledge from the books placed in front of him. Had he
been able to, he wouldn't need to try to struggle through
these books.

As he began to puzzle through the pages, he realized
something: these were written by the prior Utu Tonah. This
wasn't some book that he had used for research; this was a
journal of sorts, a record.

Tan slowed as he began to puzzle through the pages. Not
only a record but a comment about the bonds that he had
taken. The first pages were more descriptive, detailing the
effects of adding the bonds and the way that he suddenly had
access to more shaping strength as he forced them. The
descriptions were written in a clinical way, with such a
distance to them and no regard for the elementals.

Had Tan not known what kind of person the Utu Tonah
was before, he did now.

Still, there was something compelling about reading these
pages. Not insight into the mind of the man, but Tan gathered
a sense of purpose, though he didn't understand *what*
purpose the Utu Tonah would have in forcing as many bonds
as he had.

Tan glanced up for a moment. The book should probably be destroyed. He didn't want others to see the way the

Utu Tonah described absorbing even more power. What would happen if another saw this and chose to attempt the same?

He sighed. He needed to understand the Utu Tonah. Needed to know if there *had* been a reason for what he did. Maybe there would be something within these pages that would explain why he had come to Par-shon.

———

Tan's vision had blurred from staring at the pages of *Ishthin* for the last few hours. He had discovered nothing new while reading through it, at least nothing that might help him understand the former Utu Tonah.

The farther he read in the journal, the clearer it became that the Utu Tonah had started down the path of bonding with a purpose. Tan still didn't understand *what* that purpose had been, and now doubted that the answer would be found in these pages, but the purpose that had driven him to begin with changed over time and became about gathering power. That much was clear.

Toward the end of the journal was the most recent section that the Utu Tonah had written. There he spoke of obtaining the draasin bond and claimed it would bring him into something he called Unity. There were a few references to this state, but nothing with enough clarity for Tan to understand what he hoped to gain, other than power.

He made his way to the room he shared with Amia and found her sitting by the hearth. She looked up and smiled as he entered, though it was a troubled smile and the corners of her eyes held the edge of a frown.

"I didn't want to distract you," she said.

Tan took a seat next to her and stared at the fire. As usual, saa flickered within the flames. Through the fire bond, he could almost hear the connection, but saa chose not to speak to him. "I'm not certain what I'm supposed to be doing here," he admitted. "I came to try to enforce a rule that I'm not sure the people of Par-shon need."

Amia folded her hands in her lap. "They need guidance, Tan. That's why you returned."

"But what kind of guidance? They weren't always ruled by the Utu Tonah. This place," he said, sweeping his hand around him, "was built for an invader." He held out the journal that he'd discovered, and Amia took it with a frown. "I couldn't find any sort of archive like we have in the kingdoms, but I found this."

"What is it?"

"A record written by him." Tan sighed. "He didn't begin his journey the same way he ended it. It wasn't always about power for him. Not from the start, at least."

"You saw what he became."

"That's what he became, but I don't know what he was before then." He tapped the book. "Look at his earliest entries. He speaks of the bonds in a way that is calculating, but not with animosity. He sought the power of the elementals for a reason, but one that wasn't clearly about power."

That had been the most troubling for Tan. If the Utu Tonah had not simply sought power, what else could there have been? Did it have anything to do with the darkness that Honl described?

He wished Honl would have remained behind rather than venturing off to... wherever he went. Far enough that the connection was faded and Tan had to strain to even sense him. Had Honl remained, he might have been of assistance.

Maybe Honl could even help him understand the dynamics within Par-shon. Tan struggled there almost more than anything else.

"Why are you doing this?" Amia asked him. "What's with your desire to understand the Utu Tonah?"

When Tan turned to her, she gave his hands a reassuring squeeze. There was a strength to her that he didn't possess. It was only part of the reason he cared so much for her.

"I made a mistake with Incendin once," Tan started carefully. Amia might agree with him most of the time, but she had distinct feelings about the lisincend after what they had done to her family. He understood how she felt, and struggled with it at times as well, but had he only understood the reason that the lisincend attacked, how much would have been different?

Was it the same with the Utu Tonah?

Tan wondered if he should have taken the time to understand him better, to learn why he abused the elementals as he did. If he had, maybe they could have avoided the attack.

"Sometimes there is darkness for no reason," Amia said softly. "I know that you want to explain *why*, but there might not be a why. The world is full of people who don't think as you do, Tan. Most struggle to even consider the needs of the elementals, even to realize that they exist, yet you not only understand that they live among us, you speak to them and try to understand them. What you do is powerful, and it's why you are so well equipped to lead."

He sighed. "I don't know that I'm equipped for anything. I don't understand the people of Par-shon, I don't know how to forge trust, both for them with me, and for me to be able to trust them. Without that, I don't think there's anything I can do."

She patted his hand. "There are ways to rule until you create that trust."

"Not that will have a lasting benefit," Tan said. "I don't *want* to be Utu Tonah. And until I can be comfortable that whoever takes my place will rule in a way that doesn't abuse the elementals here…"

He trailed off. It wasn't only Par-shon that he had to worry about, was it? Within the kingdoms, he had fought against something similar, and there he had done it without authority. He might have been named Athan, but that meant nothing compared to the level of authority he possessed with his current title.

How had he managed to sway the people of the kingdoms?

It hadn't been about convincing each individual person. Rather, he had worked with Roine and his mother, Cianna, and Ferran. Shapers who had taken the lessons of the elementals and begun to understand them. All had started with the conversation with the elementals.

Could the same be said here? Was that the mission that he would have to achieve?

The council wanted nothing to do with him. They wanted him gone from Par-shon and hated the fact that he would change things. But maybe he had approached it in the wrong way.

"You're not the only one given power and authority you don't want," Amia said.

Tan held her hand and turned back to the fire, thinking through what he could do.

He might want to understand what had motivated the Utu Tonah, but that was in the past. The present was a new challenge and one where shaping would not solve the problem. Shaping might actually have caused *more* problems for him.

Settling back in his chair, he began to think through how he could reach those on the council. What he intended might be difficult, but he had an advantage and the only one where shaping might help. With spirit, he could understand the moods and the attitudes of those he tried to reach. Tan wouldn't force spirit on them; doing so felt too much like what Althem had done. But he *could* use it to help him understand the differences, and wasn't *that* the lesson he had taken from Incendin?

Only, he didn't know how he would get through to certain people. There were enough of the Par-shon leaders that he struggled to understand, but Elanne in particular worried him. How would he get through to her, when her entire role was to encourage the forced bonds?

## 9

## KOTA'S HUNT

The air had a bitter hot scent to it, one that once would have put Tan on edge, a scent that reminded him of Incendin and the heat and dangers found in those lands, dangers he no longer felt the same about. Now, the scent only helped him realize that he needed to search more closely.

"You don't sense anything, do you?" Amia asked.

She leaned back against a tree, watching him with amusement, her deep blue eyes catching the light of the sun almost as much as the wide circle of gold around her neck. She crossed her arms over her chest, covering the brightly striped jacket she wore, the only other sign of her Aeta heritage.

Tan tried using earth and spirit but came up empty.

"You still haven't answered," Amia said.

Tan rubbed his hands together in frustration. "Because I *can't*. There's something here. I know there is. But I can't pick up on what it might be."

*Perhaps I was wrong about you.*

Tan looked over to see Kota, the massive earth and fire elemental, come bounding to a stop. Asgar had brought her to Par-shon to help with the *other* reason that he'd come to Par-shon. He needed to understand what other elementals the Utu Tonah had created. When he'd discovered the journal, Tan had hoped that he would find answers, but there was nothing about the elementals.

What if that hadn't been the Utu Tonah's domain?

But there wasn't any sign of someone who was Master of Elementals that Tan had discovered unless he had missed something. It was possible that he had; that was part of the reason that he remained, needing to learn if Par-shon would repeat the same behaviors now that the Utu Tonah was gone, or if they would attempt something else.

Yet, seeing Kota, he realized that not *all* crossings had the same negative outcome. Once, he had called her kind hounds, but that label didn't fit. They were creatures created by the ancient shapers for reasons Tan still hadn't discovered, but twisted by the creation, much like the great serpent of fire, kaas.

Using the fire bond, Tan had realigned the hounds with fire, and they had changed. Most had grown larger as if the twisted connection to fire had stunted them. But more than size, the keen intellect had changed. Kota might be the best example, but she was not the only one.

*You are too insensitive,* she went on.

Amia laughed. Tan shot her a look, but she only shrugged. She could often hear the elemental as well as him. It wasn't the same with each of the elementals, though she could hear Asgar when he allowed it. But Kota she always heard clearly.

*What have you found?*

Kota pointed with her nose. *To the south. If you were any real hunter, you wouldn't need for me to guide you.*

Tan touched his sword. *I can show you a hunter.*

*I have witnessed you with that weapon. I think I am still safe.*

Amia laughed again, and this time, Tan could only shake his head. Even with the resistance that they'd faced so far in Par-shon, it was good to have her at peace, especially as being here delayed the celebration they both wanted.

More than Amia, Kota had changed. Since the Par-shon defeat, his bonded had become more self-assured. Considering how long the hounds had been twisted by fire, and the effort that it had required of Tan to pull them from that, he was pleased that they would be able to know anything other than suffering. Now, were he to let her, Kota would be his constant companion, closer to him in some ways than Asboel ever had been, though the draasin had always been merely a thought away.

"Do you sense anything now?" Amia asked.

Tan shifted his focus to the south, stretching with awareness of each of the elements, adding spirit as well. Spirit wasn't necessary but usually felt right, and this time was no different.

But he still sensed nothing.

*Are you certain?*

Kota turned deep black eyes on him. *You should have learned that you do not need to question me.*

Tan approached Kota and ran a hand along her rough fur. *Take me there?*

*Like the draasin says, I am no horse.*

With that, Kota bounded off, leaving Tan with Amia, suppressing his laughter.

"What would you have done had she allowed you to ride?" Amia asked.

"I think I might fall over from shock," he said and pulled her against him as if he needed her strength to keep from pitching onto the ground. Instead, he pulled them into the air until they drifted on a shaping of wind mixed with fire.

Tan tracked Kota as she raced across the countryside. The land had changed since he had defeated the former Utu Tonah. Life had returned to places where it had been lost, much like life had begun to return in Chenir after Par-shon had been defeated and the shapers of Chenir were allowed to return, drawing the elementals with them.

When he reached Kota, he found her sitting, staring at the horizon. Her body was completely still, but he recognized the tension within her.

Much as he once had been able to do with Asboel, Tan reached through the bond and watched through her sight. Something was out there that had her attention.

*Do you see it, Maelen?*

*Not on my own.*

Her ears flicked, the only part of her that moved. *In the distance. Earth and wind. I cannot tell more than that.*

He knew of no elemental that was a combination of earth and wind. But now that Tan knew what he was looking for, he had a better chance of seeing what Kota saw. Other than Honl, none of the wind elementals had any form. Even before Tan had rescued Honl from kaas, the elementals had nothing more than a translucency to him. Tan had been able to make out some of his shape, but nothing like it was now.

Earth, on the other hand, was different. Kota and the hounds were elemental crossings, but of earth and fire. In that way, they were much like kaas, only kaas was predominantly of fire while the hounds were predominantly of earth.

Tan listened for earth, using his connection to Kota and strained to detect the elemental that she saw. There was *something*, but it was a faint sense and one that he couldn't reliably detect.

What of wind?

Tan sensed the wind and drew through his connection to the wind elementals. Not only Honl, but the elemental wyln of these lands. He detected a fluttering of movement, but nothing more.

Could he use a combined sensing to detect the elemental?

Tan used wind and earth, sensing for it. Knowing that it was out there, knowing that there was *something* that he should be able to detect, made it easier, but the connection was still much more tenuous than what he possessed with any of the other elementals.

And then, like a rough whisper across his mind, he detected it.

It was raw, nothing like the refined connection that he possessed with ashi or the other elementals of wind, and nothing even like the connection that he managed with golud, or the other earth elementals. There was a sense that this elemental was young, almost infantile, which, as he considered, it might be. When he'd held the power of the combined shaping, he had the ability to repair all of the damaged elementals formed by the Utu Tonah. There were many, and Tan had made a point of trying to find those that he could, but this had been the first one they managed to track.

He debated whether to reach out to the elemental before deciding against it. The potential to actually cause harm to it was too great. Better to leave the elemental as it was than force something before the creature was ready.

Instead, Tan used a shaping of spirit, pulling through Amia and letting her guide him so that he could send a reassuring sense to the elemental.

There came a flurry of movement, and a winged creature took to the air and streaked toward the south.

Using Kota's sight, Tan noted how small and compact the creature was, but there was strength to it. Mostly wind, but the connection to earth was there as well.

"What happened?" Amia asked. She took a deep breath, as if willing to move now that the elemental had been scared off.

"An elemental of wind and earth, one of the crossings."

"Did you speak to it?"

Tan shook his head. "Not this one. It was too young to connect to. There was something wrong with attempting to force a connection, especially knowing how they were created. It was enough to know that it isn't twisted as some of the others were." Had the elemental remained twisted, or if it even had been, Tan wouldn't have been able to heal it. That ability had only come when he was so deeply seated with the power of the Great Mother, when he had combined the shaping of each of the nations as they brought that power to him, to allow him to unify the people against the Utu Tonah. In that way, *he* had served as something like the artifact, bridging the shapings together.

*You were wise to give it time. That one will need time, but I sensed great strength in him.*

*Earth strength?* Tan had detected strength with wind, and it must have had enough strength to be able to fly, but he hadn't *really* known.

*There is earth strength in that one,* Kota confirmed.

Tan took a deep breath. *You will hunt?*

*That is why you brought me to this place.*

*I didn't bring you. You let the draasin carry you.*

Kota bared her fangs at him, but Tan petted her. The dark brown and black speckled fur was rough beneath his hand, and he felt her great strength. *Careful, Maelen, or I will not hunt.*

Tan chuckled and pulled Amia to him on a shaping of wind as he prepared to return to Par-shon. If nothing else, having Kota here gave him a sense of relief.

## 10

## THE MISTRESS OF SOULS

Tan shaped himself above the city, trying to stay out of sight of the people making their way along the streets. He'd found that a shaping of wind obscured him while traveling above, much like a shaping of earth gave him the ability to hide while on the ground.

Distantly, he sensed Kota as she prowled along the shores of Par-shon. With her here, he had a different understanding of the landscape. She'd come across two more crossed elementals, and each time he reached them, Tan had realized that they were too young for him to risk connecting to.

What would have happened had the Utu Tonah forced them to bond?

Or had he already?

Those were questions that he wanted to pose to the Mistress of Bonds, but first he had to find her. So far, she had managed to elude him.

And now, rather than finding Elanne as Tan had hoped, he found Marin by accident.

The Mistress of Souls made her way down the street flanked by three younger men. They each carried a basket and had clean-shaven heads. Simple, dark brown robes matched her robe.

When Tan landed in front of her, she looked down at the ground. "My Utu Tonah," she whispered.

The men with her lowered their baskets and bowed. "Utu Tonah," they repeated as one.

Tan looked down the street. Hadn't he sensed Elanne here? Spirit and earth had shown him the connection to her, but he didn't see her anywhere. He needed answers about the bonds.

"Your ministry goes well?" he asked. He reached out with spirit and couldn't find Elanne where he thought she had been. Tan added earth, but even that didn't help. Either she was no longer here or, more likely, something had changed so that he couldn't reach her.

Given all the bonds that he knew existed throughout Parshon, he suspected that she hid somewhere he couldn't reach her. There might even still be someplace like the tower had once been, a place where the tiles with runes meant to obstruct his ability hid her from him.

"We serve the people," she said softly.

Wind swirled around his feet, and Tan glanced up, thinking of Honl and wondering where the elemental of wind had gone, but Honl wouldn't have needed to find him. He could simply reach through their connection.

"You still haven't shared with me what it is you do, exactly," Tan said. "How long have you served in your role?"

She tipped her head. "My role, Utu Tonah?"

Tan nodded. "I've spoken with the others on your council, but you keep avoiding me," he said, forcing a smile as he did. It wasn't so much that she avoided him, but she certainly had not gone out of her way to try to help him. None of the councilors had, really, and Tan didn't blame them, but he thought that their concern for his title and the fact that he had defeated the previous Utu Tonah would forge a certain level of respect.

With some, he had. Leon, the Master of Coin, had demonstrated immediate deferential respect, but then, Tan suspected he feared to lose that authority. The Master of Trade, a carpenter by the name of Aled Throns, had taken some time, but Tan thought he had a potential ally there. Garza had turned out to be the Mistress of Shaping, a position where Tan had some natural credibility. Only Elanne and Marin had proven to be difficult, and he thought he was making some headway with Elanne. Or had, when he could find her.

"I have not avoided you, my Utu Tonah," Marin said, keeping her voice soft. "The people need stable guidance. That is my role."

"Not the role of the Utu Tonah?" he asked.

He noticed her tensing and, with water sensing, noticed how her heart began to flutter. Tan attempted a spirit sensing with her, but couldn't detect anything. Either she knew how to block him—something the warrior shapers had learned to do against the archivist spirit shapers—or she could shape spirit herself. Tan would have doubted that likely, especially knowing what he did of Par-shon and their ability with spirit.

"I would not presume to tell you your role, my Utu Tonah."

"That's not what you said when we last spoke. I would hear your thoughts," Tan said.

Marin swallowed. "The Utu Tonah leads the people in this life," she said carefully, "while the Mistress of Souls guides them toward the next."

"You haven't attempted to guide me."

She looked up. "You would seek guidance?"

Tan sensed an undertone of something more to the question. "I always seek answers and understanding. That is how I was able to reach the elementals and how I understood that they were not to be forcibly bonded."

He said the last to gauge her reaction. Would she be offended by the comment, or would her heart begin to speed? He might not be able to use spirit sensing with her, but that didn't mean he had no way of detecting her mood.

But he detected nothing that suggested anxiety. Rather, there was a calm about her.

"You make bold statements, Utu Tonah," she said, "but some do not believe."

"What don't they believe? That I would not force the bond onto the elementals, or that we should work with them?"

She managed to hold his gaze far longer than she had in the past. "Yes."

"What do *you* believe?"

As she watched him, he felt a shaping building. With

certainty, he knew that she could shape spirit. Likely others serving with her would as well.

That realization only opened more questions for him. How had she escaped the notice of the Utu Tonah all that time?

Or had she?

*She shapes spirit,* he sent to Amia.

He sensed her, distant in the tower, and she responded by coming to the forefront of his mind, engaging their bond. *Are you certain?*

*There is a shaping here, but not one that I can fully detect.*

*That doesn't mean spirit. You would be able to detect a spirit shaping.*

Tan wasn't sure that he would. He would detect a *shaping*, but knowing whether it was spirit or something else would be difficult. At least with the other elements, the connection to the elementals helped him know the details.

"I believe that you have come to our lands and have asked our people to consider a different path than the one they had expected. I believe that you intend to lead us but don't yet know what motivates you."

One of the men with her gasped, and Tan suppressed amusement. He'd been trying to convince the people around him to stop treating him as if he had to be feared, but they had no reference for that. To them, he was the Utu Tonah, possibly no better than the prior one, and powerful enough to have killed him.

Marin let out a controlled sigh. "I am sorry if I speak too freely, Utu Tonah, but you asked what I believe."

Should he attempt a shaping of spirit on her? If he were strong enough, or even if he used a subtle enough sensing, he might be able to understand what she hid from him. There was no doubting that she did.

Worse, although it should not affect him as it did, someone able to shape spirit would be harder for him to trust. The experience with the archivists had taught him that. And if she attempted to shape him with spirit, he knew that he couldn't trust her, not really.

But he needed to understand. To do that, he would have to find a way to bridge a level of trust.

"Would you show me how you guide the people?" Tan asked.

Marin watched him as if expecting his request to be something of a joke, but when Tan didn't respond, she nodded. "I will show you the people, Utu Tonah, and you can see if you will still lead."

She nodded to the men with the baskets, and a quick shaping built. With it came the realization that something passed wordlessly between them. Tan didn't press, but he would find out whether she truly shaped spirit, and if she did, whether she had somehow influenced the Utu Tonah. If she did, it was possible that she had suggested he go after the Aeta, or even possible that she had suggested a way to defeat Tan.

The alternative was equally possible. She might have tried preventing him from learning about the connection to spirit. That would be powerful information if true.

They walked through the city, moving past shops and

buildings, many of which were in various states of disrepair, before passing into a part of the city where there were larger buildings. Children ran through the street, many wearing nothing but a wrap around their waists and most without anything on their feet. In spite of that, they sounded happy, their shouts and cries as they chased each other the universal sound of children at play.

Marin watched him. What reaction did she expect of him?

He'd seen poor sections of Ethea, but there weren't nearly as many as in Par-shon. Or maybe he chose *not* to see them in Ethea. When he was there, he had access to the university, the archives, and the palace, all places that the average citizen of Ethea would not be able to reach. Wasn't it the same in Par-shon? As Utu Tonah, he spent most of his time in the tower, or the sprawling estate that had been the previous Utu Tonah's, and rarely out among the people.

"There will be many who won't want to see you," she said to him carefully.

"Why?"

She shrugged. "They see you as the Utu Tonah. To them, you are no different than the one before."

"I am very different than the one before," Tan said. "They will have to see that."

Marin studied him and then nodded. Tan hadn't noticed a shaping building, and maybe she hadn't built one. He doubted that she could shape him with spirit. Since learning of his own connection to spirit, and with the bond to Amia, he had been protected from a spirit attack. Even the First Mother hadn't been able to shape him, as far as he knew.

"You must show them if that is what you would have them know."

Marin led him to the door of the building, the three men with baskets following behind. Tan held onto a connection to earth, reaching out to try and understand how many were around him, and stopped counting when he reached the thirties. Dozens of people occupied the courtyard outside the building.

Many were young, much younger than those he worked with at the tower.

Tan noticed that as soon as he entered the wide courtyard, children screamed as they ran through, coming up to Marin so that she could pat them on the head and whisper a few words before they went running away. A few older kids stopped by as well and waited for her to speak to them softly. After she was done, he realized that the men with baskets handed them something before they disappeared.

"What are you saying to them?" Tan asked.

"That is between them and the Night."

"The Night?"

Marin barely glanced in his direction. "You are not of Par, Utu Tonah. You do not understand our beliefs."

"Help me, then."

He didn't think that she would answer, and maybe it would have been better had she not.

As a larger man with thick arms and broad shoulders approached, Marin spoke so softly that only his ability to shape the wind let him hear. "So that you can turn them against us?" Marin said.

The large man wrapped her in a hug and then bowed to her. She traced a finger along his forehead in a pattern that felt familiar. For a moment, Tan thought she might be forcing a bond, but there was no flash of power and no painful drawing from the elementals. He thought that he would manage to detect if there *was* any forced bond.

Then the man straightened, and his gaze turned to Tan. A flash of red raced through his cheeks and tension swelled within him. Tan barely had to possess any connection to spirit to know the anger within the man, if not the reason behind it.

"Mistress," the man said in a hushed whisper, "you know that I would never question your judgment."

"Isan, the Utu Tonah asked to understand my role."

As she said his title, the sounds in the courtyard around them fell silent. A few others shuffled over toward Isan, and they lined up behind him. All had much of the same agitation that Tan detected from him, but he didn't understand the reason.

He decided to use spirit. This was the reason that he'd come to Par-shon, wasn't it? So that he could understand the people and prevent the same attack from recurring?

Starting with Isan, he started to layer a connection of spirit through the man.

And felt pushed back.

Tan frowned and glanced at Marin.

What was this? Had she provided some level of protection to these people? But protection from what?

"You didn't need to bring him here, Mistress. After what he's done—"

Tan was surprised at the way they spoke. It was nothing like the respectful way others within the city had spoken to him. In some ways, it was refreshing.

"What did I do?" Tan asked, stepping forward.

Marin shook her head at him in a silent warning.

Isan glanced from Marin to Tan and then bowed his head. The gesture was slow and deliberate as if he intended to make it clear that he was not *forced* to bow. "You are the Utu Tonah. You may do as you please."

Tan stood in front of Isan. The man smelled of sweat and smoke, but mostly he reminded Tan of the way his father had smelled. A healthy scent, and one that carried the scent of hard work.

"Have I offended you in some way, Isan?" Tan asked. "You would rather have the other Utu Tonah, the one who forced bonds on the elementals?" Tan turned to Marin. "Is that what this is about? Your people miss the power they had when the Utu Tonah allowed them to bond?"

He felt his anger building and suppressed a shaping that threatened to spill out within him. Shaping unintentionally wouldn't serve the purpose he had in coming here. But he couldn't allow the people to think that the old ways could return. Somehow, he would have to convince them that there was another way for them to understand the elementals.

Maybe trying to talk them through it wouldn't work and he would need to be more forceful. He hated the thought that it would be necessary, but seeing this man and sensing the agitation within these people, he began to wonder if there *was* another way.

"If the Mistress agrees that you can be here, then I cannot object," Isan said.

Marin looked from Tan to Isan, and then to the others gathered in the courtyard. All seemed to block him from getting any closer, as if they intended to keep him from the building behind. "Perhaps, Utu Tonah, it would be best if you did not enter this place until you have proven yourself. If you are indeed interested in what you claim, then let the people have the peace they seek. Only then should you attempt to enter."

Isan crossed his arms over his chest, a gesture that was mimicked by many others in the courtyard, almost as if every person wanted to prevent Tan from passing. Whatever the prior Utu Tonah had done still lingered. None trusted him, and Tan wondered if there were anything that he could say or do that would change that. Forcing his way past was a sure way *not* to succeed.

Tan decided to take a step back, and he bowed his head in respect to the Mistress of Souls. Of all those on the council he'd met, she had at least treated him with a modicum of respect so he would do the same to her and her people. She might be the key to helping him get through to the people of Par-shon and finding a way to reach them.

"I will wait," he said to Marin. "But I would like to continue our conversation."

The edge of a smile tugged at the corner of her mouth. "I would like that, Utu Tonah."

With that, Tan backed away, unable to help how it felt like a retreat.

## 11

## A BOND RESTORED

The wind gusted more strongly through Par-shon than usual, and Tan shaped a small protection around himself to avoid it. There was a hint of warmth to it that reminded him of the ashi wind elemental, but he knew that in Par-shon, ashi wasn't the primary elemental. Here, wyln served as the primary elemental, much like how in the kingdoms, ara blew the strongest.

"You don't have to follow me, my Utu Tonah," Elanne said.

"I told you that I only want to understand your role." It had been hard enough to find her after leaving Marin, and he didn't want to lose her quite yet.

"And you think to do that by following me."

"Working with you, perhaps, would be a better way of putting it." Tan hadn't been sure how to approach her but decided that the best way would be to come at it from a direction of seeking to understand. If he did that, everything else would fall into place. Or so he hoped. "Tell me again what you're doing."

Elanne, stooped over a small wall near the edge of the city, looked up. The wind blowing over the top of the wall sent dust and debris swirling around, and he shielded his mouth. Elanne had the sense to wear a scarf wrapped around her mouth, which kept most of the dust from bothering her. Only her dark eyes were visible.

"As I have said, I am ensuring that our protections are in place." She turned away from him and focused on the wall again, tracing her fingers through a series of patterns etched into the stone.

Tan looked over her shoulder and watched her work. These weren't the same runes that had been used in the jewelry, or on the bonded shapers themselves. These were a different type of rune, one that appeared more like those used on the buildings that he'd seen elsewhere in the city, and similar to those that he'd found in the kingdoms.

Tan focused a trickle of shaping energy and sent it into the rune. This mark was for wind, and as he shaped wind into it, the gusts surged and sent Elanne's scarf blowing.

She swore under her breath, and her eyes went wide, and she glanced over at Tan, as if afraid of how he might react. He offered her a smile, one that he hoped was reassuring.

"Sorry about that," he said.

"That was you?"

Tan touched the rune, feeling the power bubbling beneath it. This was not a mark that forced the elementals here; rather, it was one that called to them. In the kingdoms, runes like this had summoned the elementals, not trapped them. What purpose would there be having a rune for wind along the wall?

"That was me," he said. He trailed his fingers along the mark, pushing with a hint of wind, feeling the way it settled beneath his touch. There was no harm to the elemental in what he did here, but once the mark settled, the swirling and gusting settled as well, calming.

"Great Mother," he whispered. Had the wind actually *wanted* him to help fix the rune?

"You have a gentle touch," Elanne said. "There are not many able to modify these marks. Most are very old, and from a time before Par-shon, before Par."

Tan studied the rune and wondered if there was a connection to the ancient shapers, even here. "How is it that you can repair them?" he asked her. To know what needed to be done, he had used the connection to wind and let the elemental guide him. But Elanne wouldn't have that same benefit.

"I don't shape if that's what you're asking," Elanne answered. "There is a texture and a shape to these. Only the most skilled with bonding can understand."

"This isn't bonding," Tan said. "Bonding was forcing the elementals to connect to the shaper, something the elementals did not want. This... this is something different."

Elanne shrugged. "This is the same, at least in Par-shon. The purpose might be different, but the shape of the marks and the need for caution when making them is the same." She stood and dusted her hands along her clothes. She was dressed in something like a wrap of fabric with muted colors streaking through it. Elanne had pulled a part of the wrap up over her chin and breathed through it, keeping her mouth covered. Now that the wind had settled, there was less of a need, but she still didn't lower it. "That is the reason we have a Master of Bonds. This person is responsible for many things, but one of the greatest is ensuring that these bonds remain around the city. When they are lost... strange things happen."

"What do you mean that strange things happen?"

She nodded over the wall. "You sensed the way the wind blew before the bond was repaired. It is that way with the others."

Tan studied the rune—not a bond, regardless of what she might call it—and wondered what purpose it might serve. There was no denying that the wind had eased the moment that he had fixed the rune. What of the other marks throughout the city? Would they be the same? Were there others that needed repair?

"How many of these do you maintain?" Tan asked.

She cocked her head to the side and closed one eye, her mouth pinched together as she seemed to consider. "There are nearly a thousand throughout the city."

"How many were placed before the Utu Tonah arrived?"

She blinked and turned back to him. "All were here before the Utu Tonah."

A thought came to Tan. "How many were damaged in the time after he arrived?"

She thought about it and shook her head. "That is not for me to know. I was not Master of Bonds at that time. There are many bonds now that need repair, enough that I am too busy to be..." She trailed off as if realizing again that she was speaking to the Utu Tonah. "I should not speak so freely, my Utu Tonah."

Tan shook his head. "You can speak freely. And all I want is to understand what you're doing, not interfere."

"You could not interfere, Utu Tonah—"

Tan silenced her with a wave of his hand. "You've already shown me that you have a skill I don't understand. Please, Elanne, I would like to see the other... bonds... you repair."

Using her word for it was particularly difficult, especially since he didn't agree with the way that Par-shon had used them in the past, but the Master of Bonds could teach him something, and if he wanted to understand Par-shon, and if he wanted to know what might have motivated the Utu Tonah, then he would need to be willing to listen and learn from those he didn't agree with. Recognizing that need and succeeding were difficult challenges.

Elanne shifted the wrap and uncovered her mouth. "You do not need to waste your time on this, my Utu Tonah, but I will show you."

---

Tan followed Elanne through the city, stopping periodically at buildings or walls or even once at a holding pen for sheep that reminded Tan of friends he'd lost when Nor fell. Thinking of Cobin and his daughter Bal reminded him that he should have sought them out long ago. So few had survived the fall of Nor that he should have taken the time to find them. By now, they would have moved on and hopefully had no idea of the challenges that Tan had faced. As far as he was concerned, he preferred to keep anyone else from knowing the dangers he experienced. That meant that those without the ability to shape were safe, protected from the horrors of the initial Incendin attack, or from what Par-shon had done.

The only thing that he *couldn't* hide was the release of the draasin. They hadn't been seen in a thousand years and now flew freely. There were only four remaining now that Asboel had died, and without the greatest of the draasin, Tan wondered if there would be others. That was a question for Sashari sometime when she had finished mourning, if she ever would.

Each time they stopped, Elanne would trace her finger along the runes, either deepening the etching or modifying it in some way. Tan chose simply to watch. With each pattern she repaired, the elemental behind it surged, strengthened by what she did. He thought that he could sense her process and had enough connection to the elementals that he might be able to recreate it, but there was a delicate artistry to her work.

"How did you learn to do this?" he asked as she repaired the third pattern. They stood next to a small building near the edge of town. It had a low, sloped roof and a faded sign hanging in front of it that he couldn't read. The scent of burnt oil drifted from within. "These bonds," he clarified. "How is it that you know how to do this with them?"

Elanne had grown more comfortable with him watching and didn't refer to him by title every time she spoke, but remained deferential. "These are the bonds," she said patiently as if explaining to a child.

"What you call bonds are different," Tan said again. He wanted to understand, not to argue, because what she did now was not what he would have expected from Par-shon. "The bonds the prior Utu Tonah used were different."

"Those were not of Par. Those bonds were Par-shon."

"I don't understand."

Elanne traced a small length of sharp steel across the pattern. This one only needed to be more clearly defined, not modified. Tan could sense that without touching it and thought that he could manage it with a simple shaping of earth, but doing so would only diminish what Elanne did.

"This is Par-shon," she said.

Tan nodded.

"But it was not always." She hesitated and lowered her eyes, looking away from him. In all the time that he'd been watching her, she had never really been this obsequious.

"You can speak freely," he urged.

She swallowed and met his eyes. "Before the Utu Tonah, this was Par. Before that… I do not know. The records do not speak of it."

"Records?"

She nodded. "The records of the land. We don't have anything from before Par. When the Utu Tonah came, he destroyed much, but the records remained, though they are difficult for us to fully understand. Par remained. But the time before Par, that is gone."

Tan had searched for archives throughout Par-shon and had not found anything. He had thought that the tower would hold the answer, but there had been nothing other than the journal written by the Utu Tonah. There was insight hidden in those pages, but not the answers that he sought. He wanted to know whether Par-shon was a place of convergence and whether the people had known. From what he'd discovered, they *must* have known, but there were no other records that he could find.

"Where are the records?" Tan asked, careful not to sound too eager.

Elanne looked down again, avoiding his eyes. "Utu Tonah… I have said too much."

He shook his head. "No. I would like to understand Par and would like to know the history of this land."

She took a deep breath. Emotions warred through her before her back straightened. "You want us to believe that you are a benevolent ruler, but you are no different than him. You come and destroy our heritage, much as he did. Would you force me to reveal what remains?"

The force of her anger took him aback. "I only want to understand."

"Understand. So that you can use that to destroy even more of our past? Have you not done enough, Utu Tonah?"

She clapped a hand across her mouth as she froze, then she turned away and ran down the street.

Tan stared after, thinking that he should do something,

chase after her, but what would that accomplish? She would only fear him more. All he wanted was to understand, but when he tried, he seemed to fumble. How many more mistakes would he make?

He looked down at the bond that she'd been working on and noted that she'd dropped the short, sharp length of metal that she used for repair. Tan took it and noted that it had patterns along the length of it, much like his warrior sword, but smaller and more compact. Using a gentle shaping, he probed the runes and found that they held shaped power. At least he understood how she managed to work the repairs.

Tan turned his attention to the pattern. On this building, it represented water and pulled on the elemental. He ran his fingers across it, tracing it, and realized that there was more to it than simply a mark for water.

He tipped his head but couldn't decipher it. Amia might be able to help, or Honl if the wind elemental ever returned from wherever he'd gone. But now Tan had to come up with answers without their help.

What he needed was a way to copy the pattern. If he had paper and charcoal, he might be able to create an etching. He would have to return. Besides, there were other patterns that he could study.

Tan stared at the rune a little longer. Understanding the part that he missed seemed just out of reach, and he thought that if he could just study it a little longer, he might grasp what he couldn't see. But nothing came.

He might rule in Par-shon, but he didn't understand the people. Marin told him he needed to know more before he could understand how she served. Tolman worked with him, but reluctantly. And Elanne feared him and what he might do to her people. In that way, how was he any different than the prior Utu Tonah?

With a sigh, he turned away.

## A NEW PERSPECTIVE

Tan stared at the rune on the wall inside the tower. Much like those outside, the ones that he'd watched Elanne repair, he detected something else in it but couldn't quite see it. Even shaping it didn't help; it only left him with a sense that he missed something.

Pulling his eyes away from it, he stopped at the door in the hall, and behind it, the reason that he'd come. Voices drifted through the door, most excited and chattering away. In spite of the welcome that he'd received elsewhere in the city, the children, at least, seemed interested in hearing from him. Part of that was because he was the Utu Tonah, but Tan had caught the attention of a few of them—like Fasha or Mat —that went beyond his title.

He considered turning away and leaving them to the happiness they clearly had without him disturbing it. Hadn't they been through enough without having to face the new

Utu Tonah as well? Did they deserve him coming in and disrupting their peace?

But he had returned to Par-shon for a reason. He needed to ensure that there would not be another attack, and doing so meant that he needed to lead. He might not be comfortable with what was required of him, and he might not *want* the title, but he could not turn away from the responsibility.

As he opened the door, the children fell silent.

Tan studied the room. It was a large space with a dozen chairs, a rectangular table, and a hearth along the back wall. Most of the older children sat to the side nearest the hearth, while the younger ones wrestled or chased each other around. A carefree energy filled the room, one that Tan regretted stealing from them.

"Utu Tonah," one of the older children said. He stood nearly as tall as Tan and was thin, with the first traces of hair growing on his chin. His dark hair was swept back and hung to his shoulders, a style more common in Par-shon than in the kingdoms.

Tan nodded. Those sitting stood, and the children wrestling and chasing the others stopped and hurried over to stand in front of him.

Why had he come again? He thought to teach, but what would he be able to show them? These were children accustomed to the forced bonds, and though they might know the elementals, there was a different understanding here than what he would like. Exposing them to Asgar had frightened some and emboldened others.

He glanced at Fasha and saw her standing near the edge of the older children with her arms crossed over her chest. Her black hair was braided today, and she wore a dark wrap that reminded him of Elanne. She met his eyes with much of the same defiance that he saw from Elanne.

"Come with me," he decided suddenly.

He turned and led them out of the tower and through the city, not bothering to watch if they followed. Earth and spirit sensing told him that they remained behind him, close enough that he didn't have to worry about losing them.

Outside the city, he stopped. A wide road led away. Tan had only shaped himself here but had taken the road once, when he first had been captured. Tolman had been there and had been the more compassionate of those who had captured him.

"What do you see?" he asked. He stretched his senses out around him, letting the awareness of all the elements fill him. Away from the city, different senses took over. He detected the trees ringing the city, some with flowers budding along them. Squirrels and rabbits and fox and other creatures that he had no name for scurried through the trees.

He realized that the last time that he'd been here, when he'd been carried through on a shaping, flown here using the elementals in ways that he hadn't conceived, there had been an absence of life. The trees had been diminished, and the surrounding wildlife had been silent. The only place where life had remained had been within the city. Near the place of convergence, he realized now.

With the Utu Tonah gone and the bonds separated, life had returned. More than his ability to simply sense it on the air, he could smell it, could practically *feel* the change.

"Trees, Utu Tonah," one of the children called to him.

Tan smiled. "Trees. Do you see anything *on* the trees?"

A young girl stepped forward. Her hair was parted on either side and bound with bright orange string. "Flowers," she said softly.

Tan bent toward her and pointed to the nearest copse of trees. Sitting in front of the trees was a small rabbit. "Do you see anything other than the flowers?"

One of the youngest boys gasped and clapped his hands together, scaring the rabbit away.

"I saw it, Utu Tonah!" he shouted.

"When was the last time any of you were outside the city?" he asked.

They stared at him for a moment, no one answering.

"You must have left the city at some point," Tan said.

A few of the younger ones started murmuring softly to each other, but no one looked over, almost as if making a point to avoid his eyes.

"Mat," he said, looking at the boy who'd demonstrated earth shaping ability. The boy blanched when Tan called on him, and the others around him parted, giving him space. "When were you last outside the city?"

Mat swallowed and looked at the ground. "We weren't allowed, Utu Tonah."

Tan suppressed a sigh. Not allowed. Was that how the

previous Utu Tonah controlled them? "The rest of you? When were you outside the city?"

For long moments, no one answered.

"I left earlier in the week," Fasha said. A smile started to spread across her face. "On his draasin."

A couple of the children laughed, but they looked at Tan and it died off.

Tan focused on Fasha. "What did you see when you sat atop his back?"

Her eyes went distant. "Everything is so small from there."

"A view from there lets you see the world is different than it looks here, doesn't it?"

She nodded.

The older boy who had refused to sit on the draasin shot Fasha a glare. "Not all of us can ride the draasin. Can we, Fasha?"

"You were given a chance," she shot back. She blinked and turned to Tan. "Wasn't he, Utu Tonah?"

Tan didn't want there to be arguments about the draasin. Asgar had been willing to allow Fasha to ride on him in order to make a point, but there might be something that Tan could do that was similar.

"What is your name?" he asked the boy.

He shuffled his feet and didn't meet Tan's eyes. They all treated him the same way, and he wondered if the Utu Tonah had not allowed them to look at him. "Henrak, Utu Tonah."

"We call him Hen."

Tan looked up to see who had spoken and saw a younger boy whose face had flushed. "Thanks," he said. To Henrak, he said, "Hen, would you like to share the same view?"

His face went white. "I... the draasin..."

Tan shook his head. "Not with the draasin. Let me show you."

He held out his hand, and Henrak took it carefully.

Using a shaping of wind and fire, Tan lifted them into the air, sending them higher and higher until they practically stood on the clouds overlooking the city. "What do you see, Hen?" he asked.

The boy trembled. "My Utu Tonah?"

"Look down. It's okay. I won't drop you."

"How can you hold me here like this? When I was bonded, I could barely hold myself above the ground."

Tan hadn't considered that some of the children may have been able to shape themselves into the air nearly as well as he could. With the bonds, they would have control over the elementals, and that control would have given them the ability to travel in a similar way. Not the same, not unless they were warrior shapers, but close enough that they would have been able to see the world from this perspective.

"When I first began to shape, I could barely carry myself," Tan admitted. "Time and experience showed me that I could do much more than that. Now, we can talk of shaping from the ground, but what do you see up here?"

Hen leaned over. His face screwed up as he studied the ground. "I see the city."

"Look beyond the city," Tan instructed. "What else do you see?"

"Nothing but the land around Par-shon. And the water."

Tan nodded. "Water. What do you think is beyond the water?"

Hen looked up at him. "That's where you come from, isn't it?"

"There's that, but can you see that there's more than only Par-shon?"

From up here, Tan had always had the sense that there was more to the world than his small part of it. That might be the greatest gift the Great Mother had given, sharing with him the ability to have a perspective where he could see from up high and realize that he was only a part of something greater. Too often, he didn't slow down and take the time to appreciate that fact. Especially now, when he was asked to do so much, and when he traveled on a warrior shaping, moving too quickly to really have the opportunity to slow down and see the world below him.

That had always been the advantage of traveling with Asboel. There had been a peacefulness to riding with the draasin, a sense of the draasin's part in something greater.

"I can see," Hen said.

Tan sighed and carried Hen back down to the others. They waited, and a few of them accosted Hen and asked what they had done.

Tan realized that he would have to show each of them the same.

"Next one," he said.

———

Back in the tower, Tan was studying one of the marks when Tolman caught up to him. Elanne had called them bonds, but that didn't seem the right term for them. They were different than runes, though. Tan was certain of that, but not quite sure why.

"My Utu Tonah," Tolman said as he approached. He bowed his head and kept his eyes fixed on the floor. "You were with the young ones today?"

Tan glanced over. "I thought they could use a different perspective."

Tolman swallowed. "They tell me that you carried them to the sky?"

Tan pulled his attention away from the rune. Amia still hadn't had the opportunity to study them with him. She had a different understanding of runes, and he suspected that she might be able to help him. What he really wanted was to be able to reach Honl, but the wind elemental still didn't answer when Tan tried to reach to him.

"Was that a problem?"

"Not a problem, Utu Tonah, only that you don't need to burden yourself with working with the students. I have agreed to teach as you requested. You have enough to do otherwise."

Suppressing a sigh, Tan smiled at the other man. "I will

make time for those with potential, Tolman. They need to understand a better way to use their abilities."

Tolman nodded and clutched his hands together. "Of course, Utu Tonah. I don't mean to imply that you can't work with the students, only that I understand you have other demands of your time." He hesitated. "Was there a reason you chose to carry them above the city?"

"I wanted to show them a different view than the one that they get down on the ground." More than that, he had wanted to have a chance to simply interact with them and had used the opportunity to get to know them better. Most still viewed him as the Utu Tonah, the man who killed the previous Utu Tonah, but a few began to see him differently. It was those he thought to reach, especially as he continued to struggle with understanding Par-shon.

"I notice that you've been studying these lately," Tolman noted, motioning to the runes.

Tan reached toward the rune, sending a shaping through it. Was it coincidence that the rune that had sat overtop opposed this particular element, or had the Utu Tonah placed that here for a different reason?

"Par-shon has many of these throughout the city," he said.

"These are the ancient bonds," Tolman said carefully. "The Mistress of Bonds could tell you more about them, I think."

Tan pulled his hand back and looked down the hall. Another of the same type was located farther down the hall. Much like this one, there was more power to it than what he saw at first. But what was it? More than simply the effect of the rune, what pattern was he missing in it?

"The Mistress of Bonds does not want to share what she knows with me."

Tolman gasped softly. "She should share with the Utu Tonah."

"She claims that I'm interested in destroying the history of Par." Tan sent another shaping into the rune, determined to understand the secret that he detected within it. There *had* to be more to it, but what exactly? "Why would she feel that way, Tolman?"

The man looked at the ground. "Utu Tonah, I don't believe that I can answer for the Mistress of Bonds. If you would like me to bring her here…"

Tan shook his head. "No. I don't think that will be necessary."

Tolman nodded with a relieved expression and shuffled his feet, leaning away from Tan. The message was clear.

"You may go," Tan said. But as Tolman started away, Tan raised a hand. "Tell me, where would I find the records for Par?"

Tolman blinked. "The records, my Utu Tonah?"

Tan nodded. Elanne didn't want to share with him, but she had more of a spine than Tolman. At least, it seemed that she did, but what did Tan really know?

And Tolman surprised him. "There are no records," he said. "The Utu Tonah did not want records of a time before Par-shon."

"What do you remember of the time before Par-shon?" Tan asked. "What can you tell me about Par?"

Tolman flicked his eyes to the wall briefly before looking

away and staring at the ground in front of Tan's feet. "There is nothing that I can tell you, really, Utu Tonah. That was a difficult time for all of us. Better that we simply forget."

"You would forget your history?"

Tolman's brow wrinkled in a pained expression. "We would forget the torment, my Utu Tonah. We would forget what was done to our people, and how many were lost. We would forget what it was like before—" He swallowed. "I am sorry, Utu Tonah. I get ahead of myself."

Tan studied Tolman. Here was a man who could shape, one who could use earth with reasonable strength, but he feared what Tan would do to him. "What do you know about him?" Tan asked.

Tolman looked up. "Who?"

"Him. The Utu Tonah." Tan inhaled slowly, thinking of what he'd seen of the previous Utu Tonah. He'd been so determined not to be killed—and not lose his bonds—that he knew nothing other than that the elementals referred to him as the Bonded One. The title suited him as well as Utu Tonah, two words that had some vague meaning in ancient *Ishthin*, but not so much that Tan could translate them easily enough to understand why the title had been chosen. Maybe Amia could help; all of his knowledge of *Ishthin* came from the shaped gift of knowledge that she'd shared with him. It was possible that she'd shared everything that she knew, but Tan figured it was also possible that there was more than what she had shared. "What can you tell me about where he came from before he came to Par?"

That much he had worked out, as well as some of the

events after the Utu Tonah had come here and begun forcing bonds. As he gained power, there wouldn't have been anyone able to withstand him, letting him grow even more powerful and forcing more and more bonds. But there had to have been something before he came to Par. The more that he considered it, the more certain he was that was the key to understanding the Utu Tonah.

"We never learned much about who he had been before," Tolman said. "When he came... He showed strength with fire, much like you, summoning flames and performing shapings of such strength that many struggled to believe that what he did was possible."

Tolman glanced up and met Tan's eyes.

Maybe that was the reason they feared him as much as they had feared the previous Utu Tonah. Didn't Tan come with the same connection to fire? And wasn't what he was capable of doing just as impossible, especially given the connection he shared with the elementals?

Had he gone about reaching the students the wrong way? He thought that by demonstrating fire and showing his connection to the elementals, they would understand that there wasn't a need for a bond, but maybe they feared him even more because he didn't require the same type of bond as the Utu Tonah. At least with him, the bonds were visible, and they could see how heavily bonded he was, even if they didn't know what it meant.

"Do you know why he came to Par?" Tan asked.

Tolman shook his head. "Perhaps some of the council will have known, but most lost their lives in those early days."

Tolman forced a smile and nodded to Tan. "He brought order, and Par-shon was better for it."

Tan sniffed. "But Par was not." He nodded to Tolman. "Thank you. You have given me much to think about."

Tolman bowed his head as he took a step back. "Of course, my Utu Tonah."

# A SEARCH FOR UNDERSTANDING

T an sat alone in the home that had once been the previous Utu Tonah's. No fire burned in the hearth, and he pushed away the sense of the elementals, searching for a sort of silence and solitude, wanting nothing more than a sense of emptiness around him.

He needed to understand what had brought the Utu Tonah to Par-shon. There had been *something* that was more than about the elementals here, though he couldn't find it in the journal.

The journal lay open in front of him, and he had pored over it again, searching for answers and thinking that they might be found within the pages of the text that the Utu Tonah had left behind, but the only thing that he found was the detail of his desire to reach for the elementals. Not so much desire, he realized, but a need for the connection, for the power that came from it, though Tan had not been able to understand what more the Utu Tonah had wanted other than power.

Closing the book, he leaned back in the chair. There had to be something more. The Utu Tonah had chased power—that much was true and undeniable—but there was something more to it than what Tan had discovered. Why had he come *here*? From what Tan could tell, the Utu Tonah had already forced several bonds even before he had come to Par-shon. To Tan, that meant that he'd come seeking bonds, but possibly something else as well.

Searching the tower yielded no clear answers, not where Tan thought they would have been. When he had been trapped here in Par-shon, the Utu Tonah had occupied the tower. But that wasn't the sense that he had now that he'd returned. The Utu Tonah might have spent some time in the tower, but it wasn't the only place he had occupied.

That had been this home.

Would he find any answers here, or would there only be more questions?

With a sigh, he left the room and made his way down the hall. The need to understand his predecessor drove him, even thought he recognized that he might not be able to. The people of Par-shon—most of them at least—didn't necessarily *want* him to remember. But Tan needed answers.

The longer he searched, the more he began to wonder if he should have left the former Utu Tonah alive. At least then Tan would have been able to question him. With the man gone, there was no way for him to know—to really know—what his goal had been.

What did the runes scattered all around the city mean? Were they tied to the reason the Utu Tonah had come or was there something else? And why were so many in a state of disrepair?

The sprawling estate was massive compared to the small home that he shared with Amia in Ethea. There were dozens of rooms, many for the staff assigned to serve them, and a massive kitchen. Tan had searched all the rooms in the estate, but so far had not found anything that would help him understand.

As he passed another servant in the hall, he paused. "Maclin," Tan said, turning to face the man.

The servant stopped, his back straightening with tension. "My Utu Tonah," he said carefully. All of the servants moved cautiously around him now, especially since he had destroyed the runes in their jewelry and their clothing when he'd first arrived. He began to suspect that had been a mistake, but how could he do anything to repair that?

"You served here with the previous Utu Tonah."

Maclin nodded. "Yes, my Utu Tonah."

"What was he like?"

Maclin finally turned to face Tan. He kept his eyes lowered, and his chubby cheeks were flushed. Like all of the servants in the estate, he wore a long, gray robe cinched at the waist with a length of black silk. "I am sorry, Utu Tonah. I do not understand the question."

"The previous Utu Tonah. What was he like? What did he do when he wasn't at the tower?" *Or off trying to steal bonds from the elementals*, Tan chose not to say.

Maclin's head bobbed, and he gripped his wrist in front of him and swayed slightly. "He was a powerful man, much like you, my Utu Tonah. As you said, he spent much of his time in the tower, but not all."

"Where else did he spend his time?"

Maclin shook his head. "We never learned. He would leave Par… Par-shon," he corrected himself.

Tan suppressed a smile. There weren't many who still referred to the island as Par, which meant that maybe Maclin was older than Tan even realized. If that were the case, he would have a different understanding about the Utu Tonah and what had changed once he came.

As far as Tan knew, the Utu Tonah had others he trusted, some nearly as bonded as he had been, who had been responsible for securing Doma and Chenir. They likely acted on his behalf, but Tan doubted they had done so under his direct guidance. Would Maclin know who they might have been?

"What can you tell me of Par before?" Tan asked Maclin.

"Before, my Utu Tonah?"

Tan nodded. "Before the Utu Tonah. Before Par-shon. What was it like here before all of that?"

Maclin's eyes narrowed slightly, and Tan sensed a growing distrust at the reason behind the question. It was the same distrust that he sensed from Tolman, though why would Maclin feel the same way? Tolman had lived the Utu Tonah's rule, had experienced the torment firsthand, but Maclin? How had the Utu Tonah treated his servants?

"Why would you ask of what is gone, my Utu Tonah? There is nothing remaining, not that matters. He took everything. Our temples, the protection of the land, and even the hearts of the people. Now we are Par-shon. Some say that it is better."

"Some? What of you, Maclin?" If the Utu Tonah had forced the people to believe differently, it was possible that some remained who had not. From those, Tan would be able to reach a sense of understanding, wouldn't he?

"I am here to serve, Utu Tonah."

He bowed his head and with barely any spirit sensing, Tan could tell the fear that bubbled to the surface. Like the others Tan had encountered, Maclin didn't trust him. They feared him, and that fear brought a certain respect, but they didn't trust him. And Tan couldn't blame him. What had he done other than come to Par-shon and destroy the bonds that might not even have held the elementals, and demonstrated his desire to rule? In that, how was he any different from the Utu Tonah who had come before him?

"Thank you, Maclin." Tan left him standing in the hall, not wanting to press any more than he had. Likely it wouldn't work anyway. Like so many others that Tan had encountered, Maclin wanted to protect himself, and that meant not saying anything that might get him into trouble with the new Utu Tonah.

Leaving the estate, he stopped and breathed in the temperate Par-shon wind as it gusted in from the north. Salt lingered on the air, and it was humid, reminding him of Doma in so many ways.

What did he know about Par? Not Par-shon, but what had been here before the Utu Tonah had ruled? That was the place he needed to return these people to, not to the darkness and fear that had come with the Utu Tonah. But how, when he knew so little?

Yet, he knew about the bonds, the runes placed on the buildings around the city. That had been Par, not Par-shon. The bonds had some meaning to the people of Par, and might even be the key to understanding what the Utu Tonah had been after, if only he could discover what that might be.

With a shaping of wind, he carried himself to the center of the city. Dozens of people passed below. Tan stopped above the street, landing on a building. A sense of earth seemed to draw him here. Moving on, he jumped to an alley below, keeping himself shielded so that he didn't scare anyone.

There was a temptation to listen to those around him and observe the people of Par-shon, but as much as that might help him understand the people, it wouldn't help him understand *Par*. More than anything, he suspected that was the key and the secret to understanding *why* the Utu Tonah had come here.

He turned up the street and listened for the sense the runes made on buildings around him. On one, he recognized the call of fire. Though he had no bond to fire anymore, he remained as connected to it as to any of the elementals. Tan stopped at the corner of the building and studied the pattern. It represented fire, and from the smells coming off it, the building was a baker.

The pattern felt strange. Almost rough and worn in a way that implied age and time had degraded it. But there was more to the sense than that. Not only time but something else had been done to it. Touching it carefully, he noted how the pattern only *seemed* to be degraded by time. There was more to it, the addition of a subtle change to the shaping that he would have missed had it been any element other than fire.

Pushing a shaping of fire into it, he felt a strange sort of resistance. He'd sensed it before when trying to repair them and had thought that it was because he didn't know the purpose of the patterns themselves, but this time, he realized there was more to it than what he'd detected before. Someone had placed a subtle change to the pattern, intending to damage it.

With a surge of fire, adding earth as it called, he forced the rune back into place. With a pulsing of light, the bond took hold.

As it did, Tan felt the way that fire was called by it. Not forced, but called. And saa, so prominent in these lands, answered willingly.

He had seen it before but hadn't made the connection before this. The intricacy required for these patterns, and the almost loving way that they were crafted, told him all that he needed about the way the ancient people of Par felt about the elementals. These people had not abandoned their connection to the elementals. They had revered them.

Was this why the Utu Tonah had come to Par? Not only the convergence but because of these bonds?

If so, why would the bonds on these buildings have remained damaged? Elanne and the other bond masters would have repaired them, wouldn't they?

Unless Elanne didn't want them repaired.

He had thought that she had been repairing bonds, but maybe he had it wrong. When he found her, she must have been damaging them. That would explain why she seemed so upset when he had appeared.

Tan heard noise down the street and felt the pull of shaping. In Ethea, it was a common enough occurrence, but here in Par-shon, there were few shapers, so he should not detect anything.

He started down the street, making his way toward the shaping he detected. Few others were out on the street, and Tan made an effort to keep himself shielded using his connection to earth, borrowing strength from Kota. None seemed to notice him as he hurried along.

The commotion came from a crumbled building. Three people milled outside, looking up at the damage and speaking softly to each other. Two of the walls had simply split, letting the roof collapse.

That seemed strange enough, but what was even more so was the way that Tan sensed earth. Something had changed here. For a moment, he thought that someone might have forced a bond, but that wasn't what he detected. With his connection to Kota, he suspected he would know whether earth was used in a way that the elementals found distressing. This… this was as if earth had simply given out.

Holding onto his shielding, he crept along the edge of the street and searched the stone. He thought he knew what he was looking for, but wasn't certain that he would find it. Par-shon was an old city, and it was possible that the building had simply collapsed because of time, rather than anything more nefarious.

But near the front of the building, he found what he had suspected. A rune—or a bond, according to Elanne—was worked into the stone. Tan touched it, tracing his fingers across the pattern and searching for the sign that it had been damaged like the others. At first, he sensed nothing amiss, but then he found it.

The pattern had a subtle change. There wasn't much to it, barely only enough to detect, and nothing like the clear sense that he'd had when working with the pattern for fire.

For the building to collapse meant that earth had simply given out.

That, combined with the shaping he had detected, suggested to Tan that whatever had been done had been recent.

He looked around but saw no one in the street other than the three people from the building.

Yet he detected a sense of shaping, though he couldn't tell the direction or the target. It was near, and he had the sense that someone watched him, as if they saw him in spite of the shielding that he used.

Tan unsheathed his sword and made his way through the street, searching for the sense of shaping that he'd detected, but it was gone. The sense faded, and whoever had damaged the building was gone.

## 14

## SUPPORT FOR PAR-SHON

The tiles thudded beneath his boots as Tan hurried through the tower. He would have answers. There was enough dancing around his questions and not enough cooperation with what he needed to know, and now there were buildings falling in the city because a faction still attempted to damage the bonds, as if they wanted to wipe away the last remnants of Par. Tan wanted to know *who* had attacked the rune, but he also wanted to know *why*.

Worse, Amia had returned to the kingdoms, summoned back by the Aeta. Thankfully, Asgar had brought her, but that left Tan without her guidance. After what he'd seen, he needed her.

The answer had something to do with Par, of that he was certain, and Tolman would answer him this time.

Only, he couldn't find Tolman.

Rather than Tolman, Tan found Garza, wearing flowing robes that covered her bulk. The Mistress of Shapers role had diminished by placing Tolman in charge of the students, and she strode through the hall until she saw Tan. When she did, she froze and bowed deeply.

"My Utu Tonah," she said.

"Come with me, Garza," Tan said.

He didn't wait to see if she would follow, making his way through the tower until he reached the room in which he had first encountered the previous Utu Tonah. It seemed fitting that he would question Garza here since she had been the one to bring him to the Utu Tonah all those months ago.

Taking a seat on the chair in the center of the room, he fixed her with the hardest stare that he could muster. He would not harm her, but then, he *would* have answers, something he did not so far.

Garza gripped her hands together, keeping her eyes lowered.

"You're the Mistress of Shapers. Where is Tolman?" Tan asked first.

"My Utu Tonah, I do not know where he would have gone."

Tan frowned. This would have been easier had Tolman been here. He felt that he could persuade Tolman in ways that he couldn't with Garza. She could be intimidated, but that wasn't what he wanted, either.

"I would know whether you support Par-shon."

Garza frowned at him. "My Utu Tonah?"

Tan leaned forward. This had been troubling him since returning after finding the blacksmith destroyed. There had to be a faction in the city that supported Par—that was why the bonds remained on the buildings, even if they should have failed over time—and there was a faction that supported Par-shon and whatever the Utu Tonah had represented to them. He would know which was which.

"I would know if you support Par-shon."

She swallowed and cast her gaze back to the floor. Garza had been something resembling decent to him when he had been trapped, but she had still followed the Utu Tonah. All had. Tan had the sense that most followed willingly, searching for the power that he offered through his connection to the bonds with the elementals, but began to wonder if not all had supported him as he had thought.

"I support Par-shon, my Utu Tonah," she said.

Tan layered a spirit sensing on her and detected fear and anxiety, both of which he expected. But there was something else there as well, something that she hid from him. With enough of a spirit shaping, he could determine what that might be, but then, Tan had no interest in harming her. He wanted answers, preferably freely given.

"You support Par-shon and not Par?"

He said it softly and watched her.

Even if he were not able to sense spirit, he noted the way her pulse bounded with slightly more force and could practically hear her heart begin to race.

"My Utu Tonah?"

"I have come to discover that there is a faction of people who still support ancient Par," Tan said. "I would know if you are among them."

"Par has been gone for many years, my Utu Tonah. We are Par-shon only now."

Tan sniffed and stood. He made his way toward Garza and kept his guard up, fully aware that she was a potent water shaper. He detected nothing from her that told him she prepared to shape, but he wondered if she had discovered some way to shield her shaping from him much as he did with earth.

He stopped in front of her and leaned forward, close enough that he could smell the distinct odor of grass and leaves, the scents of her garden. "You understand that I can shape spirit," he said.

Garza swallowed and nodded.

"And you know that I can use spirit to detect whether you are truthful with me?"

Her eyes widened slightly, and he realized that she didn't know that.

"Now again, Garza, do you support Par-shon?"

She raised her head and met his eyes. "Do with me what you will, Utu Tonah."

Tan smiled. "Not 'my' Utu Tonah?"

"The Utu Tonah was never mine."

Tan smiled. "Good."

Garza blinked. "Utu Tonah?"

Tan turned away from her. "I am tired of everyone showing me false loyalty, Garza. You appear to be the first willing to say what you feel." He reached the chair and faced her. "I need to know how many still support Par."

"You can do with me what you want, but I will not reveal that."

"I could simply take the information I want." Tan had no intention of actually doing it, but he could use the threat of what he *might* do to persuade her. And he needed to know who supported Par and who supported Par-shon. The difference seemed minor, especially when he first came to Par-shon, but the implications were much greater than he could have expected.

"Then do what you will," she said.

"I am not the same Utu Tonah as the one who came before me," Tan said. "And from what I've found, the people of Par do not value the same as what Par-shon and the Utu Tonah valued." He sighed. "It seems that Par values much of the same as *me*."

Garza met his eyes and shook her head. "You say the right things, Utu Tonah, but we have suffered much. The last Utu Tonah came to Par making similar claims."

"What claims are those?"

Garza hesitated, and Tan wondered if she would answer at all. She sighed. "He claimed that he sought only the safety of the elementals and that bonding to them protected them and allowed us to understand them better."

Tan realized that he shared much the same philosophy, only his was born of a true connection to the elementals, one forged from the very first time he spoke to them when he nearly died and the nymid had saved him. From that moment onward, he had come to appreciate the elementals and recognized their unique potential. They were to be protected and understood, not attacked.

"And you fear that I am no different than him," Tan said.

Garza sighed. "There were some who thought that you would not return. That you were content to rule the lands across the sea."

Tan nearly snorted at the comment.

"And then you did return. The first thing that you did was destroy centuries of Par's heritage. How could you be any different?"

Not the destruction of the tiles, those runes that prevented shaping in the tower and throughout the city. That had been added and were new enough that Tan knew they had come from the Utu Tonah. But the destruction of the bonds that he'd seen the Council wearing, bonds that he had mistakenly believed represented forced elementals bonding. Had he only taken the time to *ask*.

"I didn't know," Tan said softly.

Garza watched him.

"It probably doesn't matter to you," Tan went on, "but I didn't know anything about Par. I knew only Par-shon. And Par-shon forced bonds, something I oppose. Since coming here, I have seen the way the bonds have been placed on the buildings throughout the city and have seen how they call to the elementals, not forcing an answer, but asking for their help. That is not the act of a people who would harm them."

"Not harm, Utu Tonah," she said.

Tan sighed. There had to be a different way to reach them,

but if he couldn't even reach out to Garza, how could he
expect to be able to reach the rest of the people of Par-shon?

"What *can* you tell me about Par?" he asked.

"As I said, it doesn't matter what you intend, Utu Tonah.
You will not destroy the rest of Par's heritage."

"I'm not the one you have to worry about."

"What do you mean by that?"

"Only that there is someone—or some*ones*—placing
marks on the bonds throughout the city. Whatever they do
damages them."

Garza frowned. "There are none in Par who would do
something like that. The Mistress of Bonds would prevent it."

"I *saw* it, Garza. A blacksmith with a mark for earth that
had been damaged." Tan wondered how long that blacksmith
had stood. Could it be like some of the other buildings
around the city and have been here for centuries? Or had it
been a more recent addition to the city? Either way, the
destruction of the shop was likely because of whatever
damage had been done to the rune. "And what if the Mistress
of Bonds was the reason it happened?"

Garza shook her head. The folds under her chin shook
with the motion. "That is impossible, Utu Tonah."

"Impossible? As impossible as your Utu Tonah being
defeated?"

Garza's wide face clouded, and Tan could tell that he was
getting through to her, but not as completely as he would
have liked. "You are more capable than he expected."

"Did you ever wonder how I managed to defeat him?"

Would telling her help? Tan didn't necessarily need

Garza's help, but he needed someone who understood what
Par had been like to be willing to speak to him, to work *with*
him, especially if he were to understand what it was that the
Utu Tonah intended by coming to Par. And now, if there was
something to the fact that these bonds were damaged, he
needed to understand who might be doing it—and what they
intended.

"You were stronger than him. And he underestimated
you. When you were here..." Her eyes widened, and Tan
suspected that she remembered she had been a part of his
capture here. "He thought only of the draasin," Garza went
on. "With that creature and his failure with what he planned
here, he thought that you would be able to bring him
that bond."

The final bond. Unity was what he called it, though Tan
had no idea what that meant. The Utu Tonah had bonded to
so many of the elementals, but that still hadn't given him an
understanding of them. He was connected to them, but it was
forced, nothing like the shared connection that Tan possessed
with them.

With the way that he had forced the bonds, Tan wondered
if the Utu Tonah would ever understand something like the
fire bond. Asboel claimed that no shaper had ever reached the
fire bond before, but was that because they didn't have the
capacity or because they were not willing to submit to the
needs of fire?

"What failure of what he planned here?" Tan asked, realizing that there was something more to what Garza said. That
might be the most important piece of what she told him.

"You don't know?"

Tan shook his head.

"That is not for me to share, Utu Tonah."

"Garza—"

"I cannot. The Mistress of—" She cut herself off, clapping her hand to her mouth, and then turned and ran from the room.

Tan let her leave, not wanting to chase her and doubting that it would change anything if he did. But she hid something from him that was more than simply about Par. Understanding what she hid was key to understanding the Utu Tonah, he suspected.

But what?

He needed Amia with him, but she had returned to the kingdoms. Asgar would see her back when her task was completed, but until then, he was alone in Par-shon. Even Honl would be helpful, especially given all that the wind elemental seemed to have learned, but Honl remained distant. Calling him would only distract him, and there was no real need at this time. Only a desire to not be alone, which was how he felt.

For the first time since forging the first bond, when he had sealed himself to Asboel and known the connection to the draasin, Tan felt alone.

Amia was there as she always was, distant but at the back of his mind. Kota and Honl, too. Even the nymid were there, though his connection to them was different. But none were ever-present, not like he was accustomed to with Asboel when he had essentially shared Tan's mind during his last days. There was a stark solitude, and Tan wasn't sure that he wanted it.

Standing alone as he tried to understand a strange land, he missed his friend more than ever before. Even were he to reach into the fire bond and pick on the memory of Asboel that existed there, it wasn't the same, and it never would be again.

Tan lowered himself into the chair that the Utu Tonah had once occupied, praying for answers. None came.

## 15

## FIRE CHOOSES

Tan used earth sensing to alert him when Tolman returned to the palace, though he could just as easily have used water sensing, he realized. Knowing Tolman the last weeks, he had become attuned to him in ways that he wouldn't have realized was possible before. Tan made a point of seeking him out.

"Where have you been?" he asked.

Tolman stopped and turned carefully toward him. "My Utu Tonah?"

"I have questions for you."

The other man's face blanched. "My Utu Tonah?" he repeated.

Tan debated what he intended to ask Tolman first. There was the question of Par and Par-shon, but Tan thought that he knew what he needed to do there. He would find Elanne and ask why she had been destroying the bonds throughout the city. But other than that, and assigning a new Master of

Bonds, one who might actually be willing to work with him to help him understand the intricacies of Par, there was the other comment that Garza had made that left Tan with questions. She knew something about what the Utu Tonah had been after here in Par.

"You served the previous Utu Tonah, did you not?"

Tolman bowed his head. Tan was growing weary of everyone avoiding his gaze. "I served, my Utu Tonah."

"What can you tell me of what the Utu Tonah planned for Par-shon?"

They stopped in front of one of the runes. Tan could tell that there was something else to it, though not *what*. Power surged from it, along with a calling to the elemental that would have been silenced by the tile the Utu Tonah had placed over it.

"I was not part of the inner council, my Utu Tonah."

"But you were a part of the council."

"That is for Par..." Tolman looked away, and his face flushed. "My Utu Tonah. I was not part of the previous council. I do not have answers to what you seek."

"You can't tell me what the Utu Tonah was after?" Tan asked.

"He sought bonds and gifted them to those loyal to him," Tolman said.

There was more to what the Utu Tonah had wanted than that, Tan felt increasingly certain. Not only from what he'd read in the Utu Tonah's journal but from Garza's comment. There was something about Par that had brought him here. Maybe it was only that this was a place of convergence. Garza mentioned a failure, but Tan hadn't discovered any failure of the Utu Tonah in his time here.

"There must have been something other than bonds," Tan said. "Why else would he have come to Par?"

"We never learned, my Utu Tonah."

"Some must have. You must have seen something that would tell you what he was after. Why else would Garza refer to his failure?"

The flush quickly faded from his cheeks, and he sucked in a breath.

"You know something."

Tolman shook his head. "Nothing, my Utu Tonah."

"I grow tired of the secrecy, Tolman. You told me that I was Utu Tonah. You allowed me to lead, but I can't do it with the secrets. I know there's a disagreement between those who still favor Par and those who follow the Utu Tonah. I have not decided which side you fall on."

"There is no side, my Utu Tonah."

"From what I have seen, Tolman, there is a side. I've already asked Garza which side she is on. Do I need to ask the same of you?"

Tolman didn't have the chance to answer. One of the children—a young girl by the name of Molly—raced into the hall. "Utu Tonah!" she shouted as she saw him and came skidding to a stop in front of him.

"Is everything well, Molly?"

"Yes. Yes!" She glanced at Tolman and then turned her attention back to Tan. "I need your help."

"Mine?" Tan asked.

She nodded and started down the hall, waving for him to follow. Curiosity as much as anything spurred him to follow. Earth sensing told him Tolman followed and helped him visualize the concerned look on the man's face.

At the end of the hall, Molly led them inside a room Tan didn't recognize. That wasn't unusual; Tan didn't recognize most of the rooms in the tower. Molly pointed to a blackened chair in the corner.

"Look," she urged.

"What am I looking at?" Tan asked.

She pointed at the chair again, but Tan still didn't know what it was that she wanted him to see.

Tolman seemed to recognize what Molly wanted to show them and walked to the chair, running his hand along the armrest. He brought it away and up to his nose. He sniffed his hand. "This was you?"

She nodded, her head bobbing enthusiastically. "Yes, Master Tolman."

"What is this?" Tan asked, making his way over to the chair. He touched it as Tolman had and found the armrest warm. Using fire, he sensed the blackness to the wood and realized that it had been shaped, and recently. A slow smile came to his mouth. "You shaped this?" he asked.

He held onto the fire sensing, letting the awareness of it linger. There was something more to the shaping, almost a strength that he wouldn't have recognized had he not been as skilled with the elementals. But this wasn't only a shaping. This came from the elementals.

"Utu Tonah?" Molly asked.

He'd already checked each of the children and noted that none of them had a bond forced on them, so that wouldn't explain the heavy presence of saa in the shaping. "Can you shape, Molly?" Tan asked.

She shook her head. "Not like you, Utu Tonah."

Tolman touched his arm and jerked his hand back, as if afraid that he'd dared to touch the Utu Tonah. He nodded to the other side of the room, so Tan followed him over. Tolman leaned in and lowered his voice as he spoke. "That one didn't have the same potential as the others," he said to Tan. "That was why she had her lessons here. For her to do this…"

"She speaks to saa," Tan said.

Tolman's shoulders tensed, and he shifted his feet as if to block Tan from reaching Molly. "If she did, my Utu Tonah, it was not like before. Please, you cannot tear it from her—"

"Tear what from her?" Tan asked.

Tolman looked terrified, but Tan couldn't understand what it was that would make him so nervous. Certainly not a young shaper of Par-shon, and a powerful one in these lands, learning to speak to the elementals.

"Please, Utu Tonah," Tolman said. "Let her keep…"

Tan stopped listening and focused on saa. The elementals would be powerful here, and he'd already spoken to fire in these lands. It shouldn't surprise him that another would be able to speak to the elementals in Par-shon, and especially not to saa. Something had changed in the kingdoms as well, and elementals that had not spoken to anyone for years had begun to speak once more, even to the point of forming bonds. The same would happen here, he suspected.

*Saa,* he called, reaching through the fire bond. *Did you speak to this girl?*

The steady crackling flame sense that he associated with saa returned. *Maelen. You object to this one?*

Tan could saw saa as a thin streamer of smoke as it swirled around Molly. He smiled. *I don't know anything about this one. Does she burn brightly?*

*Ah, Maelen. You know that fire could not bond if she did not.*

Tan chuckled. Tolman stopped whatever he was saying and looked at Tan.

"You would laugh at my concern?"

"Not at you, Tolman, but at what saa says about Molly." He went over to Molly and knelt down. "What does fire say to you?" he asked her.

A smile spread across her face, and she looked him in the eyes. It was refreshing to have someone actually look at him, and not with fear or anxiety about what he might do. "You said that they listen and that they will bond to us," she said.

"You haven't bonded."

She shook her head. "They tell me that they can't yet. But they *talk* to me, Utu Tonah! Just like you said they would."

Tan couldn't help but smile at her. "Saa thinks you have potential," he said.

"You speak to them too?" Her voice fell to a whisper.

"Molly, I speak to all the elementals, but I'm connected to fire the strongest."

She bit her lip and glanced over to Tolman. "They said I should tell you. That you would want to know. Master Tolman..."

"What about Master Tolman?" Tan asked.

She looked away from Tolman. "He said... he said it was dangerous to tell you if we were able to speak to any of them. That you would want to take them from us."

Tan patted Molly on the head. "You were right to tell me. And I won't take saa from you. That isn't for me to do. Besides, how will I know how brightly you can burn if you don't get the chance to speak to them?"

She beamed at him. "They called you something else, but I knew what they meant. It's easier when they talk inside me."

"What did they call me?"

She shook her head. "It was a strange name. Not a word I recognize."

Tan smiled. "Was it Maelen?"

Her eyes widened, and she nodded vigorously. "That's it! What does it mean?"

"It's an old word," Tan said. "And a name given to me by the draasin. Maelen were small creatures, but were said to be fierce." She laughed and covered her mouth. Tan smirked and nodded. "Sort of like you, I suspect. And now you know as much as I do about the name."

"That's a funny reason for a name."

"The draasin are funny creatures," Tan said. "Keep working with saa, Molly. If they say that you have potential, then you need to keep working." He nodded at the blackened arm of the chair. "And if that is what you can do when you work with saa, then I would agree."

She nodded again, "I will Utu Tonah... I mean, Maelen!" She giggled again and ran back over to the chair.

Tolman waited by the door, and Tan waved for him to follow as they left Molly to keep working. In the hallway, Tan leaned in to Tolman. "You told them not to tell me if they could speak to the elementals?"

"My Utu Tonah..."

"No. This is enough, Tolman. How can I work with them if I don't know what they are capable of doing? These children must learn to work with the elementals, but they need to do it in the right way. Someone like Molly, already forming a connection to the elementals, tells me that there is much potential here. You can't hide that from me, not if I am to help them understand what they can do and how to use it."

Tan didn't bother to tell him that it wouldn't matter if he tried. Tan's connection to the fire bond would tell him. He had known about the others who had bonded through the fire bond.

"My Utu Tonah, I am sorry. I will accept whatever punishment you have for me."

"Punishment?" Tan repeated. "I don't want to punish you. I want you to work with me to help these children learn. And I don't want to separate bonds that form naturally. The elementals would not choose to bond if they felt the shaper would abuse the bond."

Tolman swallowed. "I... I think I misunderstood you, my Utu Tonah. Perhaps I have underestimated you as well." He glanced at the now-closed door.

Behind it, Tan could hear snippets of Molly speaking to saa, though he didn't listen to the conversation. With the fire bond, Tan thought that he could hear what was said, but he didn't want to eavesdrop. Tan had the sense that Molly would share anything that he needed to hear anyway. But what he did recognize told him that she was learning aspects of shaping from saa, lessons that would be more powerful and meaningful than anything that she could learn from fire shapers, especially if she were bonded to saa.

"Do you really speak to *all* of the elementals?" Tolman asked.

Tan turned back to Tolman. "That's what I keep telling everyone. After everything that I've done, you still question my ability to speak to them?"

"There are some who question whether you are able to speak to them as you claim. They think that you defeated the Utu Tonah because you were able to secure more bonds than the other Utu Tonah."

Tan shrugged. "I was able to defeat him because I am able to speak to all the elementals. They strengthen me even without bonds. And it wasn't bonds that defeated the Utu Tonah; it was the shaping of all the lands across the sea working together that stopped him. I only used those shapings."

Tolman studied Tan a moment, squeezing his eyes shut as he took a few breaths. When he opened his eyes, he nodded. "This is something you must see, my Utu Tonah."

## 16

## WHAT PAR HIDES

They stopped at the edge of a steep slope. Far below, Tan saw craggy rocks that hadn't fully recovered after the Utu Tonah had drawn the elementals from the land. That restoration would take time. Even in Chenir, where the shapers there knew ways to speak to the elementals, to draw them back into the land, Chenir hadn't fully recovered.

"What do you want me to see here, Tolman?"

To the north, the land sloped downward and toward the sea, the crashing of waves audible. South stretched toward a river that probably had once taken up much of this ravine.

Tolman stood at the edge of the rock and pointed. "There," he said. "You must use fire. I… I have no strength in fire."

Tan searched with earth first, figuring that if Tolman could detect anything, it must be with earth, but there was nothing. Switching to fire as the other man suggested, he detected a nagging sense at the edge of his senses, but not one that he recognized. "What is it?"

"You asked what the Utu Tonah sought while in Par."

Tan nodded.

"This is what he sought. Only, he was never able to find it."

Tan sucked in a breath. "You hid it from him?"

"Not me, my Utu Tonah. All of Par. It was a quiet rebellion."

"Why show me now?" Tan wondered what he would find. What would be so important that they would protect it from the Utu Tonah and keep him from discovery?

"You... If you speak to the elementals, you would learn eventually."

"What is it?" Tan asked again.

"This is something that you will have to experience on your own."

Tan wasn't sure that he liked that answer, but there didn't seem to be any way for him to find out without simply going and looking.

If Tolman claimed a connection to fire existed down below —and Tan had detected that there was—then he would use that as a guide. Holding onto the sense of fire, he followed the faint sense, dropping down the side of the rock on a shaping of wind and fire until he was nearly to what he detected. Whatever it was had been buried deep within the ground.

Tan glanced up, wondering if Tolman played some kind of prank on him. Reaching any farther from here would require him to shape through the stone, but using earth sensing, Tan detected a massive void deep beneath. Whatever Tolman intended for him to find would be under there. Maybe it was nothing other than a strange cavern, but maybe there really was something. Without his connections to fire and earth, he doubted that he would have detected anything. Not only earth but the connection that he gained through Kota.

*What is this?* Tan asked her.

He sensed her loping across the rock as the hound raced toward him. A mixture of curiosity and a sense of uncertainty radiated from her. Whatever he was about to go after had her nervous.

*Careful Maelen,* she said. *I cannot reach there. Another protects it.*

*Another?*

*Of earth. They are strong and do not care for my intrusion.*

An earth elemental protected whatever was in the cavern, and Kota couldn't reach it. That piqued his interest more than anything else.

Using a shaping of earth that he mixed with a touch of fire, he burrowed a hole through the rock, straining for the cavern that he sensed deep below. The shaping required him to push with more effort than he would have expected, and Tan added a rumbling call to the earth elemental that he suspected was involved in hiding the cavern from him, requesting the elemental's help.

Tan doubted that he would have been able to reach the cavern had he not attempted to connect with the elemental. Whatever was there was meant to be difficult to reach. The longer he held onto the connection, the more he became aware that there was something else protecting the cavern. There was a connection there, one that he wasn't expecting to find but one that he had sensed throughout the city. Bonds. Runes that called to the elementals, asking for their help. And in this place, they answered gladly.

Not only earth but all the elementals worked here to protect this secret. When Tolman had said that Par had protected this place, he might have downplayed the strength that gathered here.

Tan sent a call out to all the elementals that he could reach. Par-shon possessed much strength in many of the elementals, not only fire with saa, but also of earth, the silent but powerful elemental that he detected here, and wind, with wyln gusting through, and even water, with udilm connected to these lands nearly as much as it was to Doma.

He could speak to them all, and did, sending his call for help.

As he did, he asked them to recede, to leave the cavern, if only long enough for Maelen to enter.

The response came slowly, but it did come. The elementals departed, pulling away, all but earth and a trace of fire. Saa made it clear that it *needed* to be there.

If he hadn't been interested before, Tan was definitely now. For saa to want to remain, even when earth was so prominent here, told him that there was something to this cavern that he really *had* to discover.

Using a shaping of earth, Tan pushed earth to the side. With fire as prominent as it was here, he decided to add more of it to his shaping, ultimately mixing fire and earth in equal measures. An opening formed, slowly widening. The walls glowed from Tan's shaping, enough for him to see that the tunnel led down—far down to the cavern below.

*Can you tell what it is?* he asked Kota.

*That way is still blocked to me.*

*When I go down, can you join me?*

*I do not think I will be allowed.*

Tan had suspected as much, given the tight way that the earth elemental he detected here controlled the cavern, but descending below placed him at some risk, didn't it?

He looked up and saw Tolman lowering himself on a shaping of earth. He eyed the tunnel Tan had shaped into place. "I can see that I was right. Had I kept this from you, you would have discovered eventually."

"What is below?"

"As I said, you must experience that yourself."

Had Tan not been so intrigued by the sense of fire he detected in the cavern, he might not have attempted to reach it, but he wanted to know. He practically *needed* to know.

"You will come with me."

Tolman shook his head. "Not here. Earth is strong here, but not for me. There would be others if you do not wish to go alone."

Tan sighed. Others. And more questions about Par versus Par-shon. If only he had a clear answer, but then that was the reason that he came here, to gain a clearer understanding of what Par hid from Par-shon and the previous Utu Tonah.

"She will watch you. Do not think to betray me." Tan

nodded to Kota, and his bonded flashed her fangs. Tolman turned and saw her and his eyes widened.

Without waiting to see how Tolman would react, Tan jumped into the tunnel.

Heat pressed against him, but he no longer feared heat. Fire was a part of him and would not burn him. In spite of his effort to maintain a uniform width to it, the tunnel narrowed as he descended. He dropped quickly, practically sliding through the earth.

And then he stopped. Tan had reached the cavern. Curiosity filled him. All the elementals had worked together, much like they had at the place of convergence when Tan had rescued Asboel. That much collaboration between the elementals surprised him.

Tan shaped fire, drawing on saa. A ball of light sparked into view, and he fed the flames with a shaping of fire, adding more and more until the flame took hold on its own, not needing him to add anything more to the shaping. He released control and saa fed it, filling the cavern with light.

It was a massive space. Walls of smooth stone surrounded him, and he knew that they had been shaped. Power radiated from somewhere nearby, filled with the strength of fire.

Tan made his way toward the sense of power. Earth sensing didn't give him any insight as to what he might find, and neither did fire. Wind and water left him with no more answers.

Could there be something of spirit here?

Tan didn't think that was the case, but what, then?

He reached an array of stones, each nearly up to his waist,

with ribbed sides layered in striations of color: black and deep blue and scarlet. They were almost perfectly oval but had a wider section on the bottom. All were about the same size, and they clustered in something like a circle, nearly two dozen in all.

This was where Tan detected fire, but he didn't understand why he would. There was noting about the rock that seemed like he *should* detect fire from it.

He laid his hand on the first stone. The rough edge was hot, much hotter than he would have expected. The cavern stone seemed to draw away the heat, but why would it do that? The other elementals seemed to add to the effect, helping the stone pull away the heat.

Tan frowned. With a powerful sensing of fire, he reached for the stone.

And felt pushed back.

It was the first time fire had repelled him.

But he was connected to the fire bond. He didn't have to rely on his ability to sense only.

Focusing his mind as he had learned to do when connecting to the fire bond, he reached for it. Once there, he felt the connection, the drawing sense of fire, and pulled through that to determine what hid from him in these stones.

A great stirring answered him, and he nearly lost his focus.

"Draasin?" he whispered.

The word reverberated through the cavern.

He made his way around each of the stones and realized

that each of them were not stones as he had thought, but draasin eggs.

Great Mother. *All* of these were eggs. But how?

Had Asboel known? Tan had never asked whether there was any way for the draasin to remain viable now that they had returned to the world, and Asboel had never spoken of it, but Tan had feared that with the passing of his friend, the draasin would eventually fade from the world as well. But what if Asboel had known that there was a collection of eggs like this?

At least Tan understood the reason that Par felt strongly about protecting this place. With as much as the former Utu Tonah had sought the draasin, claiming the need for a bond that would bring him to Unity, having it so close to him, where he would have needed nothing more than to discover a way for the eggs to hatch... that would have made him incredibly powerful, especially if he managed to force bonds to *all* of these draasin here.

*Did you know?*

He sent the connection through the fire bond and on to Sashari. She remained in the kingdoms with Cianna, and he recognized that she was distracted hunting, but this was too important not to question.

*Maelen.*

She came from a long way away, and it seemed muted as if the shaping that protected this place also limited his ability to reach her.

Tan pulled an image of the eggs into mind and sent that

through the fire bond to Sashari. *Did you know that so many remained?*

There was a delay before she responded. *So many. We had hoped…*

*You didn't know?*

*We didn't know, Maelen. So much had been lost in the time that we were away.*

Away. Tan noted that she did not remind him how the draasin had been trapped and forced to be a part of the shaping that had hidden the artifact. Sashari didn't hold any more anger about that than Asboel had near the end. The draasin could hold their anger deep, but they had come to understand the need for their service. The anger that drove Asboel at the end had been directed toward those who thought to use the draasin against the elementals, not against the ancient shapers who had used him to protect the artifact.

*You knew there would be eggs?*

*That is how it has always been, Maelen. A clutch is buried, and some are lost. Fire would not let the draasin light extinguish.*

*Will there be others?*

Sashari didn't answer at first. *It is possible that these will be the last.*

Tan ran his hand over one of the eggs. Deep within, he felt a subtle stirring that reverberated against his connection to the fire bond. With enough fire and enough coaxing, Tan suspected that he could convince the egg to hatch.

Was that part of his purpose now? Honl spoke of how the Great Mother used him, at first to free the draasin, and then to show that Incendin should not be feared, and finally to defeat the Utu Tonah. Maybe she was done with him yet. And he didn't mind, especially when he was used like this.

Now wasn't the time to attempt to hatch the eggs. Before he did that, he would want Sashari, Enya, and Asgar nearby. The other hatchling still hadn't taken her name, so Tan didn't think that she would be of much use with the eggs. And the eggs would need to be moved from Par-shon.

*No, Maelen. They cannot hatch anywhere but the land they were laid. They will not be viable.*

*There are nearly two dozen here. These are all of Par-shon?* Or Par, since they were from the time before the Utu Tonah had come.

*Not all. The colors are wrong for that land. You must learn where they belong and return them to that land to hatch.*

There were so many! But for the draasin, especially given everything they had done to help him, and save the people of the kingdoms, Tan would make whatever sacrifice they demanded of him.

*How will I know?*

*The fire bond will show you.*

Tan started toward one of the other eggs. It was lighter colored and streaked with black. In many ways, the egg itself was beautiful. As he made his way toward it, the walls of the cavern began to rumble.

*Maelen!*

It was Kota, and the urgency in her voice surprised him, as did the difficulty she had even reaching him. Tan glanced at the eggs, concern for them growing with the continued rumbling from the ground, and sent a shaping to the earth, asking the elemental within the rock to come up and protect the eggs. The floor shook and then, slowly, the rock began to form around the eggs, sealing them in place.

*Thank you*, Tan sent to the earth elemental.

There came a deep response, almost too difficult for him to understand, that reminded him of a drumming, much like what the shapers of Chenir used.

Then the walls around him began to shake.

Tan listened to the earth and felt the ongoing shaking. It would collapse in moments.

He started into the tunnel, sending a surge of heat toward the rock that now covered the eggs, pulling saa into the protection. He drew on wyln and udilm as well, not certain they could do anything to help the eggs here, but they had provided some protection before Tan had asked them to withdraw.

There wasn't a chance for him to know if they answered.

The tunnel began to collapse around him.

## 17

## BORN OF FIRE

Tan shifted his focus to earth, forcing it back and to the sides to keep from getting buried in stone. He pushed heat and flame that he drew from saa at first, and then from the fire bond itself against the rock. With enough force, he pressed up and up, streaking ever higher through the tunnel.

Walls began to collapse on him, but Tan continued to push, using shapings that he controlled, not calling on the elementals. When that failed, he added the strength of the elementals to his shaping, drawing from Kota, from fire, and from wind. All of it boosted him and sent him skyward.

But he wasn't fast enough.

The rock collapsed, sending him backward.

Tan dropped, pressed down by massive amounts of stone and wind, all pushing down on him, attempting to crush him. Only by the strength of his shaping did he manage to keep from getting crushed under the weight of the rock.

At the bottom of the cavern, he rolled to the side as rock and debris crashed into the cavern with him. He shaped a barrier of earth and wind around him, buffering the impact of the stone. Even then, he barely held out against it.

The rock stopped moving.

Tan stood, pushing away the rock that had fallen around him. Little room remained in the cavern: rock filled it. He reached with fire sensing and detected that the draasin eggs were intact, and let out a relieved sigh. Whoever had attacked him had failed to damage them.

At least there was that victory.

But now he had to get free of the rock.

He moved slowly, finding that each step was difficult. The rock piled all around him, and he had to crush it with a shaping of earth and wind, pulverizing it so that he could move freely.

He glanced around. The tunnel should not have collapsed on him. He had shaped it with earth, using fire to augment his shaping, but something had failed. Was there something that he missed? A shaper stronger than he realized? Or had Tolman misled him?

He would have answers.

First, he had to get free.

What had once been a massive expanse of a cavern was now full of loose rock. Tan shaped his way toward the draasin eggs, careful to shield his shaping as he went. If there were someone above ground who had attempted to harm him, he would not have them know they had failed. But what better way to rid Par-shon of the Utu Tonah than to crush him beneath the ground?

Not Tolman, though. Tan didn't think that the earth shaper would have betrayed him, not considering his connection to earth and the fact that he had revealed the draasin eggs. That meant that there was someone else here who intended to harm him. And perhaps not only him, but the eggs as well.

He continued to crush rock, leaving it as little more than dust that he swept away on a shaping of wind as he made his way toward the draasin. Fire sensing told him that they were intact, but they had survived in this cavern for at least a thousand years. He would not have them damaged the moment that he discovered them.

When he reached the eggs, he found the rock around them had practically melted. Saa had done its part to protect them, granting them the heat from the elemental. The earth elemental here had absorbed most of the impact, but there was one egg where the rock around it had failed and where the heat from saa had slipped through, heating it to a glowing red.

Tan approached carefully, holding his hands out in front of him. *What happens when saa heats the egg?* he asked Sashari.

*Saa would not do something like that.*

*Not intentionally.*

He sent an image of the collapsed tunnel and the way that the rock and saa had worked together to try to protect the eggs. Through the fire bond, he sensed Sashari's agitation at that, and a few for the unborn draasin.

*That one must be fed, Maelen.*

*I don't understand.*

There was a delay as if Sashari had to push to get through the connection, making Tan wonder if whoever had attacked had somehow managed to impact the fire bond, but then she answered.

Her answer came in images, much like what Tan had been sending to her.

When she mentioned feeding the draasin, he imagined hunting for food, as Sashari had done for her hatchlings until they were old enough to hunt alone. But that wasn't what she had meant at all. The draasin didn't need food at first, but to be connected to fire and the fire bond. They were of fire, but the initial moments after birth were essential for tying them to fire.

And this egg, heated as it was by saa, would hatch.

Another draasin would join the world. It would be Tan's responsibility to see that it lived.

He grabbed the egg in both hands and sent a shaping of fire through it, reaching for a connection to the hatchling within. The sense of it was weak but grew stronger. Saa maintained a connection as well, understanding that now that the draasin egg had started to hatch, fire must remain in contact with it.

Tan added his shaping to it, filling the egg with a shaping of fire that came from him but also from the elemental energy he sensed around him. The draasin hatchling began to stir. Slowly at first, but with increasing movement, striking at the shell. The heat softened the shell as well.

Sashari pushed on him, guiding him how to feed the draasin, showing him how to send even more fire to it. The draasin became more active, pushing on the shell.

And then Tan felt it within the fire bond.

No longer was it some vague sense of fire. This was an elemental of fire, born into the bond. There was power here, and he needed to bring it to life.

Tan continued to draw on fire, pulling more, borrowing first from his own stores and then from saa around him. When that began to be depleted, Tan started pulling from the connection he sensed with the draasin, pulling from Asgar and Sashari and Enya, who each gave freely. Then he sensed that beginning to fail, and Tan pulled from the fire bond itself.

He had never pulled on fire through the bond before. Had he not been wrapped as he was in the shaping, needing the strength of fire in order to help the draasin egg, he would not have tried. But he had the sense that the egg would not survive if he did nothing.

The attack that had collapsed the tunnel had required the help of saa and the earth elemental, but this egg had been damaged and had started the process that would lead it to hatch.

Wrapped in the fire bond, he felt the overwhelming greatness of fire. There was the memory of Asboel within it, and he imagined that his friend guided him, though he had only spoken to Asboel through the fire bond once since his friend had died.

Power flooded him.

But Tan was not the vessel and was not the target of the

fire he summoned. He poured it into the egg, in massive amounts, and heat and flame flooded it.

Even that began to fail.

His strength was not enough to feed the draasin and save the elemental of fire. The egg, and the potential of the draasin, would die.

*Use the Mother.*

The suggestion came from somewhere. Perhaps saa, or Asgar, or Sashari. But it sounded like Asboel once again guiding him.

Tan added a shaping of spirit.

At first, he drew on a small shaping, but then he pulled on more and more, the fire bond telling him that he *needed* to use more spirit. He exhausted all the spirit that *he* could pull, and then reached through his bond with Amia and began pulling on that as well. She gave to him gladly, suddenly aware of what did and what he attempted.

Spirit flooded from him, joining the shaping of fire, as it began to sink into the egg.

The shaping failed.

The egg cracked.

Tan sagged and fell against the nearest egg.

His body ached. His mind throbbed.

And he felt the egg shaking.

Tan turned to the egg. The shell had a long split down one side of it, and what had been a black shell with streaks of gray now glowed a red so dark that it might still be black.

A small claw poked out of the shell and began pulling at shards. Wings unfurled.

Tan watched, mesmerized by the way the draasin hatched. Long forelegs crawled out of the egg and then the long snout pressed out, piercing the shell.

Small, yellow eyes blinked open.

The draasin snapped and hissed a breath of steam at him.

It crawled from the egg and fully unfurled its wings. They were deep black, much like the shell. The draasin flapped its wings but couldn't fly.

Tan stood and didn't try moving toward the draasin, not wanting to frighten it.

The draasin started forward, flicking his wings and sniffing at the air. With each breath, it snorted steam, and then it managed to shoot fire.

Reaching through the fire bond, Tan connected to the draasin, sensing the connection there. The draasin resided within the fire bond, but only weakly. The connection grew stronger with each moment, pulling on fire, *feeding* on the bond.

Now he understood what Sashari had meant about feeding the elemental.

*You have done well, Maelen,* she sent to him.

*What now?*

*The hatchling must feed. Then it must eat.*

*How will I know when it is ready?*

Sashari sent a sense of amusement through the bond. *You will know.*

Tan looked around the cavern. One of the hatchlings had survived. Another draasin was born into the world. And he had aided in that.

*Is that what it was like for you with the hatchlings?*

*Each is different. This one will be strong. Much fire was needed to feed the hatching, and the feeding is not yet complete. He will rival even Asboel.*

But first, he had to survive.

And that meant that Tan had to get free of the cavern and then find a way to protect the draasin. The hatchling was small, no larger than a puppy, and it completed a circle around the other eggs, sniffing at them as it went. When finished, the draasin curled up on the ground in front of Tan, wrapping its wings around itself.

"Time to get you out of here," Tan said to it.

The draasin tipped his head back and looked up at him, blinking with its two yellow eyes. It snorted a streamer of steam as if to answer.

The draasin would not be strong enough to make it out of the cavern on his own, and Tan didn't want to leave it here, not while it continued to feed on the connection with fire and still needed to eat.

"Will you come with me?" Tan found speaking aloud to the draasin easier. He could attempt to reach it through the fire bond, but given the size and the fact that the draasin continued to feed on fire, he didn't want to distract it from the bond.

The draasin stood on thin legs. If Sashari was right and the draasin would eventually rival Asboel, the creature would grow to an enormous size, but right now, it was small and frail. It would need protection.

Tan lifted the draasin, who crawled up his arms and looped around his neck, settling in there. Tan didn't have to hold it this way, and it managed to secure itself there.

Having the draasin riding him was a strange sensation. Even stranger was the fact that the draasin rode him in nearly the same place that he did when riding on Asboel or Asgar.

Through the fire bond, he heard an amused laughter from Asgar. *Now you're the horse for him.*

Tan ignored him.

He stopped where he had landed when the tunnel collapsed. The ground showed the impact of his landing, and he'd left a trail in the pulverized stone as he made his way toward the draasin. Getting back out meant that he would have to shape his way free from the tunnel, but after feeding the draasin, he wasn't certain that he had the necessary strength to manage that.

But the elemental might be able to help.

Tan focused on the power that he sensed within the stone. The elemental continued to provide protection for the draasin eggs, supported by saa.

*Help me get this hatchling to safety,* he sent to the earth elemental. *You have protected him for long enough; it is my turn to do what I can.*

The ground trembled softly in response.

Above him, rock pulled apart, separating into a crack wide enough for him to get through. Tan pushed up on a shaping of wind and fire, into the crack, trusting that the elemental would allow him to get free.

Unlike the tunnel that he had shaped that had narrowed the closer he went to the cavern, the crack remained the same size all the way along. The draasin barely moved, radiating a comforting warmth. Tan recognized the way it continued to feed on the fire bond, though the draw became less and less, as if it was getting full.

The rock was smooth all the way through.

Tan shot through the crevasse formed by the elemental.

Then he emerged.

He stood upon a shaping of wind, anger coursing through him at the fact that someone had thought to attack him while he was beneath the ground, thinking that they could harm him as he sought to understand what happened to the draasin, that they would endanger the draasin that had been protected by this cavern for centuries. They would find that he would not fall easily.

Lightning crackled from the sky, summoned by his shaping.

The draasin stirred on his back and sent a single huff of steam.

Tan surveyed the ground around him, but there was no sign of whoever had attacked, causing the tunnel to collapse.

What of Tolman?

He rose higher and higher until he reached the top of the rocky overlook that led down into the ravine. Once there, he searched using earth and spirit.

Then he saw Tolman.

The shaper's body lay bent and twisted on the ground. Blood streaked around him, soaking into the earth.

Tan dropped next to him and reached for the pulse in his neck. It was there, but thready and weak. Using water, he stabilized the injuries, but water shaping was not something he had much skill with. Tolman needed a healer.

But would he be able to find Garza and convince her to help?

18

THOSE WHO SUPPORT PAR

The draasin curled in front of the hearth, soaking in the warmth of the flames. Saa burned brightly, filling the air of the small room in the estate with his strength. Tan paced, watching the draasin and marveling at how *small* the creature was, but already he detected strength from him. In that, Sashari might have underestimated what it was capable of doing.

Tolman lay on a cot in the back of the room. He hadn't moved since Tan returned him to the estate, but at least the bleeding had stopped. His injuries were severe. A deep gash across his face had bled heavily but wasn't nearly as dangerous as the hole in his stomach, as if someone had speared him. That had required more strength to control the bleeding. Had he not fed the draasin, he might have had enough strength to help Tolman himself.

Tan looked up at the soft knock on the door.

When it opened, Maclin poked his head inside. "My Utu

206

Tonah," he said with a bow. His gaze swept across the room, noting Tolman lying on the cot and then the draasin curled up in front of the fire. He sucked in a sharp breath and pulled his attention back to Tan. "You summoned the gardener?"

Tan nodded. When searching for Garza, he hadn't known any other way to reach her other than asking for Maclin to bring him the gardener. As he hadn't seen any other gardeners in Par-shon, he thought it a safe gamble.

Garza came into the room. Tan sensed the irritation within her, but it evaporated as soon as she saw Tolman. Unlike Maclin, she didn't notice the draasin lying next to the hearth.

"What happened to him?"

She didn't bother with any title or honorifics, and Tan was grateful that she wanted only to get to business.

"I don't know. He was attacked after *I* was attacked."

Garza glanced over at him. "Who would attack you, Utu Tonah?"

Tan snorted. He wasn't entirely certain who had been behind it, but he could think of several who might have. The first on that list was Elanne, and a desire to prevent him from reaching the draasin eggs. Once he found her, he would discover what exactly she intended.

"Can you help him?" he asked.

Garza had already set her hands on him, and her shaping built. Without looking at him, she asked, "Why could you not heal him? I assume that you're capable, especially given the fact that you destroyed your predecessor."

"I can heal, but I was distracted with another task that required my energy."

Garza grunted and continued her shaping. "He was seri-
ously injured. You must have done something to help him, or
he wouldn't still be alive."

Tan chuckled. "I did something," he agreed.

She continued to work, not saying anything more as she
did. Her shaping was complicated and nearly as talented as
what he had seen from Wallyn. Unlike Wallyn, her shaping
came in waves, sweeping through him and then receding. As
it receded, Tan noted how the water shaping pulled away the
injury. When it crashed into Tolman, she sent healing waves
through him.

Tolman's injuries stabilized and his breathing became
more regular. His cheeks were pale, but some of the color had
returned to them, more than had been there before.

Garza stepped away and rested her hands on her belly. "It
is done. He will live."

"Good. Then you can send word to those for Par-shon that
the attack on Par failed."

Garza jerked her head around at the statement. "What do
you mean?"

Tan stepped toward her. "The attack came when Tolman
revealed the secret you alluded to, the one the Utu Tonah
failed to discover."

He moved to the side to reveal the draasin lying next to
the fire. As he did, it uncurled, stretching his wings. Tan
couldn't be certain, but it seemed to him that the draasin had
already grown larger than when he had hatched. He certainly
produced more heat than when he hatched, radiating warmth
that came from all the fire that he'd fed on.

"You found it," she whispered. She glanced past Tan to Maclin, who stood at the door, watching silently.

"I was guided there."

Garza looked down to the resting form of Tolman. "He took you there? He should not have!"

Tan sniffed. "Maybe he recognized that it wouldn't matter if he didn't share with me, that I would discover eventually. I have not lied about my abilities, Garza. I *do* speak to the elementals. I do not command them, but they listen and will often cooperate. That is the reason I was able to defeat the Utu Tonah."

Garza started toward the draasin, but it breathed out a small streamer of fire, and she stopped, stepping back. "You should not have been able to reach that place. None has managed to do so since Par was founded."

That would explain the difficulty that Tan had in reaching it.

"The elementals granted access. *That* is the reason I reached it. Now. You will send word?" Tan asked.

Garza pulled her gaze off the draasin. "You would really want me to share what you did?"

"Not what I did, but how one of your own was attacked. I may not know much about your heritage, but I have learned this much: Par shared many of the same values with me. If anything, I will see that Par is restored."

Garza swallowed. "You would do this?"

Tan smiled tightly. He hadn't known what he intended to accomplish in coming here, but now he thought that he understood. He *would* restore Par, though he might not know what that meant. In time, he would. "I will do what is necessary," he said.

Garza watched him a moment and then nodded before leaving.

Tan sighed as looked upon the fallen shaper. He sensed Maclin's approach, and the man bowed to him again, his gaze sweeping back to the draasin. "Would you pardon a question, my Utu Tonah?"

Tan nodded.

"That... creature. Is it yours?"

He stepped toward the draasin. He should have been more cautious about revealing the draasin here, especially knowing how the prior Utu Tonah had attempted to reach them. Even with Garza there had been risk, but with her, the risk had been greater that she wouldn't be willing to help Tolman. With Maclin... he didn't know what Maclin would do or what side he fell on.

What would happen if Maclin knew how to force bonds? Would he attempt to do so with this draasin? The elemental was too young to safely take a bond, and if he did, he would be powerful.

"The elementals belong to no one," Tan said.

Maclin blinked. "Of course, my Utu Tonah. Only I... I had not expected to see one so young. You will bond it?"

Tan doubted that he would bond fire again. Since losing Asboel, a part of him missed the bond and wished to have the connection to one of the fire elementals, but now he had a connection to *all* the fire elementals through the fire bond itself. It was different than what he had shared with Asboel—

there was not the guidance that he once had received from the draasin—but Tan no longer needed the same level of advice. He had changed so much since he first had bonded to Asboel, and the nature of the bond had changed during that time as well. Now Tan found his guidance elsewhere, through the fire bond or from spirit or even from the other elementals. But he doubted that he would find the same connection to fire again.

"This draasin will take no bond unless he decides," Tan said. He put the force of spirit behind his words, wanting there to be no question to Maclin, or whoever Maclin might tell about the draasin, of what Tan's intentions were for the creature.

Maclin remained quiet for a few moments before letting out a long sigh. "You truly are different than him, aren't you?"

There was no *Utu Tonah*, and no fear in the way that Maclin asked, only curiosity. Tan noted how the servant no longer stood with a deferential pose but held his hands clasped in front of him, seemingly at peace.

Was the answer to his question about Par versus Par-shon in front of him the entire time?

"I am not the Utu Tonah," Tan said. Perhaps it was time for the people of Par-shon to see that. If he were to remain here and lead—and given the need that he'd seen and the fact that there were draasin remaining for him to protect, he suspected that he needed to remain—he would take on a title of his choosing. And there was only one that he could think to use. "I am the Maelen."

His bonded elementals responded to his statement with something that seemed almost a cheer. All referred to him as Maelen, but Tan had never really shared that openly. Why would he now, other than it simply felt *right*.

Maclin nodded. "There will be others who will seek to defeat you, especially now that you have brought—" he nodded to the draasin, "—back to Par. But the Lasithan will now know you, and they will support you."

"I take it from the statement that you lead the Lasithan?" The word had some familiarity, as if it had roots in ancient *Ishthin*, but Tan didn't recognize it.

Maclin took a breath and nodded. "There have always been some who knew and understood. Even when *he* came, we watched, and waited, and did what was needed to keep the past safe, knowing that the future would depend on it."

"What past were you wanting to keep safe?" Tan asked.

"There is the past that is known, and the past that is unknown," Maclin said. "The Lasithan aim to keep both safe, though the unknown past is most relevant."

Tan wondered what Honl would say if he had a chance to speak to Maclin. Would the wind elemental, especially with his newfound interest in understanding the past, feel as compelled as Maclin? Would Maclin know something that Honl had not discovered? Maybe Maclin would even have answers to the strange darkness that Honl seemed convinced existed.

"Then you are of Par?" Tan asked.

Maclin glanced to Tolman. "Of Par, preceding Par." He

shook his head. "Both answers would be similar, I think. The Lasithan have served."

"Did you know?"

Maclin tipped his head to the side and frowned.

"Did you know what he intended when he made his push across the sea?"

"Ah. You still think this is all about a quest for power."

"Wasn't it?" Tan glanced at Tolman and felt the pull of the elementals in the room. Once, such awareness would have failed him in Par-shon, but then, the elementals had failed everyone in Par-shon.

No, he decided, that wasn't quite right. The people of Par-shon had failed the elementals. Had they not, the Utu Tonah never would have pushed hard enough to damage them. He never would have grown strong enough to force Tan to confront him. But then, Tan would never have needed to come to Par-shon and learn about the draasin eggs here.

Asboel had often claimed that the Great Mother had a plan for him, and that was the reason that Tan was asked to do as much as he was. Tan wondered how that could possibly have been true, but then, he had been the only one to realize that the lisincend could be saved. Tan had been the only one willing to give the hounds a chance at redemption. What would have been lost had he simply attacked them like so many others had over the years? Elementals would have been lost, and so many already had been.

It was the same with kaas. Had Tan not searched for an alternative, another way to stop the creature, he would have been forced to destroy the elemental. He wasn't even certain it was possible for him to destroy kaas, but had the twisted elemental continued to attack the people and elementals of his homeland, what other choice would Tan have had? Yet it almost seemed as if the Great Mother *had* brought him face to face with kaas, as if she *wanted* Tan to be the one to help, knowing who he was and what he believed.

And if that were the case, how could Tan *not* continue to search for what role the Great Mother might have for him?

"You saw that there was more to his plan," Maclin said. "I can see it in your face, Maelen."

It was strange, yet also fitting, to have someone other than the elementals refer to him as Maelen. When the elementals did it, it always reminded Tan of his connection to Asboel and the nickname that the draasin had placed upon him. With Maclin, it felt like more of a title, yet no less appropriate.

"What was this Unity that he sought?"

Maclin sighed. "You ask what others were not able to determine. As much as we wanted to know his mind, to understand what drove him, we were never able to determine what it was that he truly wanted. At the beginning, most thought it nothing more than power, but that desire changed over time."

From reading the Utu Tonah's journal, Tan didn't think that it had been about power, at least not at first. It might have become about that, but when he first came to Par, there had been more of a curiosity than anything else, and a desire to understand the elementals through bonding to them. He had wanted power, but it was not power for the sake of power. To Tan, that seemed different.

But something changed for him, and Tan wasn't sure when it had.

"Garza said he failed. And Tolman told me that he had wanted to find the draasin."

"He knew that draasin still existed. Fire would have changed had the draasin truly been eliminated entirely. That it had not told him that somewhere, there was a potential for them. When he first arrived, and we began to suspect what he was after, the Lasithan worked especially hard to hide their existence. Some feared that he would bond enough elementals that it wouldn't matter. I admit that I was among them. But then the draasin appeared across the sea." Maclin nodded to Tan.

"They were restored to this world," Tan said. "And I don't regret the fact that I did."

Maclin smiled. In the time that they'd been talking, Maclin had dropped his subservient demeanor and had adopted a more confident manner. This was a man accustomed to leading.

"You should not regret returning fire to this world. I think that without it, *he* would have succeeded in reaching them eventually. In that way, you and your connection to them prevented a much worse catastrophe."

Freeing Asboel had given Tan the connection to the draasin, and through the draasin, to the fire bond. That, as much as anything, had been the way that he'd managed to defeat the Utu Tonah. "What will your Lasithan do now?"

"Now, Maelen?" Maclin still managed to make the title respectful. "You mean now that you have demonstrated the ability to reach the draasin that was long promised to return? Many assumed that it would be someone of Par, and I think few truly believed that you had the ability you claimed, but for you to have reached the draasin... There would not have been another way."

He indicated Tolman, who appeared to rest comfortably. "And for him to have shared the location, something that only the strongest among us had ever learned, tells me that you managed to gain his trust." Maclin glanced over to the draasin near the fire. The small fire elemental stretched his wings and shifted his slender tail so that it better curled around him, leaving the barbed end pointing away. "I admit to curiosity about *how* you managed to convince Tolman."

"I don't know what I did, but it had something to do with the students, I think. He was afraid that I would use them and try to find the bonds they formed naturally, I suspect because he assumed I would steal them. And there is one of his students that saa thinks highly of. It was after working with her that he brought me to the draasin."

Maclin sighed and stepped up to the cot holding Tolman and squeezed his arm. "Old friend, you risked much with your decision," he said softly.

*Tolman blinked his eyes open. A smile spread across his face. "You survived."*

"What happened?"

"When you descended, there was a disturbance in earth. That place has long been protected by bonds, so such disturbance should not have been possible, and certainly not with such strength, but..."

"My tunnel collapsed," Tan said.

Tolman nodded. "I was attacked. I did not see who it was, only that they were powerful."

"Someone does not want Par to return. They prefer the ways of Par-shon," Maclin said.

Tan let out a frustrated sigh. He suspected that he knew who it had been, but not *why*. What would Elanne and those under her gain by continuing to bond? She had seen how Tan had destroyed the bonds and had heard him discuss his unwillingness to force bonds on the elementals, and maybe that was all the reason that she needed to try to end him. She might not be able to defeat him directly, but if she could collapse the earth on top of him, she wouldn't have to do it directly.

And if it was Elanne, Tan had to understand how to stop her.

"I need you to tell me all who support Par," he told Maclin.

The other man locked eyes with Tolman for a long moment before looking at Tan. Then he nodded.

19

# FEEDING THE DRAASIN

The bond on the building didn't hold with the same strength that it once had. Tan used that fact, hoping to draw Elanne out, not willing to damage the bond further but wanting to find some way to coax her out of hiding. Since finding her in the street, apparently repairing bonds—though now he wondered if that really was what she had been doing—he had not seen any sign of her.

The bond that he crouched near in the shadows was one for fire. Fire would be easier for him to track and to modify the bond if needed.

The draasin curled around his neck again. Like before, he had the amused sense from Asgar when the hatchling crawled up his neck to settle in before they left the estate. Tan found it easier for the draasin to ride with him this time and hadn't really wanted to leave him behind, not with his uncertainty around who might be willing to help and who might be interested in harming the draasin.

He *thought* that Elanne was the one who still supported Par-shon, but he wondered if maybe he might be wrong. There were enough others in Par-shon who had done well under the Utu Tonah, and enough who missed the bonds that he had forced on the elementals, valuing the power that came with bonding to them.

A few people wandered the streets, but not as many as the last time he'd been in this section. There was a wax-worker nearby—probably the source of the fire bond—as well as a baker and butcher. The mixing of scents made his mouth water.

Not only him. The draasin perked up as they waited, sniffing the air.

"Are you hungry?" Tan asked the hatchling.

It nipped at his ear and hissed fire. Tan winced. He might be impervious to draasin fire, but sharp jaws would tear flesh. The idea of being part of the draasin's first meal didn't appeal to him.

*Kota, can you help with the hunt for the hatchling?*

The earth elemental clucked deep in his mind, the sound of her laughter. *Maelen, you would like me to be the hatchling's mother? We would work together to teach the draasin to hunt?*

*I think the draasin will teach the little one to hunt, but right now it's not so much about the hunt, but about the food. The draasin said that he would need to eat after he fed.*

*Fire fills this one, Maelen. I see why the Mother chose for him to hatch.*

Tan smiled. The longer that he'd been around the hatchling, the more he recognized that this one was indeed well connected to fire. He filled with fire and grew stronger with each day since he had connected to the fire bond.

As he sat there, he sensed nothing. He debated how much longer he should watch. If only there were a way for him to search without having to be here. But there might be.

*Kota. If you won't hunt for the draasin, will you hunt for me?*

*What would you have me hunt?*

*I would search for the woman Elanne.* He sent an image of her and tied with it the sense of earth that he'd detected when around her. *Do you think you can remain hidden and help me find her?*

*Why must I hide, Maelen?*

*You would frighten the people of Par-shon.*

Kota clucked deep within his mind again. *They would frighten easily.*

*They have suffered much.*

*As have I. If you need it, then I will search for her.*

Tan decided to leave the bond, but not before he used a shaping of fire to repair it. As he did, he added a flair of his own, modifying it in such a way that it would be stronger and call to saa with more conviction. With the bond in place, he felt an appreciative sigh from saa.

Strangely, as he worked with the shaping, adding fire in increasing force to repair the bond, he felt an echo of his shaping from the small draasin. He remained curled around Tan's shoulders and didn't really move during the shaping, but there was movement within him, from the connection he shared to the fire bond.

"You shouldn't be copying that," Tan said to him and

touched him on the nose. The draasin nipped at him again, and he jerked his hand back.

Food for the draasin.

If he didn't find it, he suspected that he would become a snack whether he wanted to or not. And with the butcher nearby, he could find something for the draasin.

Using a shaping of fire and earth, he masked the draasin. Keeping him hidden was easy enough with fire alone, but adding earth made it more stable.

The butcher shop was an older building, and Tan suspected it came from a time long before Par-shon had been founded by the Utu Tonah. This was a building of Par. A small, squat man eyed him as he entered, peering down his long, bulbous nose at him, taking in his dress and then his sword, before turning his attention to Tan's face. Reddened cheeks flushed as his eyes widened.

"My Utu Tonah!" he said with a gasp. "You honor me with your presence here."

"The honor is mine," Tan said. He glanced to the back of the butcher shop, where massive slabs of shaped ice kept the meat cold. Most were wild deer, with a single boar visible from where he stood. The selection was different than anything that he would find in the kingdoms. Of course, Tan was more comfortable hunting for his own food than turning to a butcher to prepare it for him.

Growing up in Galen, he had learned to prepare most of his food himself and rarely had to depend upon going to the town market for fresh cuts of meat. His home of Nor didn't have water shapers able to freeze slabs of water, which made maintaining freshness more challenging.

"I'm looking for a man who can be discreet," Tan began, again looking around the man's shop. As the only customer, he had no one else to worry about overhearing. The shop was clean, but the lack of business raised concern that the butcher's business was not thriving. He might be able to use that fact as he searched for a way to feed the draasin. He could have asked Maclin, but after everything that he'd seen and discovered, he no longer really knew who he could trust.

And maybe the answer was no one. As an outsider, he might not be able to trust any of the people of Par or Parshon. Given what he'd now discovered, there was much at stake, more even than he would have imagined when he first decided to return to these lands. He had thought there might be elemental crossings and had found a few, but a clutch of draasin eggs was far more valuable than anything else he might find.

"Discreet, my Utu Tonah? I am sure that you have nothing to fear from someone so lowly as Balsun."

"I hope not, but I have learned that Par-shon is more complicated than I realized."

Balsun nodded as he pressed the tips of his fingers together over his belly. "Par-shon has always been complex, my Utu Tonah. Having the blessings of these lands requires it to be complex, but then, you must understand that."

"I understand that my knowledge has limitations." The draasin shifted on his neck and Tan had to pull on the shaping that masked him, finding a way to keep him hidden from the butcher. He fought the urge to grab the draasin and push him back off his neck as he made another attempt at Tan's ear, but he realized the draasin seemed to be playing rather than truly attempting to harm him. He forced a smile, needing to turn the focus of the conversation. "That is not why I've come. What I need is a supply of your best venison," he said.

It probably didn't matter to the draasin if it was the butcher's *best* venison, but he figured it wouldn't hurt to make the request seem more important by asking for it. Besides, it might make him think that Tan had something prestigious planned for it.

Or maybe he'd try to poison it. Given Tan's position in Par-shon, he didn't really know which of them it would be. And he hated that he questioned.

"Ah, my Utu Tonah, you are in luck. Balsun has acquired quality venison. I have hunters who secure nothing but the best for me, and I am well known for my ability to provide only the best cuts. Are there any in particular that you would like to see?"

Tan wanted to tell him that it wouldn't matter, especially since the draasin would likely roast the meat himself and tear it apart, but he smiled at the butcher. "I am interested in seeing how skilled your cuts might be. If they are satisfactory, I will return."

Balsun smiled widely. "You will bring great fortune to Balsun!"

Would he? The reception that he'd gotten in Par made that unlikely, and maybe he would bring the wrong kind of attention to the butcher. Tan hadn't considered that. If there were members of a faction loyal to Par-shon, and essentially loyal to the prior Utu Tonah, then it would make sense for them to have an interest in harming anyone Tan favored.

"How much will you need?"

Tan considered the draasin's appetite and decided that he might need an entire deer. "I'll take as much as you can spare. A few stones will suffice for now."

Balsun bobbed his head and made his way back toward the meat storage.

Tan fought to keep a smile on his face, wondering if he really had made a mistake. Keeping track of the varying political dynamics was harder than he would have expected. When dealing with Incendin and then with Par-shon, he had only needed to convince Roine. Even that hadn't always been necessary, especially as Tan had taken to doing what he felt was needed. Always, he'd done that with discussion and counseling. What did he use to guide him now?

Nothing. Not even Amia.

That was something he would need to change. Hopefully, the issue with the Aeta was mostly wrapped up, or would be soon so that he could have her return to him. Having her with him not only provided guidance, but she also gave him a sense of comfort. Nearly dying here had left him feeling particularly *un*comfortable.

*You were never in danger of dying.*

It came from Amia, and he smiled, this time not needing to force it. *What do you mean? I was nearly crushed by an entire mountain of rock.*

*After everything that you have done and you feel the need to exaggerate? I think the elementals will agree that you were never in any real danger.*

Tan felt the clucking laughter of Kota and pushed her away. *I would still like to have you with me.*

*Then I will come.*

*Have you finished... whatever it was that you needed to do?*

*Nearly. But I will come if you will come for me.*

Tan didn't think that he could safely leave the draasin behind, not since it was so young. Not only might he need to feed, but there was the risk that one of the people who had tried attacking him when he was in the cavern might return, and if they were capable enough to nearly collapse the entire rock of the cavern onto him, then they would certainly be capable enough to harm the draasin.

Worse than that, though, was his fear of what would happen were the hatchling to be forced to bond. More than anything, he feared to leave the draasin here for that reason, but also feared to take him anywhere that he might face danger. Around Tan, there might not be anyplace that was really safe.

*I will see if Asgar is willing to come for you again. Asgar?*

*Maelen, I will help your mate, but only her,* the draasin answered. *Besides, I am interested in meeting this little one.*

Tan glanced at the draasin hidden beneath his shaping, obscured from Balsun—at least, so he hoped. It pulled on Tan's neck, shifting as if trying to find a more comfortable position. It wouldn't be long before he could not sit on Tan's shoulders, but for now, Tan figured it was as safe a place as any, even if he did have to use a hint of earth shaping to support him.

With it settled that Asgar would return with Amia, Tan returned his focus to the butcher, doing so in time for the man to make his way from the back of his shop carrying a stack of venison steaks wrapped in thick paper. The draasin smelled them, for he moved and sniffed. A trail of steam erupted from his nose, and then he nipped at Tan's ear. He struggled *not* to jump, imagining how he would explain that to Balsun.

"Will this suffice?" the butcher asked.

Tan took the offered stack of steaks and nodded. "I think that will be more than enough."

Balsun nodded happily.

"Balsun," Tan began, deciding that he needed to know more about this man if he were to use him to supply the draasin, "how long have you owned this shop?"

"Ah, Utu Tonah, my family has been here since the Founding," he said. His demeanor changed, and he touched the tips of his first two fingers to his chin, bowing his head slightly. "An Alasand butcher has worked this building since the first days of Par... Par-shon."

"Only Par-shon?" Tan asked. If Balsun had been here for years, Tan suspected that he would support Par. Maybe that was his clue to how to know who to trust and who might need extra attention, though he began to suspect that was unreliable. Elanne had come from families of Bonders—at least, that was her claim. But he didn't know that he could trust her.

Balsun glanced at the ground, unwilling to meet Tan's

eyes. "Par-shon, my Utu Tonah," he said. "Of course Par-shon."

"Send the rest to my estate if you would," Tan said, suppressing the urge to sigh as he began to understand another aspect of the challenge facing him. Not only did he have to confront the difficulty of Par versus Par-shon without knowing who was on which side, but he also had to deal with the struggles of those who'd lived here during the Utu Tonah's reign.

Would he ever manage to juggle all of that?

Not only juggle all of that, he thought as he made his way out of the butcher, but there was the issue of doing what he could to protect the draasin eggs. With the new hatchling, he had one more elemental to protect, and this one even more frail and fragile than any that he'd needed to protect before. Beyond that... he had an entire clutch of eggs, and all had the potential to hatch.

He hadn't given much thought to it yet, but if he managed to succeed, he could see the draasin returned to the world. Not as three that he'd returned after thawing them from the ice, but truly returned, with the skies filled with them, something that had not been seen for over a thousand years.

If he did that, there would be no way that he could keep them all safe. He would have to relinquish the thought that he could even try.

The draasin crawled along his neck, nestling in as he tried to get more comfortable. He stirred long enough to try to bite at Tan's neck and ears before drifting off again. Tan would like to laugh at the draasin, but he felt too much obligation to the creatures to laugh. The elementals depended on him, and if he couldn't understand the dynamics in Par-shon, then he would have to worry about something more mundane than not managing to help the draasin: he wouldn't be able to help the people of Par-shon.

As he made his way back toward the estate, he wished he better understood how to help these people. If he could, and if he understood who might be working against his attempts, he might be able to figure out just what he was supposed to do.

It was the reason he looked forward to Amia's return. Until she did, he would wait, and feed the draasin, and try to come up with a way that he could help the people of this country, including those who might not *want* his help.

## 20

# ROOM OF TESTING

The room of testing had not changed since Tan was last here. After returning the Utu Tonah's body, he had made a point of coming to this room and destroying each of the tiles with runes that would prevent shaping. Now they were all cracked but remained in place, untouched for months. A layer of dust hung over them, with nothing but his footprint to tell that anyone had ever been in this room.

He stood in the doorway, looking inside. The other tiles had all covered runes; would this be the same?

Using a shaping of earth and fire, he burned the remains. The char left a bitter stink in his nose which he swept away with a shaping of wind. Beneath the tiles were runes much like those he'd been seeing around town, the ones he was concerned that Elanne had broken.

"Did you know that they would be there?" Amia asked.

"I thought they might."

Tan started to step into the room but decided to carry himself on a shaping of wind instead. He wanted to see the runes and didn't want to risk further damage to those that had been hidden by the tiles the Utu Tonah had placed.

Amia stayed at the door watching him. "What do you see?"

The runes in this room were different than those on the buildings around the city. There he had found patterns that were tied to the elementals, a promise of something more in them, but these were not shaped like the elementals at all. These were sequences set into a pattern. Words written. A record.

Many of the shapes made sense, but not all of them. These weren't the same as what he'd seen of *Ishthin*, and the pattern was different than what he'd used for the elementals in the past. Tan didn't know *what* this spelled out, but it was clear there was something here.

"You should come in here," he said.

Amia surveyed the room before taking a step inside, sticking to a narrow path along the wall where there weren't any marks laid out. "This is older than *Ishthin*," she said in a breath.

"You can't read it?" Tan asked.

She shook her head. "Many are the same as the runes you've used for the elementals," she began and looked up at him, "but you knew that."

Tan nodded. "They're similar, but not the same."

When they had faced Par-shon, a Rune Master had been part of the Utu Tonah's forces. When Tan stopped her, she had taught Tan about the ancient shapes required to trap elementals, but that was all she had been able to teach him. What was in this room was about more than trapping elementals, of that he was certain.

Thinking of the Rune Master left him wondering how there could have been so many who sided strongly with the Utu Tonah when now he found only those afraid of him.

"What is it?" Amia asked.

Tan looked around the room. Elanne might be able to help him understand, but he'd have to convince her that she wanted to help. "There were some who were committed to the Utu Tonah," Tan said. "One man had bonded nearly as much as him or the Rune Master." He shook his head. "Some might have been forced or coerced, but not all were."

"You knew that before."

"But that's not the sense I've had since we've been here," he explained. "There might be those who were coerced, but there is a sense of anger at what happened to them."

"Even if he forced others to follow him, some still did gladly. Those are the ones you need to worry about. They're the people who derived joy from what they did."

He lowered himself to the ground, studying the patterns. He didn't understand the runes but knew that learning how to decipher them was important. And understanding the Utu Tonah was important as well, mostly because he saw the impact he had on the people of Par.

"I don't know how to find them," he said. "I came to Par-shon thinking that everyone followed the Utu Tonah and that no one disagreed with him, but that hasn't been what I've found at all."

Amia leaned forward to study the runes. "If only there were some way that we could discover who to trust," she said, smiling as she turned to him.

Tan shook his head. "I've already tried spirit sensing. That hasn't helped any more than reading through the Utu Tonah's journal. Even the people who seem like they support me can change their mind, and those who deny that they supported the prior Utu Tonah could change their minds. Short of simply *shaping* them with spirit, it's unreliable." He sighed and turned away, leaving the testing room and waiting for Amia before pulling the door closed behind them.

"I feel like I need *more* than what I've been able to learn so far," Tan said as they started down the hall. They reached the roof of the tower; the city spread out below them. It was a different vantage than he had even when shaping himself in the air. From here, he was not so high up that he couldn't see people moving through the streets, and not high enough to view the distant ocean. From here, there was only the city.

Wind whipped around him, fluttering his jacket and pulling at Amia's hair. She held it in place. Tan refused the urge to shape the wind and control it, letting the natural gusts blow over them.

Making his way around the top of the tower, he realized that there were four runes set into the stone sides. Each had crumbled, damaged by time or by the actions of the Utu Tonah. Tan thought about calling Elanne to repair these as well but decided that *he* could repair them just as well as she could. He might not understand what purpose they had, but at least he could restore the patterns.

Stopping in front of the one most like wind, he ran his fingers across it. The stone forming the etched shape had cracked, leaving barely enough for him to detect. Power still trickled through it. Tan used a shaping of wind and added a touch of earth to fix the rune. As he did, he felt the shape correct itself, practically not needing his guidance.

The wind around them fell still.

"What did you do?" Amia asked.

"Nothing more than what I learned earlier." He traced his hand across the repaired pattern, feeling the pull of wind through it. This was not a forced bond, nor one that trapped the elemental within it. Adding a small shaping of wind, he strained for understanding before the answer hit him. "This is how they spoke to the elementals," he gasped in wonder, turning to Amia to share the discovery.

"What do you mean?" She crouched next to him, studying the pattern. It was for wind, but much like the others, there was something else written within it, though Tan couldn't decipher it.

"There's the calling for wind," he said, pointing out the pattern, "but then there is the extra, what I haven't really understood. It's bothered me since I first realized the patterns meant something more than a way to trap the elementals, but I haven't known what it was. But I do now. These *speak* to the elementals."

"If you know what it says, maybe we can figure out how to read those runes in the testing room."

Tan made his way to the next rune, one for fire. Much like he did with wind, he shaped fire and added water to it, the shaping guiding him which element to add to fix the rune. With something like a hiss, the pattern was repaired.

"This one is fire," he explained. "Wind is harder for me to reach in Par-shon. Wyln is the prominent elemental. But saa… I can reach for saa."

Tan shaped fire and called to saa.

The elemental of fire responded, surging toward his summons. *Saa. Does this pattern speak to you?*

*Maelen,* saa answered with something like the crackling of flames within his mind. *These are the voice of the ancients.*

Tan stared at the rune. This was different than some of the others he'd found in Par-shon, but the differences were subtle and hard for him to decipher. *What does it say to you?*

*These were requests, Maelen, made before any learned to speak to us.*

*What kind of requests? There are others like this, and I would like to know how to translate them.*

*Translate?*

*Read them. Understand the ancients.*

Flames surged around the pattern, not harming it. *This one is a call for warmth.*

*Why warmth?*

*These lands have not always been warm, Maelen.*

*What of the place of convergence? A place the Mother calls to you.*

*This is such a place,* saa answered.

Tan sighed. That fit with what Honl had shared, and he

thought it was at least partly the reason the Utu Tonah had come. Tan turned to the other runes and stopped before the one for earth. Like the others, he used a shaping to repair it and was surprised to learn he needed to add fire as he did. Once the rune was repaired, the tower itself rumbled softly.

The last rune was for water. Tan managed to fix it much like he had the others. A sense of rolling waves washed over him as he completed it.

Then he stood and looked all around the top of the tower. Other than the wind fading, nothing else had changed meaningfully. Amia trailed around the tower, studying each of the runes before moving on to the next.

"These are for each of the elements," she noted. "What of spirit?"

Tan hadn't really thought of that, but Ethea had runes for spirit. So had the place in the mountains around Galen. "Do you sense anything here?"

She stopped at the last pattern she studied, her fingers trailing across the pattern for earth. A shaping built from her, massive and more complex than any shaping of spirit that he could create. He had strength with the elements, and the ability to use each of them, but Amia had finesse with spirit in a way that he couldn't begin to replicate.

The shaping released from her with something like a sigh and settled over the tower itself.

For a moment, she stood without moving, her eyes closed as she appeared to listen. Then she stood.

"Take us up," she said to Tan.

"Up where?"

She pointed into the sky. "Up."

Tan obliged and used a shaping of wind and fire to lift them above the top of the tower, where they floated. Wind buffeted around them, but Tan ignored it, pushing back with a shaping of air. "What did you want to see from here?"

She pointed toward the top of the tower.

Its stones had a certain pattern that came from variations in color. What seemed random and simply due to time or the choice of stone had a distinct shape from up above.

How had he not seen it before?

But then, he hadn't been looking before. This time, he came with the frame of mind that he wanted to find what patterns the ancient people of Par-shon might have placed. And this, the largest that he'd found, was clear.

A rune for spirit. The shape was slightly different than those of the other elements, as if it had been added later.

"There's something about it," Amia started before trailing off.

She began a shaping that Tan could tell was meant to probe into the rune.

He copied her shaping but added each of the elements to his. Doing this saved him because Amia gasped as her shaping struck the pattern. She convulsed in his arms.

Tan nearly lost her. Only through his connection to the elementals was he able to hold onto her. He dropped back to the top of the tower and lowered her to the ground.

"Amia?"

She didn't answer.

With a shaping of water, he reached through her,

searching for what might have injured her. He detected nothing.

Tan switched to spirit. She had been shaping spirit when she had suddenly started to tremble. Whatever happened to her was tied to that, but Tan didn't know what that could be. His connection to spirit was strong, but hers was stronger.

Still, he could trace the shaping that she'd used and how it had probed the rune. A connection had formed, one that threatened to overwhelm her.

Was there anything that he could do to help?

Not without risks. He'd tried using spirit in the past and had nearly killed Cora when he had. If he attempted something similar and failed, Amia would suffer.

She started convulsing again.

Tan couldn't do nothing.

Using spirit, but layering each of the elements into it as well, he created something of a shielding around her mind, separating her from the connection she'd shaped to the rune on the tower.

The convulsions stopped, but she didn't open her eyes.

Tan smoothed her hair, struggling for answers, but none came.

Shaping—at least *his* shaping—would not be able to help her.

## 21

## AN INJURY AND A CALL

T an placed Amia on the bed in the sprawling home of the former Utu Tonah. She still breathed, but the color in her cheeks had faded. Even some of the luster to her hair was diminished. Worse, she hadn't woken up.

He had used water but hadn't been able to find anything else wrong with her. Whatever had happened was from spirit and her attempt to probe the rune. The shielding that he'd placed over her mind seemed to help, but it did nothing more than keep her mind safe. It didn't fix the problem.

Without answers, he wouldn't be able to help her, but where would he get the answers he needed?

Not here, and he didn't want to risk carrying her across the sea and back to the kingdoms. He could summon Aeta spirit shapers, but he had learned as much of spirit as most of them. Water shaping might be helpful, but his sense of water told him that nothing was amiss.

*Honl.*

Tan sent the request on a shaping of wind, summoning a deep strength and drawing on the elementals around him. He needed Honl's knowledge. There might not be anything that he could do, but he could help Tan understand whether there was anything that *could* be done.

*Maelen.*

The response came as a distant call.

*I need you. The Daughter needs you. She is injured.*

There was a pause. Then, *I will come.*

Tan sank back into the bed, cradling Amia against him. The connection that had formed as she shaped the rune on the top of the tower moved with her, almost like something alive. Tan *felt* the connection but didn't understand what that meant or why he should be able to.

Anger threatened to well up inside him. Had they not come to Par-shon, she wouldn't have been injured. Had he not wanted to understand, she wouldn't have attempted to shape the rune. Like so much else, this was his fault. Because of him, and because of his desire to believe there might be more answers than what they had seen, Amia was injured.

"This is not your fault."

Tan looked up and saw Honl standing at the edge of the bed. He had taken on even more form than before, as substantial as Tan. Only his floating above the ground revealed the fact that he wasn't.

"She shaped spirit into a rune," he explained.

"Shaping into the ancient patterns can be dangerous, Maelen."

Tan smoothed her hair. A sheen of sweat had broken out on her face, and he wiped it away. "I had done the same. There are... patterns set throughout the city," he explained. "At first, I thought they were bonds like the Utu Tonah used, but they aren't. They call to the elementals and speak to them. Saa claims they are the way the ancients spoke to the elementals before anyone could truly speak to them."

"What of the pattern that struck the Daughter?"

"I don't know. We had repaired the patterns on top of the tower, and she was determined to find one for spirit. When we took to the air, we saw it. She tried shaping into it..."

Honl stretched a wispy arm toward Amia and brushed through her body, as if reaching *into* her mind. He stood for long moments like that, and Amia's breathing sped up as he did. Then he withdrew his arm.

"There is something very powerful to her shaping," Honl said.

"It seems like she's connected to the rune, as if her shaping did..." He didn't know what the shaping had done, or how the rune had connected to her. "Had I not wrapped her mind in this shaping, I wouldn't have been able to stabilize her. She kept convulsing."

"I think you did what was needed. But I need to see this rune."

"I don't want to leave her here."

"Maelen, she is stable. You can show me and then return."

Tan touched her hair and sent a shaping of water through her again before standing. Nothing had changed for her. The shaping that had taken her, and connected to her, remained unchanged. Somehow he needed to find a way to separate that connection.

He sealed the door to the room with a shaping using each of the elements, and then led Honl to the top of the tower, taking to the wind once outside. It felt strange and comforting to have his bonded wind elemental with him again.

"It has been too long, Honl," he said.

"You don't need me the way you once did, Maelen."

They stopped above the tower, hovering there. Honl swirled in the wind, becoming insubstantial as he touched each of the runes that Tan had repaired before returning to stand next to him on the air.

"There is much strength to these patterns. You repaired them?"

"They were degraded," Tan said. "Time and..." He wasn't sure what else had led to the degradation. Had that been the result of the Utu Tonah, or had he even known what they had here? Tan doubted that he truly understood, or else wouldn't he have covered them with tiles as he had with the others inside the tower? "What of the spirit rune?"

Honl studied the top of the tower where the rune took shape out of the stone. "This is subtle work," he commented, "but it could not be the only such pattern. There would be too much strength for it to be alone."

"This is the only one."

"Do you sense it?" Honl asked.

"Sense what?"

"The energy. The summoning call. And now there are others."

"It's the only one that I've found. The rest were all carved into the stone."

Honl swirled above him, disappearing for a moment before reappearing to the north of the tower. Tan followed him and turned to face the tower.

"Do you see it, Maelen?"

Tan stared at the tower until it came into focus. Much like the pattern on the top of the tower, the stone along the side had variations in color as well. From above, he had barely made out the shape of the pattern, but from the side, it was even more difficult, as if whoever had constructed the tower had done so with an eye toward using the pattern in its building.

"That's earth," he said with a whisper. The shape of the rune stretched the entire length of the building, using the tower's shape to guide it. Toward the base were the two parallel lines that formed the prominent part of the symbol.

He'd never seen it before, but then, he hadn't been looking. Without knowing that it was there, he simply could ignore the subtle changes to the contour of the stone, but now that he knew it was present, now that he understood, he couldn't see anything else.

Tan made his way around to the next side of the tower, and there was water. A circular pattern with something resembling waves rolling through. The pattern was distinct for Par-shon but similar enough to the one that he saw in Ethea as well.

On the opposite side of earth, he found fire. And then air.

All of the elementals, even spirit, represented on a grand scale built into the stone of the tower itself. And he had never seen it.

"This has been here all along," Tan said, turning to Honl. "Did you know?"

The elemental studied the wall, focusing on wind. "Now I feel the pull of the pattern."

"Not before?"

"There was no drawing sensation, Maelen, nothing that would not be expected in a place like this."

"What kind of place?"

"We have already spoken how this is a place of convergence. This is a place of the Mother, much like your home."

A place of convergence, but one that was different than in Ethea as well. Something had been done that obscured the elemental draw, but Honl was right: now that Tan knew it was there, he could *feel* the pull of the elementals.

"This is different than the other patterns," he said. "Those were designed to speak to the elementals." Tan felt certain of that now, especially now that he knew what the patterns could do and had felt the strange draw. He needed to examine the other runes to see if they were the same, and now with Honl, he might be able to understand, but that was for later, *after* he figured out what had happened to Amia.

"They are different, Maelen, but the ancients who designed this place were not ignorant to the ways of the elementals. There is understanding at work here that I am not entirely certain about."

"Will you stay to help me understand?" Tan asked.

Honl looked troubled, as much as a creature of wind and spirit *could* look troubled. "I will stay, Maelen, but I fear any delay allows the darkness time to grow."

"That's where you've been? That's why you won't answer when I try to summon you?"

"Do not place blame on me," Honl chided.

"Had you been here, this might not have happened!"

"If I do not search, none will know to prepare." Honl turned and looked to the northwest, the direction of Incendin and the kingdoms. "I have wondered at my purpose. Why would the Mother create a being like me? I am no longer ashi, but something else. Perhaps greater, or lessened, I don't know. But I wonder why. I think I have come to understand."

"What did you come to understand?"

"That I have a purpose. We each have a purpose. Yours is to prepare, to train, those who will oppose the darkness while mine is to understand." Honl appeared to smile and turned back to face Tan. "It is the reason that I can absorb the centuries of knowledge contained in your records. With time, I can piece it together, to help you, guide you as you prepare."

"I don't think that's my purpose, Honl," Tan said softly. "I can speak to the elementals and can teach how the elementals must be treated, but that is the extent of my purpose. That was why the Mother granted me the gifts that she did, so that I could defeat someone like the Utu Tonah. So that I could bring the draasin back from extinction. More than that…"

"Maelen, *you* are meant to be the Light."

He said it as if there was some title behind it.

"I don't know what that means."

Honl laughed, a sound that disappeared on the wind. "Neither do I, but that is why I must study. And I cannot do that here, confined by these lands."

"What of the Daughter?"

"Look at these patterns. There is an answer here, if we can understand it."

"Honl, she has *bonded* to the pattern of spirit. I feel how it trails from the top of the tower, like a physical connection to her."

Honl tipped his head to the side in the strange way that he had taken to doing, and then floated to the top of the tower. When Tan joined him, Honl dropped and floated just above the surface, the effect disconcerting. He looked like a man and was dressed like a man, but floated like an elemental. So much had changed for him in the last few months.

"A connection?" Honl asked.

"Yes. Why? Does that mean something to you?"

"How did you heal her mind again?"

"I used a shaping of each of the elements to wrap her, and then separated her from spirit." Tan hadn't taken the time to consider what that shaping would do, other than the fact that it had protected her and kept her from the convulsions. Had he not, he feared that she wouldn't have survived. He'd only seen one other person die from a shaping like that, and when the First Mother had done it, Tan suspected she'd chosen her fate. This... this was more like an attack.

"Would the same thing happen to me if I shaped into the stone for any of the other elements?"

Honl shook his head absently, the gesture so human. "You have already bonded, Maelen. You would be protected."

Tan frowned at the choice of words. "What do you mean by that?"

The wind elemental looked up and met Tan's eyes. "These patterns," he said, motioning to the top of the tower. "They are meant to summon. Surely you must sense that."

Tan considered what he sensed of the patterns. Now that Honl pointed it out, he *did* detect a drawing sensation, a force practically pulling him to the tower, as if he were compelled. But it was not a uniform sense. Rather, he felt most strongly drawn to fire. "I feel the drawing of fire, but nothing else."

Honl tipped his head. "Fire. You do reach the fire bond, so I suppose that makes the most sense. In that way, you are nearly a creature of elemental energy yourself."

"I still don't know what you're getting at, Honl."

"These patterns are meant to call to the elementals. There is no coercion, not like what the Bonded One had used, but simply a calling. It is an ancient pattern, one that is found in your home."

"Where in my home..." He trailed off, realizing that Honl meant the archives. The patterns were found there, most clearly in the stone, but also *beneath* the archives, where the other elementals were drawn. Tan had always believed that places of convergence happened naturally, but what if the elementals had to be summoned there? "You're saying that the ancient shapers asked the elementals to create these places?"

"I haven't been able to determine that yet," Honl answered, "but that is the most likely answer. There is the power of the Mother there, but to reach it, the others must be present. It is different here."

Tan's breath caught. The power of the Mother. The source of spirit shaping.

And he had thought that Par-shon had no knowledge of spirit, and that the Utu Tonah had only learned of it after discovering Tan and attempted to use the Aeta to help him access what he could not. But what if that assumption was wrong?

"What did you mean about the bond?"

"You have bonded. You could not form a bond to the elementals these patterns draw."

"Honl," Tan began, realizing where he was going, "there is no elemental of spirit."

Honl tipped his head to the side again. "We did not believe that there was, but what if there is?"

## 22

## SEARCH FOR HELP

Tan drew through a connection of spirit and earth, straining for Marin.

He needed someone who understood spirit in Par-shon. From his connection to the other elementals, he'd learned the response to the elements was different in every land he'd visited, from the way the wind blew in Galen versus Incendin to the way he managed to find earth. Each place had its own rules and rhythms.

Par-shon would be no different than the others. And he wasn't certain, but it was possible that this extended to the connection to spirit.

For Amia, he would find out if there was anything that would explain what had happened, and how to fix it. The only person he could think of in Par-shon to help was Marin.

Only, Tan didn't know if she would be willing to give him assistance.

He returned to the place she'd taken him. As far as he

248

could tell, it was something of a place of worship, where the Mistress of Souls guided the people she served, leading them through her connection to spirit.

It was empty.

The fading sun sent streamers of light into the plaza. No children moved within or along the street, almost as if they had been removed or brought somewhere else.

Using earth and spirit, he reached again for Marin but still couldn't find her. Frustration bubbled within him. He needed to understand if there might be something to what Honl had suggested. What would it mean if there *was* an elemental of spirit, and if there was, had Marin known?

Tan could speak to the elementals and had used that connection to reach to the Great Mother, binding together his connection to them so that he could access even more strength, so that he could practically tap into the Great Mother herself, and *he* hadn't known about an elemental of spirit.

Unless what Honl suspected was wrong.

That was what he wanted to learn from Marin.

He stopped at one of the pillars occupying the middle of the room. There was nearly a dozen, arranged in such a way that he was forced to weave through the empty room. When he'd been here before, he hadn't known that the bonds had any additional piece to them. Knowing gave him better insight to the people, but he still didn't know how to use that information.

And Amia depended on his learning. At least Honl watched over her. It gave the wind elemental a chance to study her as well. But he needed to find answers so that she could recover. If he didn't... Tan didn't want to think about what would happen.

The nearest pillar had none of the runes some of the buildings did. Tan circled around it, hoping for answers, but found nothing. He moved on to the next, but there was nothing more for him there, either.

Near the center of the room, he found the first marking on the pillar.

Tan crouched close and traced his fingers across it. It was different than some of the others he'd seen in the city, and as he shaped into it, he realized that it was connected to spirit.

Rather than shaping spirit alone, he used a combined shaping of each of the elements to probe it. This was the way that he had learned to shape spirit from the beginning, but that wasn't the reason that he'd chosen to shape the rune in that way. Whatever had happened to Amia had come because she had shaped spirit alone. Tan would not risk the same until he knew what had happened, and how to avoid the same happening to him.

The shaping surged into the pattern. At first, he detected a resistance, but the more that he pushed—and, he realized, the more that he used pure spirit—the better he was able to stabilize the pattern that had been here.

This reacted differently than the other shapings that he'd done when the runes were involved. With those, like the one on the buildings or those upon the tower that he had helped repair using a shaping, the shaping seemed to take hold on its own, requiring little guidance from him. This rune for spirit demanded his input.

Tan wracked his mind for what he knew about spirit runes. They weren't common, even in Ethea. Other than the uncomplicated runes that had been made by the archivists in the lower level of the archives, the only patterns that he could think of he had learned from the First Mother and Amia.

Fixing one of those runes in his mind, he focused on the shaping, and sent it into the pattern on the post, hoping that it worked. If it didn't, and if it rebounded on him, he wasn't sure if he would be injured like Amia had been.

His shaping met resistance.

Tan pressed through it, using an increasing draw of power.

The pressure against him continued and for a moment, he didn't think that he would be able to overpower the resistance. Drawing on the strength of the elementals around him, something that he hadn't had the need to do since defeating the Utu Tonah, he pulled on more strength than he could summon on his own.

The shaping built, swelling with power and force, and then it settled into the rune, taking hold.

Tan released the shaping with a sigh and stepped back to see what he'd done.

The rune was much like the one he'd visualized as he shaped, but there were subtle differences. He detected a drawing of spirit strength toward the rune, a strength that he had not felt in any other form before.

He wiped his hands on his pants and let out a shaky

breath. Once, a shaping like that would have nearly over-whelmed him, or at the least would have left him fatigued and unable to stand, but now that he could draw from the strength of the elementals, he no longer had the same chal-lenges. But he felt the strength required to perform the shaping and wondered if there had been any real purpose to what he'd done. Why would there have been such difficulty in placing this rune? It was almost as if everything here served to *prevent* him from repairing it.

*You have created the mark of the Mother.*

Tan turned to see Kota crouching in the shadows. He hadn't sensed her approaching and wondered how she made her way through the city without causing some sort of chaotic scene.

*Not the Mother,* Tan said. He studied the rune. It was different than his vision of the runes used for spirit. *This is spirit, but not spirit that I recognize.*

*That is the mark for the Mother,* Kota said again. She approached slowly, her stubby tail pointing behind her and her fur standing on edge. *Maelen, there is something else here.*

*What do you sense?*

*I do not know,* Kota said.

Tan didn't detect anything, but the hound had a different sensitivity than he did and a different connection to the elemental. *The Daughter is injured. Honl tries to understand, but we don't know how to draw her back.*

*That is why I'm here.*

*You sensed what happened?*

*I can tell the connection changed. A bond was drawn. You had asked me to search for the other, but I have not been able to find her.*

Tan clenched his eyes closed, frustrated. If this were somehow tied to Elanne, then he would know. And he needed Marin to help, especially if she could shape spirit, to determine if there was anything else that he could do to help Amia.

And he'd been unable to find either of them.

*Honl thinks there might be an elemental of spirit that bonded her.*

Kota prowled around him, her hackles raised. What did she detect that had her on edge?

*There is no elemental of the Mother, Maelen.*

*What if there are? What if we only haven't seen them? There are elementals for each of the other elements; why wouldn't there be one for spirit?*

*Maelen, the connection to the Mother comes from the shaper. You are the spirit elemental.*

What did Kota mean by that?

The shaper connected to the Mother? Tan started to think about what that might mean. There had been the possibility that they hadn't seen elementals of spirit simply because they could hide better than the other elementals, but the reason could also be that there were not any spirit elementals.

*Then what bond are you talking about?*

*I do not know, but I've seen that there is much strength in these lands. More than I would have expected from what I knew before we came.*

*What kind of strength?* Tan asked, but he already knew that the people of Par had valued the elementals. A dichotomy existed in this place, that of Par-shon and that of Par. Those who still supported Par-shon sought power, and perhaps something else. But those who supported Par… Tan didn't fully understand *what* they wanted. They protected the draasin and had done so for generations. They created bonds formed of runes older than what he'd ever found in the kingdoms and used these to speak to the elementals. Other than that… he didn't know.

*A connection to the elementals that is as great as what you had in your lands. That is why the hatchlings were here. And it must be why the Bonded One came to these lands. We must find a way to understand.*

*What can you tell about this pattern?*

*You repaired it. I can… feel it.* Surprise drifted through the connection to the hound.

*How is it that you feel spirit?* Kota shouldn't be able to detect the calling of a spirit bond. She was a hybrid elemental, one born of crossings made by the earliest kingdoms' shapers, but a hybrid of earth and fire, not of spirit. If any of his bonded elementals should be aware of spirit, it would be Honl.

*Not spirit, Maelen. As I said, this mark calls the Mother. There are others in this city, though they are damaged as well.*

Others?

Why would there be other damaged spirit bonds in the city, and why would Marin have used this place as her place of worship? He found that nearly as surprising as the fact that she wasn't here.

Unless something had happened to her.

What if Marin had been *protecting* the bond, preventing Elanne or those with her from damaging it? That might explain why Marin chose this place, and why she'd always seemed so secretive with him.

*Can you show me the others?*

*There are only two. A fourth remains undamaged.*

Four. Tan couldn't help but notice that the number corresponded to the number of different elements. Which would the pillar here represent? Possibly wind, with the way it flowed on the tall pillar, or earth.

But the others?

*Can you show them to me?* Tan asked again.

*Do you think this is wise while the Daughter lies injured, Maelen?*

Tan didn't know *what* the right thing was. Leaving Amia seemed the worst, but damaged bonds of spirit runes, bonds that Kota suggested led to the Mother, had him worried that whatever happened here might be tied to what had happened to Amia, if only he could understand what, and how.

For that reason, he *had* to find the damaged bonds.

*I think that is the only thing I can do to help her.*

Kota rubbed up against him, understanding his concern. *I will show you, Maelen.*

23

# MARK OF THE MOTHER

The hound led Tan to a place on the outer edge of the city. Before leaving, Tan had paused and spoken to each of the elementals of Par and asked them to watch over the place and keep the repaired bond from harm. Until he found Marin and understood why it was important, he would keep it intact.

This place was much like the last in many regards. It was an older section of the city, practically ancient, and far enough away from the tower that Tan could see it rising overhead like an angry finger of rock. With a single shaping, he could return, but not until he understood. If a bond of the Mother were somehow involved, Amia would *want* him to understand before going to her.

The silence between them caused a pang to echo through his soul. As much as he hated losing Asboel—and that had pained him in ways that he still didn't fully understand—

256

losing Amia would be a thousand times worse. What would he be without her?

Yet he knew how she would feel about that suggestion. Amia would tell him that he would be fine without her, that he would know what to do in time, and that he would need to trust that the Great Mother had a plan for them.

*You hear her still, Maelen,* Kota suggested.

*I don't hear her, but I know what she would tell me.*

*Then you are wise to listen.*

Tan took a deep breath and surveyed the area around him. *Where is this place?* he asked. *Did you find it while searching for Elanne?*

*The damaged bond throbs, Maelen. I cannot describe it any differently.*

Tan closed his eyes and listened for the bond. If it throbbed for Kota, would it do the same for him? Could he detect the remnants of the bond and trace it, repair it if possible? And if he did, would he be able to understand what had happened to Amia?

He used a combined shaping of spirit, drawing on each of the elements. It washed away from him, sweeping through the buildings until he found a place where it struck strangely. Almost throbbing against him.

With a shaping of fire and wind, he reached the building that housed it. The building was made of simple stone, and solid. Earth radiated from it, much like it did in many parts of Par. Tan had found that fire was strong, but that was through his connection to saa. Somewhat more surprising was the fact that earth was as potent here as it was. Even wind, under the guide of wyln, had much strength here. And udilm, the great water elemental found in the surrounding sea, had not fully departed even after Tan had severed all of the forced bonds.

As Kota suggested, Par was a place very powerful with elementals. A place of convergence.

And the Utu Tonah had come here, but still hadn't managed enough strength to be victorious.

Almost, though. He almost had managed.

Now was not the time to think what would have happened had he succeeded. All the elementals would have been forced to bond, to serve the Utu Tonah.

But Tan still didn't know the reason *why*.

He shook away the thought and the questions that came with it. They were for another time. Pushing open the door, he entered the building.

In some ways, it was much like the last. A wide open space with a hard, dirt floor and pillars rising throughout it in some sort of pattern. The damaged rune came from the midst of that.

He made his way to the rune. The last one had been on the pillar itself. This was different, worked into the stone on the ground. That made it a mark for earth. If that were the case, then the last one would have been wind. Where would he find fire and water?

And what did it mean that there were these patterns set throughout the city like this? These were different than any of the others. Much stronger, and they served a different purpose.

Tan hurriedly shaped spirit into this one. Time was short,

and he needed to discover the purpose of these patterns before Amia suffered any longer.

The rune was even more damaged than the last.

It pushed against him, like a knife slicing across his flesh, leaving it raw and exposed.

Once again, he drew upon each of the elementals of Par and poured that strength into a shaping, tying them together and adding his contribution of spirit. When he'd done it the last time, he had wondered at the purpose, but now he thought he knew. There *was* something to these bonds, and they needed to be whole. There was a reason the ancients of Par had placed them here. He might not know it yet, but he finally trusted that the people of Par had known the reason and that it was a good one.

The shaping required enormous strength, reminding him of what he had done when he hatched the draasin. With that, he was able to pull on the fire bond. That wouldn't work this time, not for this shaping. He continued to draw on the elementals, requesting more and more strength. Almost as if understanding the reason for his request, they gave it willingly, sending it flooding through him.

Tan turned the shaping into the pure white burst of light that formed the bond of spirit. He felt the original threads of what the bond had done and repeated it, pushing more strength into the bond, reforming it not as it once had been, but as he sensed it needed to be.

With one last push, a demanding draw of energy from him, he completed the bond.

Then sagged to the ground.

Kota nudged him to sit. *The Mother no longer throbs against me here. This was necessary, Maelen.*

*I wish I knew why.* He inhaled slowly and managed to sit on his own, and looked around the room. Now that the bond had been repaired, others appeared on the walls. Dozens of them... hundreds upon hundreds. Not only bonds but runes with meaning that he didn't have the knowledge yet to understand.

All had been hidden by the missing spirit bond.

*Did you know this was here?* he asked Kota.

*Earth sits strongly in this place, Maelen, but earth is strong throughout much of these lands. You must sense that.*

*I have sensed that,* Tan agreed. He might not know what that meant, other than the fact that this was a place of convergence, but he had sensed it.

He stood, drawing strength from Kota to replace some of what he'd lost in the shaping, and started a circle around the room. Each of the bonds was incomplete in some way. Some were obviously damaged, as if someone had taken a knife and simply drawn it across the runes. Others were more subtly damaged. Those he sensed more than he saw, detecting the way the energy that should flow freely from them no longer did. Whatever call would have come from the bonds had been lost.

*These have meaning,* Tan said. *But I don't know what most of them say.*

*They have meaning to these lands and this place, but the Mark of the Mother is what truly gives this power.*

Tan studied the rune for spirit. It glowed brightly, almost

as if retaining the energy that he'd used to repair it. Had the other bond done the same? Tan couldn't remember, but then with that one, the lanterns lit around the room might have obscured it.

Had there been a similar collection of runes on the walls in that place? Tan would have to go back and see, but surely he would have noticed had there been runes like this throughout that place as well.

But maybe he wouldn't have noticed. He'd been focused on trying to find Marin to save Amia, that the discovery of whatever these bonds represented hadn't fully registered with him.

*The other damaged rune. Where did you find it?* Tan wondered if it represented air or fire. And did that mean that the fourth bond was completely unblemished? That if he found it, there would be no damage to the Mark of the Mother?

*I will take you to it.*

Kota bounded outside the building. As she did, Tan felt something change.

The hound was attacked.

Kota did not take well to attack, and she roared, her angry voice thundering through the air, splitting the ground with her rage.

Tan raced toward the door, slowed slightly by the effort of his recent shaping. The elementals had mostly restored him, but depending on what he found outside, he might need more strength than what he had remaining.

Shapers waited for him outside the door. All of Par-shon.

They remained hidden, protected by the walls of the nearby buildings, but he detected the energy of their shapings. Enough shapers were here that Tan made a slow circle, fearing that he would be attacked. Fire wouldn't harm him, but what if the earth opened and attempted to swallow him? He might be able to control the wind, but would the water here work with him? Udilm was the elemental in Par-shon, and udilm had always had a tenuous relationship with him.

He raised his hand. "Stop!" he shouted. "As Utu Tonah, I command you."

A shaping built, one with massive strength and energy, enough that surprised Tan. He hadn't expected that much control from the shapers remaining in Par-shon. Most of the shapers here had been bonded, and the severing of the bond *should* have injured them to the point that they wouldn't be able to attack, but there was strength here.

Had he been wrong? Had the shapers of Par-shon not only required the elemental bonds? But if that were the case, why wouldn't the Utu Tonah have used these shapers against Tan when attacking the kingdoms?

Had he known? But why had they remained here if that were the case?

Too many questions raged through his mind. And there wasn't the time to find the answers.

*Kota, be ready.*

*Always, Maelen.*

The hound pressed into the hard rock and used the connection to earth as she did. The ground rumbled, and the elemental buried deep within the earth answered. She exuded a sense of power.

The shaping building from the hidden shapers faltered.

"You would attack your Utu Tonah?" Tan shouted. If they feared the title, he hoped that would be enough to convince them to back away. He had no interest in attacking more shapers of Par-shon, not after he finally thought the war won.

The shaping unleashed.

It was a combined shaping and coordinated.

Had he not had Kota with him, he might have struggled to fend off the attack. Kota caught the earth shaping and deflected it while Tan resisted the fire shaping. That left only wind and water, which he was able to draw away and send funneling into the ground.

Pulling on wind and water, he sent a swirling shaping, pushing against those who attempted to harm him. There was resistance, much like what he had met when trying to repair the spirit bond he'd found here, but he forced his way past that.

There came a distinct sense of separation.

Not of a forced bond being torn away, but something else.

Something worse, Tan realized.

This time, when he pushed, he recognized that a *natural* bond was there and that what he did attempted to separate that natural bond, as if he would steal it from whoever had formed it.

He swore to himself. He would *not* do the same as the previous Utu Tonah. Already he made too many mistakes and had ventured closer to what the prior Utu

Tonah had been willing to do. This was a boundary that he would not cross.

Releasing the shaping, Tan took a deep breath and stepped forward, sending a request to the elementals around him. *I do not want to harm these shapers. Help them to understand.*

Another shaping built and Tan prepared to deflect it. He could return to the estate and check on Amia, but he still hadn't discovered the purpose of the runes. Without knowing that, how would he save her? Whatever was happening to her was connected to spirit and the Mother.

*Let these shapers know who I am.*

The answer came on a breath of wind, so faint that Tan almost couldn't hear it. *Maelen...*

The shaping stopped.

Tan waited. Would they attack again, or would his connection to the other elementals be enough to convince whoever had bonded wyln that he could be trusted?

A flutter of wind caught his attention and Elanne dropped to the ground.

She held a long metal rod, so much like the one she had dropped when Tan had found her last. Was this what she used to damage the bonds, or did she truly attempt to repair them?

"Elanne," Tan said.

She tipped her head. "You speak to wyln."

"I speak to all the elementals."

"You are bonded, you said so yourself. Ashi was your elemental of wind."

Tan closed his eyes and sighed. "If you thought that I was only bonded to ashi, then you haven't been listening. I have a bond to an elemental of ashi, but I speak to all the elementals."

"They call you Maelen," she said. "What does that mean?"

"It means you should believe me. And it means you need to stop destroying these bonds. If you have bonded to wyln, then you can learn how strongly I feel about forced bonds. I know that you're still working for him, you're still trying to destroy the work of Par—"

"Maelen," she said, interrupting him. "If *you* think that I have been trying to destroy the bonds of Par, then *you* haven't been paying attention."

Tan frowned. "You truly have been trying to repair them?" he asked.

She nodded. She closed her eyes and whispered something softly. The wind blew through with a flutter of power before she opened her eyes again. "What did you do here?" she demanded.

"What do you mean?"

"To this place," she said, motioning to the building where Tan had repaired the spirit bond. "That is why we are here. I am the Mistress of Bonds. They are *my* responsibility. When you damage them—"

"When *I* damage them?" Tan asked. "The bond was already damaged, like the other bond that you'd damaged."

Elanne took a step toward him. A shaping built from her, one that sent the wind sweeping around her. "You think that I damaged these bonds? You know that I am named Mistress of Bonds. Before your predecessor, such a title was nearly the highest in all of Par. Why would I do anything to jeopardize the trust placed in me by my people?"

Her people. Par, not Par-shon.

"You didn't damage these bonds?" Tan asked. Calling to Kota, he said, *There is something I have missed. If she didn't damage the bonds that we've discovered, then I don't know who is responsible. And if we can't get the last bond repaired, there might not be any way that I can help Amia.*

*You will find a way to save the Daughter, Maelen.*

"As I have said, Utu Tonah, the bonds were not damaged by me. If you had paid attention to the work that I was doing, you would have seen how I had only attempted to repair the bonds. So many have been damaged in the days since the Utu Tonah was stopped that it has kept me busier than I can manage."

Tan released the last of the pent-up shaping that he'd been holding, realizing only now that he *had* been holding onto a shaping. "I don't understand. I thought you were the one damaging the shapings. I came here to repair a Mark of the Mother before you attacked me."

At the comment, Elanne jerked her head toward the building, her eyes narrowing. A soft shaping built and wind whistled through before departing. "You came to repair? The Great Seals cannot be repaired once damaged. We have tried —all of the Master of Bonds have tried—but none has succeeded."

Tan started into the building, deciding that he needed to settle this once and for all. Whatever else, he needed to understand what Elanne had been doing. And if it involved repairing the bonds, then he needed to understand, mostly so that he could help. If it didn't, and if there was something she kept from him, maybe it was time that he stopped worrying so much about how Par-shon saw him and do what he needed to return the Par that he could tell had once existed.

With a shaping of air, Elanne jumped in front of him. Tied to the elemental, her control was impressive. Not quite on the level of his mother, but then, Zephra had been working with the wind for as long as he suspected that Elanne had been alive.

"You may not enter this place."

"Why? Because you don't want me to?"

She shook her head and held her palm facing out toward him. As she did, her wind shaping continued to build. Other shapings began as well, all surrounding him. Tan had done nothing to find what those surrounding him had been doing, other than to note with spirit and earth sensing where to find them. Now he was acutely aware of them nearby. He recognized none but detected the way they used the elements. The only one able to speak to the elemental was Elanne. Shapers, and more powerful than he would have expected here, but not bonded.

"You may not enter because this is a sacred place."

"Sacred?"

Elanne nodded. "The Mistress of Souls teaches that only those with pure lineage may read the relics of ancient Par."

That would explain why Marin had used a place similar to this one for her preaching, and would explain why she had worked so hard to keep *him* from it when he had followed her. She had not prevented him, but her people certainly had. But his time there and finding it empty had shown him that there wasn't anything particularly special about these places other than the series of runes on the walls. That had signifi-cance, and there was knowledge that could be handed down from there, but there wasn't anything more spiritual there than a damaged rune. Would she think that he would harm that?

"Why would she abandon the one she occupied in the southern part of the city?" Tan asked.

Elanne frowned. "Southern? There is no other place like that. There are only three. This one, a place to the north, and one that has been lost to time."

"Not three. Four. One for each element. This is a place of earth. The other is wind. I know that a third is damaged, but don't know if it is water or fire."

"The elements?" Now Elanne sounded confused.

"You didn't know?" he started, and she shook her head. He motioned toward the building. "I can show you, but you'll have to let me in."

Elanne whispered something, and her face tensed. She remained silent for a while, and Tan suspected that her bonded elemental was telling her about what he'd discov-ered. If the elemental could do that, why wouldn't it just tell her what he'd found near the spot of Marin's celebration?

"You will show me," Elanne finally said.

Tan pulled on a shaping of wind and fire and slid past her, making a point of demonstrating that he didn't need her permission before wondering if maybe that might not be a mistake. It was possible that by showing that, he would lose the potential to work *with* her rather than against her.

Inside the room, he led her to the pillar with the Mark of the Mother. It still glowed, holding the retained energy of his shaping. The other intact runes also glowed softly. Only those that had been damaged remained dark.

"That is the Mark of the Mother."

"A Great Seal," Elanne whispered. "And you have restored it."

"It was damaged. I repaired it." He motioned to the marks all along the wall. "I was… wrong, Elanne. When I first came here, I didn't understand the way that your people used the bonds. There was what the Utu Tonah did, and then there is what Par did using the bonds. It took me a while to understand that they were different."

"All of this. The Records. They are recovered."

"Not all. Most have some sort of damage."

Elanne stopped in front of one of the walls and pulled out the long metal rod. Tan recognized it this time as she shaped the rod, sending a trickle of wind into it. She used this to scratch along one of the damaged runes until it fell into place, repaired by whatever she did with the rod. The rune flickered, then came alive.

"Ah," she sighed. "Not so damaged. We can restore *all* of this. This is *why* there is a Mistress of Bonds."

He had been so mistaken when he came to Par-shon. Tan had assumed that the Mistress of Bonds had been a position created by the Utu Tonah, someone who would force the bonds onto the elementals, but that had not been the case at all. Had he bothered to listen, he might have discovered this sooner. Or had the elementals not still been weak here, he might have been able to speak to them and use the elementals themselves to help him understand.

"You did this?" she whispered. "You *helped* Par-shon?"

"I helped Par. As far as I'm concerned, Par-shon is no more. Now. Will you help me with the third bond?"

"Why?"

"I don't fully understand, but there is something tied to these bonds. And if I don't repair the third, not only might Par suffer, but someone close to me will as well."

Elanne cocked her head to the side as she seemed to listen again. "I will help," she said with a nod.

## REPAIRING THE SEALS

K ota led him to the third damaged Seal on the northern edge of the city. Tan couldn't help but note how the three different spirit bonds that he'd discovered ringed the tower. Did they match the symbols for the elements that he'd seen on the sides as well?

"The Seals do not surround the tower," Elanne said when he asked. "They surround the city. They are a gift, a protection to the people of Par, and are tied to the Records, the oldest knowledge of our people."

Tan didn't argue, but these seals had something else to them other than a way to store knowledge. They *were* tied to the Records—the way that the other runes in the last archive began glowing after he managed to repair the bond told him that—but there *had* to be something more to them.

Kota crouched at an opening to a wide cavern leading down into the darkness. Much like him, the hound hesitated.

"What is it?" Elanne asked.

Tan frowned. "The last time I was near a cavern like this, I was nearly killed."

He didn't bother to explain and had made the comment mostly to gauge her reaction, but other than her eyes widening, she made no other sign that she had anything to do with the collapse of the cavern and the attempt to crush not only him but the draasin eggs.

*You will be careful this time,* Kota warned.

*I was careful the last time.*

The soft clucking from the hound in his mind was echoed by a rumbling within the earth. Elanne looked down, but Tan only shook his head. "The third Seal is here?"

"The last Seal."

Not the last. Tan was as certain of that as he was of anything. And if the third one was below ground, he suspected that meant water. There were times where he would expect to find fire burning brightly below ground, but they were uncommon.

As uncommon as draasin eggs buried beneath the ground.

His breath caught. Could *that* be the last of the Seals? The fourth and lost Seal? But... the direction was off, wasn't it? These other three all ringed the tower—or the city—but the location with the eggs was buried deeply, and not *toward* the city, weren't they?

At least he knew they hadn't been accessed other than by him. That made it unlikely that the Seal had been damaged.

Elanne started down the cavern, dropping on a shaping of wind until she was no longer visible. Tan used earth shaping to track her and jumped after her.

*Kota. You will watch?*

The hound answered by jumping down into the cavern alongside him. She changed as she did, somehow shrinking.

*I will watch next to you, Maelen.*

*A new trick?* Tan asked, holding out a shaping of fire as he walked. He expected saa to be drawn to it, but the elemental was not, at least not here. That should have warned him that something different took place here.

*This new form allows many different abilities,* Kota said.

Tan had expected a cavern much like he'd found with the draasin eggs. What he found was nothing like it.

Elanne held a wide door open. On the other side, walls of smooth stone rose twenty feet overhead. Thick timbers criss-crossed the ceiling, as much for decoration as for holding up the rock. Shaped power existed here, but not earth, as being below ground would suggest. Instead, the water seeping through the stone, glistening from the flame he held in his outstretched hand, exuded the strength of the elementals, radiating not only udilm, which he expected from water around Par, but another water elemental, one that surprised him much like the mist elemental of water had once surprised him. This was an elemental that clung to the rock, not only mixing with it but merged, a hybrid elemental, and one that he had not seen before. This elemental was older, nothing like the young crossings that he'd discovered when tracking those that the Utu Tonah had made. This, he could hear.

"It is here, Utu Tonah," Elanne said, pointing toward a spot in the middle of the cavern that was lower than any other. The damp around the rock seemed to collect, forming a small pool of water.

Tan touched the edge of the water. His finger tingled much like it had the first time that he'd touched the nymid and known what they were.

Beneath the water, he sensed the damaged Seal.

"You will need to shape the water away to reach this one," she said.

Tan had thought the same at first, but the more that he studied it, the more that his finger tingled from the elemental strength that flowed here, the more he realized that the elemental did what it could to protect the bond. Moving the water would lead to a faster decay. Likely only the presence of the water kept the remnants of the bond intact.

Instead, Tan focused *through* the water, using a combination of each of the elements to sense what had happened to the bond. As he did, it was clear to him that it was the same as the others. Unlike the others, the damage was far more extensive. And, somehow, he could tell that it was intentional. With the earth and wind Seals, he could be convinced that what had happened to them had been the result of time rather than anything else. With this, there was no doubt that someone had intentionally inflicted damage.

"I am not certain that I can repair this one," he said.

*You must try, Maelen. If the Daughter depends on you succeeding, you must try.*

Helping Amia was the only reason that he would even attempt it.

"You claim you were able to repair the others," Elanne commented.

"They were different," Tan said. It was all the explanation that he could come up with. "But I will try." Turning to Kota, he said aloud, "Keep watch over me."

The hound made a point of glaring at Elanne, turning her dark gaze upon the rune master. Elanne took a step away from the hound and built a shaping of wind. In Tan's mind, he heard a steady clucking sound: Kota's laughter.

He focused on the rune. Pulling on water would have to be first. If he used any of the other elementals, he would need to stabilize the rune while beginning the shaping, and he wasn't sure that he could do that without damaging what had been here. He might be able to repair the rune, but what he needed to do was different. To help reclaim the records of Par, he needed to restore the original bond, that which Kota referred to as the Mark of the Mother. With Amia's help, he thought that he could do that, but without her...

With a deep sigh, he sent a request to the water elemental pooling atop the rune. Whatever else, he had to connect to this elemental. His bond, that of nymid, was not found in Par the same way that the other elementals were. With udilm on the shore and the potential for an elemental like masyn near the rocks, he didn't know whether the nymid flowed through the river. And he'd never seen an elemental like this one before.

*Help He Who is Tan,* he said to the elemental.

With the nymid, there was a steady sort of movement to the way he had to speak. Udilm required a command of the sea, as if flowing with the crashing waves upon the shore. When he had reached masyn, that had been with the faintest of connections, a bonding to wind and water. This elemental was somehow both water and earth.

*Maelen.*

The elemental called to him with something like a groan that strained through the cracks in the rock and crept through, leaving the faintest of trails connected to his mind.

*I must repair this Mark.*

Tan tried to mimic the way the elemental had spoken to him but wasn't sure that he had managed with the same depth. With some of the elementals, it mattered less *how* he sent the connection, only that he did manage to send it. Others required a more precise connection, an understanding of the elemental that Tan didn't always possess.

*The Mother's call is damaged.*

*I can see that you maintain it.*

*Not maintain. Prevent the damage from spreading.*

*Why would it matter?*

*Many will suffer if this fails, Maelen. This Seal has held for millennia.*

Tan found it interesting that the elementals would use the same term for it that Elanne had used. If he had any doubt about its importance before, he no longer did.

*How long ago did it fail?*

*The Seal has been damaged for many years, Maelen, but the greatest damage has come in the last few days.*

"Days?" Tan spoke aloud. Elanne looked over with a frown. "The Seal has only been damaged for days."

She shook her head. "That cannot be. The Records here have been lost for many years. Many have tried to restore them, but have failed."

What would have changed? Tan didn't doubt that they had been damaged, but maybe they had only been as damaged as the others, a combination of time and perhaps an intentional destruction that had left them inactive. But this Seal *was* different than the others, though Tan wasn't sure why. Perhaps not in the intent behind the Seal itself, but in what would be required to repair it.

*Can you assist me in the repair?* Tan asked the water elemental. *I will need to know how it should appear.*

There was a long pause, but then he felt the elemental's response.

It came as pressure seeping through tiny cracks in the walls of the cavern, the steady drip of water from somewhere near him, and the glistening of rock that had been dry before. Elanne gasped and called on the wind, but with a request to wyln, Tan silenced it. He needed this water elemental for whatever he would do.

The only problem was that he still didn't know what that would be.

Using a shaping of water, he drew upon the strength of the elemental, connecting to it more deeply. Tan added earth to this, borrowing from the strength of earth mixed into the elemental. With wind, he summoned wyln rather than ashi or Honl, wanting to use elementals that were native to Par. Then he reached for saa and fire.

But failed.

Tan frowned. Saa was a powerful elemental of fire here, and he should be able to reach it, but for some reason, the elemental did not answer him here. Tan listened through the fire bond, wondering if he might learn something there, and was surprised to feel the pulsing strength of the young draasin hatchling. Could the draasin assist in this shaping? He was young—possibly too young—but Tan sensed that he was connected strongly to the fire bond. And there was no denying that he would be powerful.

Tentatively, he asked the draasin to assist, calling to Asgar for help as well.

Then Tan shaped.

This was a powerful shaping that required combining each of the elements together, drawing from the elementals as he did. He borrowed strength, but that wasn't what he needed the most. From the elementals, he needed guidance to understand what this Seal should have been. He hesitated drawing strength from the draasin, using the fire bond instead, but he asked the draasin for input on the form of the bond.

That wasn't enough, and Tan hadn't expected it to be. Spirit was needed—true spirit—and he pushed it into the shaping.

There came a flash of brilliant white light, then the water receded.

Colors swirled along the walls, much as they had when he had repaired the last Seal. Other runes appeared, many still intact, with only a few that were damaged and needing repair.

Elanne gasped again. "You... You did it. You repaired the seal!"

"I'm somewhat surprised myself," he admitted.

"The rest of the bonds can be repaired," she said, making her way around the cavern, looking at the runes along each of the walls. "The Records can be restored. So many years..."

Honl would want to see this, Tan realized. This was exactly the sort of thing that he'd been looking for but hadn't found while in Par. Maybe it would give him answers, help Tan to understand what had happened in Par, perhaps even explain the draasin eggs or why the Utu Tonah had come here in the first place.

"As I said—"

He didn't get the chance to finish. An explosion above them caused the ground to shake, sending a trail of pebbles cascading through the cracks. Tan lifted an arm to shield his head as he called upon Kota, drawing earth strength through her. He hadn't the need. The earth elemental reacted as soon as the explosion hit, shifting her strength through the stone and fortifying it.

*You can support this?*

*I will not need to,* Kota answered. *There is strength here.*

*Good. Then come with me. We can close it from above once we determine what happened.*

Drawing on a shaping of fire and wind, he grabbed Elanne and carried them out of the cavern. She studied his face but said nothing until they were free of the cavern and they landed near the entrance. Kota followed close behind, bounding quickly out and landing next to them.

The ground shook violently for a moment longer and then fell still.

To Tan, the elementals warred with each other.

Bonded, but not those naturally bound. These were forced bonds.

"Someone holds forced bonds," he said. He didn't bother to hide the anger in his voice.

"I thought you destroyed all the forced bonds, Utu Tonah," Elanne said.

"I did." It meant that others had been made.

Who, though?

Elanne had seemed the likely culprit, but that hadn't been what she had intended at all. He thought of others he'd met, those in positions of power, but they were either loyal to Par —something that should not have surprised him, given what he now knew—or were too weak. The only person who had any strength that he didn't know all that well…

Was Marin.

The Mistress of Souls wouldn't have the resources for this, would she? And what motivation would she have?

Answers would have to come later. Elanne turned on him, a shaping of wind building. Spirit shaping forced her to attack, used by Marin against him.

There was no doubting Marin's involvement now.

Tan pulled on spirit, twisting a shaping, borrowing what he remembered from Amia and the First Mother when he had watched them trying to heal Cora, and then from Amia when Tan had watched her with the rest of the Aeta. He layered it on Elanne's mind quickly, forming a shielding at the same time that he removed the effect of the spirit shaping.

Elanne sucked in a sharp breath and blinked. "My Utu Tonah. I don't know—"

"I do. And you weren't in control. I don't think they can do the same again."

"Who?"

"The Mistress of Souls. Marin."

"But she does not even shape!"

"She shapes just fine. She is a shaper of spirit."

"I don't understand, Utu Tonah."

Tan grunted, lifting on a shaping of wind. "Neither do I. But at least I think I finally know who was destroying your bonds, if not why."

He surveyed the city around him, pulling on earth and spirit sensing. With spirit, he detected voids where spirit shapers would be. That was how he had managed to detect the archivists. They had wanted power, but Tan had no idea what Marin wanted. Maybe nothing more than to expel him from Par, but he would have answers.

A trio of shapers formed sensory voids. Using a combination of elements, he forced a barrier over their minds, separating them from spirit as he had once separated the First Mother. Tan had known the way that being forced away from shaping felt and hated doing it, but until he understood what they did, he had no other choice.

Reaching the first, he realized it was one of the men he'd seen with Marin. "Where is she?"

The man glared at Tan, tilting his chin defiantly. He said

nothing. Tan wrapped him in earth and secured him to the ground. The man struggled, but still said nothing.

The second was no different, and Tan held him the same way.

By the time he reached the third, he didn't expect any answers, but this man was younger, and his eyes were wide when Tan landed. Tan circled him slowly. "Tell me where to find her."

He said nothing.

Tan used earth and this time added fire, heating the ground. "Where is Marin?"

"You will have nothing from me!"

"Why? Why harm the people of Par?"

Any composure the man had crumbled. "This is not about Par. This is about more! And like him who came before you, you cannot understand. She leads us to true power, and freedom—"

The man's eyes widened a moment, and then he simply stopped breathing.

Tan searched for Marin, knowing that she had to be nearby for her to have an effect like that, but saw nothing.

He leaned against a building and started to relax when a call from Honl came to him.

*Maelen. You must come. Something has changed.*

Tan looked toward the tower and the strange power that had affected Amia, and wondered what Marin might have to do with that, and what the Seals scattered throughout the city had to do with it.

*I am coming.*

## DARKNESS EMERGES

"Tell me what you sense," Tan said to Kota. They had moved outside the city and were currently gazing at the tower, hoping for a new perspective. While he was in the city, he couldn't get away from Amia and what had happened to her, but out here, the connection to her was faded. Distant, as if it had been severed —but not completely. Tan could still feel her although it was different than it should be.

Kota sat on her haunches next to him, her hackles still raised. She sniffed once and bared her fangs. *I do not know. There is a pull of earth, Maelen.*

*You sense the runes on the tower.*

*They are powerful.*

*What do they do?*

He could tell without Kota answering that the hound didn't know, only how they affected her, drawing on her, as if summoning her toward it.

*I do not know.*

To save Amia, he thought that he had to see if he could figure it out. Only, what if he couldn't? The worry and doubt that had filled him after Amia had collapsed while working with the rune hit him again. He didn't know what he'd do if something happened to her. They had been through so much already, that he didn't—he *couldn't*—think about what would happen if she didn't recover.

But he thought that he knew what he had to do to help her.

*You will watch me?* Tan asked.

*You are of the pack, Maelen. You will be safe.*

Tan rested his hand on Kota's neck and took a deep breath, wishing that there was a way for him to know what he needed to do. Even after defeating the Utu Tonah, he thought that he didn't need to fear Par-shon, but unfortunately, there was still much for him to fear.

He shaped himself to the tower and landed on top.

When he did, he was met by Honl, who appeared on a swirl of wind.

"I know what you intend, Maelen."

"I have to try. This…" he said, motioning to the rune fixed in the stone on the top of the tower, "was designed to damage a shaper."

"You don't know that."

"I know what I've discovered." And the rune on top of the tower was different than those on the sides. How had they not noticed that before now?

"What happens if it affects you the same way that it affected the Daughter?" Honl asked.

"That's a risk that I have to take."

"I'm not sure it's a risk that you can take," Honl said. "The Daughter is important to you, but you are important for so much more."

Tan sighed. "I will be no good to the elementals without the Daughter. She makes me stronger."

Honl swirled around Tan. He felt something to the connection, almost as if the elemental went through him, but rather than becoming more distinct again, he remained insubstantial and floated into Tan.

He gasped. With the connection altered this way, he felt a surge of power and a rush of wind. It tore through him on a torrent, a powerful connection unlike anything that he'd ever experienced before.

With the addition of the energy that Honl added, and connected as he was to fire and the fire bond, Tan pulled on the strength of the elementals. Connected to Kota as she watched from the grounds outside the city, he added the strength of earth to his shaping. And then water came to him, the distant sense of the nymid, so different than his connection to the other elementals but no less potent.

He drew upon them all, filling himself with shaping energy.

Then he shot above the tower.

Tan began, starting with a simple shaping of each of the elements but making it increasingly complex the longer that he shaped. His momentum carried him around the tower, slowly at first, but with increasing speed, pouring the energy that he borrowed from the elementals into the runes on the side of the tower.

The shaping carried him around and around, in increasingly rapid spirals. He focused his energy on shaping *into* the tower itself, pouring the strength that he could summon into the walls of the tower.

As he did, he had awareness of the people within the tower, and those within the city. The connection was more profound than any he'd ever had of Par-shon. In that moment, he thought he understood the needs of the people, even if he didn't have any idea how he would satisfy them. Even more than that, he was able to detect the drawing of the elemental forces of these lands. They raged deep and pure, and *strong*, so much stronger than he would have expected.

This was the purpose of the runes, the reason the earliest shapers had placed them there. They connected the people of Par-shon to the land itself in a way that they would not have been otherwise. And the Utu Tonah had come searching for this connection.

Had he known of it?

Even as Tan summoned his shaping through it, he didn't know. It was possible that the Utu Tonah had *not* known, but that meant that it had somehow been kept from him.

This connection wasn't the reason that he'd come to shape right now. He had come so that he might be able to help Amia. To do that, he needed to turn his shaping and combine the elements in such a way that he might be able to bind them and draw them down into spirit.

He would not use spirit itself. Tan wasn't sure what would happen, but he suspected that doing so would lead him to the same sort of outcome that Amia had suffered.

What he needed was a way to counter that. He could do that with the other elements, he thought, though he wasn't entirely sure that it would work.

Drawing on his elemental connection, he shifted the shaping and sent it into the rune on top of the tower.

There was resistance, much like he'd detected when he had tried repairing the rune at the place of the Mistress of Souls, but like he had there, Tan pushed, overpowering it.

He didn't know its source. It was something potent, and though similar to what he'd done while in the temple, this was different, as well. The opposition was vaster than anything there, and he had to draw on increasing strength.

The connection to Amia was there. Tan saw how it became twisted, and he drew that connection close and wrapped it within a shaping of pure spirit mixed with his combined spirit shaping.

The shaping resisted him, almost as if it were something alive.

*This is the darkness. This is what I have searched for. You must be careful, Maelen! You must be the Light!*

Tan heard Honl's voice in his head, surging into his awareness, somehow penetrating the focus that he managed to hold.

The comment almost forced him to lose control of the shaping.

*What darkness?* Tan asked.

*This... emptiness. That is what you oppose, Maelen. You are the Light.*

*I don't understand.*

*Neither do I, Maelen, not fully, but that is your purpose. You must find a way to get past this. I fear for the Daughter, and for you, if you do not.*

Tan pulled on the connection that he sensed, pulling the forced bond away from Amia. As he did, he felt the connection between them return, if only faintly.

Drawing on more energy from Honl and from Kota and, through her, to the hounds back in Incendin and Chenir, and from the nymid, and even directly through the fire bond, he pulled power. Nothing like he had used when defeating the Utu Tonah, but the strength required to pull on this bond was still enormous.

It shifted, settling on him.

Tan breathed out a relieved sigh.

Amia surged through his awareness again, the connection returned, full and intact.

*Tan!*

Her voice cried out in his mind, devastating and full of terror.

*You cannot fight this. Return the bond to me—*

She didn't get the chance to finish. Pain shot through Tan's mind, unlike anything he had ever experienced. It was sharp and brutal, reminding him of what it had been like when the Utu Tonah had tried to separate him from his bonds, but this was different, as well. There was intent to this, a desire to overwhelm him.

*Who is this?*

A voice boomed in his mind, a thunderous devastation.

Tan clapped his hands to his ears and squeezed, but couldn't push the pain from the voice. In that way, it reminded him of the draasin the first time Asboel had latched onto his mind. This was even more powerful and full of an awful intent.

*I am Tan. What kind of elemental are you?*

*Tan?* The voice repeated his name, somehow filling it with contempt. *How is it that a Tan separated my connection?*

*What connection?*

But Tan knew. This voice had connected to Amia, seeking her bond to spirit, but why?

*You will not have the Daughter.*

The comment only angered the voice. *There is nothing you can do now that I am free.*

Pain surged through his mind again, and he dropped. Had it not been for Honl watching over him, he would have fallen and might have landed away from the tower, but Honl swept him up. A shadow circled overhead, and Tan worried that this elemental had come to attack him directly, but rather than an attack, Asgar crashed to a landing on top of the tower.

His bright eyes stared at Tan, piercing through the pain.

*You must fight this, Maelen. Sashari tells me that you must, or you will be lost. All will be lost.*

*I. Am. Trying.*

Each word pained him.

Through it all, the sense of this other elemental—this other being—pressed upon his mind.

Tan realized then what it wanted. It wanted *his* connection to spirit.

If he allowed that to happen, he might fall, the same as Amia had.

He *had* to fight.

Amia joined with him, her connection granting him strength. Kota offered even more of herself. The warm presence of Honl filled his mind, and Tan felt the sense of separation the wind elemental created, a buffer within his mind. Fire, and Asgar, aided as well.

Tan screamed.

The pain was lessened, and with it, he felt a clarity of thought. He could push back, but doing so would require intense effort, and he still didn't know that it would work. The other elemental had forced itself into his mind—his, now that he'd assumed the connection from Amia—and attempted to press deeper into his mind to steal spirit.

Tan could not allow it.

Using a combination of each of the elements, drawing through the elementals, he added this combined spirit shaping to his ability to pull on spirit. It flooded from him.

This was a fight for control of his mind. Tan felt certain of that. And he could not afford to lose.

Bright white light spilled from him. The shaping was a familiar one and came every time he merged each of the elements in this way. He pulled on the warmth of the shaping, drawing strength from it, and turned it internally.

The pain within him began to lessen.

The other elemental redoubled his efforts, fighting against Tan, clinging to his mind. Tan could feel the way he attempted to hold on and slowly began to unravel the connection, pulling the forced bond from him.

And then it was gone.

Tan sealed it off, separating himself from the elemental.

He sagged against the top of the tower, exhausted and unable to stand. Honl was there, drawn out from within him. Asgar watched him, eyeing him with a worried expression that reminded him so much of Asboel. With a bound more powerful than Tan thought her capable of managing, Kota leaped to the top of the tower, using earth to assist her. All ringed him, watching him carefully. Even the sense of the nymid was there, but reserved, as if concerned that he might not be the same.

Tan stood on shaky legs and looked around at the elementals.

*Maelen?*

Tan couldn't tell who spoke to him. Probably Kota from the way she watched him, her eyes shining brightly and her flank pushing against him. Warmth flooded from her, but Tan noted tension within her muscles as she crouched next to him.

He rested a hand on her neck and ran it through her fur. "I think I'm alright," he said. He needed to reach Amia and see if she had recovered, but he didn't think that he could shape anything right now.

"I will bring her to you," Honl said softly.

"Could you bring me to her?" Tan asked.

The wind elemental looked at the others and shook his head. "Not yet, Maelen."

Tan frowned but didn't argue.

Honl disappeared, floating from the top of the tower. Tan laid his head back and simply stared at the sky. Answers would come, but right now, he wanted only to rest.

*What was that?* he sent to Kota.

*That was an ancient power, Maelen.*

*An elemental? I've never known an elemental to try to force a bond like that.* Tan was certain that was what it had attempted, but that didn't fit with what he knew of the elementals. There was aggression to the way it had tried to force itself upon him, the way it *wanted* his connection to spirit. Had that been the same for Amia?

"That was no elemental."

Tan looked up to see Honl standing next to him. He'd brought Amia and lowered her to the ground next to him. Color had returned to her cheeks, and some of the luster had returned to her hair.

She rolled her head toward him and smiled. "Tan."

He touched her face and pulled her toward him. After the terror that he'd known, the fear that he might not be able to save her, seeing her awake and able to speak to him again left him relieved.

Still frightened. He had never known an elemental that had been as aggressive. Even kaas, while dangerous, had been a different kind of danger. This…

"Why do you say that this wasn't an elemental?" he asked

Honl. "I felt the way it tried to connect to me, and the way it spoke to me."

Amia shivered. Through their bond—now restored, and if anything, stronger—he knew that she had felt the same. "It will return," she said. "Whatever it is, it *wants* to return. I think… I think that is why the Utu Tonah came to Par."

Tan sat up and looked at Honl. Of all of them, the wind elemental was the most likely to know what had happened. He had spent all of his free time studying, searching for answers. And had given Tan a warning.

This couldn't be what he had warned him about, could it?

But he thought that it could. Hadn't he felt the dark malevolence of the creature that attempted to settle inside him? Hadn't he *known* how the elemental wanted his connection to spirit?

"Not an elemental," Honl said again. The others around him hadn't moved, as if keeping watch… or holding him where he was, in case something had happened to him. "I did not understand before."

"And you do now?"

"I understand the purpose of this tower and the one in your homeland. They serve the same purpose."

"What is that?" Tan asked.

"A seal. A way to suppress the darkness."

Tan shivered at the thought, and Amia touched his arm, trying to reassure him. If what Honl said was true, there was nothing that he could say that would reassure him. "You're saying the places of convergence are a way to seal out whatever this creature is?"

Honl shook his head. "Not a creature."

"I don't understand."

"This is not a creature, not like you or these," he said, sweeping his hand toward the elementals guarding him. Tan suddenly knew that they weren't sure what he would do, of whether what he had done had worked to push back the darkness. "That is the darkness," Honl said.

"And you still think that I am the light?" Tan asked.

Honl's face took on a troubled expression. Since he'd bonded to spirit, since he had changed, however it was that he had, Honl had never seemed uncertain. That he would now… that worried Tan.

"You are a part of the light," Honl said. "Perhaps that is all that is needed."

"For what?"

Honl sighed, and wind fluttered with him. "You must repair what has been damaged. You must replace the seals of darkness. If we fail, it will come."

Tan shivered, and this time, when Amia squeezed his arm, there was nothing reassuring about it.

# EPILOGUE

T an stood among the draasin eggs, feeling the warmth radiating from them. The small draasin— well, not as small as he once had been—crawled around the eggs, nuzzling at some of them, stopping to sniff every so often.

A single lantern cast light around the cavern and Tan knelt in front of the fourth seal. Now that he knew to expect to find it, he had not been surprised to discover it at the center of the clutch of eggs. The seal, unlike the other three, was intact. Tan still didn't know what they were for, and Honl had again disappeared, leaving him without answers.

He shaped a trickle of spirit into the Seal and light exploded through the cavern, tracing through the bonds on the walls. The draasin paused and swiveled his head around, sniffing the air for a moment and then huffing with a deep breath of steam.

The Records. At least now Tan knew where to find them,

if not what they were for. Elanne and the other Bond Wardens secured the other three locations. Tan had not revealed this one to her, and would not until he had decided what he would do with the draasin eggs. Eventually, he had to share it with her. The Records of Par were not his secret to keep.

"They're so extensive," Amia said. She walked slowly and held her hand out in front of her, the way that she had since he'd managed to heal her from the spirit attack. He knew now that was what that had been: not an attempted bond, but an attack. "So many runes here. They share a story, but it's more than I can follow."

"These are the Records of Par. Elanne wasn't able to tell me what they contained. I'm not sure that she even knew."

Amia paused and turned toward the draasin eggs. "What do you intend to do with these?"

Tan watched the draasin as he crawled around the eggs and stopped in front of one. A streamer of flame erupted from his mouth and struck the eggs. Flames licked around the egg, as if caressing it, drawn into it by the strength of the fire bond.

It wasn't surprising that the draasin chose that egg. Tan hadn't known what to expect by bringing the draasin down here, but Tan had known that he needed a playmate, another to challenge him. Only, Tan didn't know which of the draasin that would be.

"The draasin need to return," he answered, making his way to the egg and setting his hand on it. Warmth radiated from the draasin egg, pulsing against him with the faint stirring of the baby within. He started feeding fire into this egg, much as he had done with the other. Like before, it seemed to pull on the fire with increasing appetite. "This was what the Utu Tonah sought. I don't know if Marin knew, or what she intended, but it had to do with the Seal. And the draasin are tied to the Seal."

If Honl was right, then Marin served a different master, one that they didn't yet understand. But he would need to understand. Now that they had been attacked—using Amia to get to him—Tan had to know and anticipate what was coming. Somehow, Par was the key.

Amia slipped her hand into his. "I worry what will happen when they fully return."

Tan continued to fill the egg with fire, letting it pour out of him. When it had been only Asboel and his family, there had been no real expectation that other draasin would return. Other than Asgar and the other hatchling, there were no others. Tan hadn't asked, but he didn't expect them to find a mate, which essentially made them the final draasin.

Now... Now there would be others. If Tan managed to find a way to hatch all of these, another two dozen draasin would rejoin the world. And then others could follow.

Finally, the draasin could fully return.

"They are elementals," he said. "We need them to return."

He would have to find someone to care for them. Tan couldn't do that himself, not entirely. With his connection to fire and the fire bond, he would be the one needed to help the eggs hatch and could start the process of feeding them, but helping them eat and providing the day-to-day care, that would need to come from someone else. Otherwise, he would spend all of his free time with them.

Thankfully, he had someone he knew fire had faith in. Molly had shown saa that she would be strong, and she respected fire. She could help.

"And what of the other?" Amia asked. "What of *him*?"

Tan had no answer to that question. Not yet, and not without Honl to help. Whatever power that he'd fought as he'd tried to save her had been more powerful than anything that he'd ever faced before. And, if what he suspected was true, it was the reason for the Seals set around the city. The tower seemed to play some role, as well.

"The ancients seemed to know about that," Tan said. Honl had called it a darkness and suggested that Tan might be the light, but he didn't know what that meant or how it was significant. He didn't doubt that it was. "We need to study and understand. I'm beginning to think that Honl is right about that."

"Where has he gone?"

Tan shook his head. He could sense the elemental, but once again, it was faint. Wherever Honl had gone was far enough away as to be undetectable.

Were it not for the draasin eggs, and the fact that Tan felt almost compelled to help them hatch, he thought that he would have gone after Honl, to find out what drew the elemental away. With his ability to shape, the world was smaller for him than it was for most. He was able to travel on a shaping of wind and reach anywhere else in the world. Not only the mainland, but he could travel beyond, using the strength of the elementals to help guide him.

Except, he didn't think that he could risk Amia on such a shaping. Taking her that far would tax even his strength, and though he might be able to draw on the elementals, he wouldn't know exactly where he was going, which meant that he couldn't use spirit in the shaping.

"Far away," he said.

He returned his focus to the draasin egg, pushing more and more fire shaping into it, drawing from the fire elementals and the fire bond as he did. The egg began to glow, and then the shell softened. A sharp claw pressed against the egg, pushing through.

Tan released the shaping of fire as the draasin hatched and began to feed on the fire bond, drawing the strength that it needed in those first moments. He sighed as he watched another draasin enter the world. Hatching the others would take time, but he would take the time needed to return the draasin to the world. As he did, he would study, and learn, and try to understand what Marin had been doing and what she had attempted to free.

Amia squeezed his hand and rested her other hand on her stomach. She didn't need to speak for him to know and feel the worry coursing through her. After everything they'd been through, both had hoped for quiet, and a chance for peace, but now... now it seemed that everything they had been through was only the beginning of something more, and possibly worse.

He forced a smile, knowing she could see through him.

But just as she could read him, he read her and realized that her worry was not for him, or even for her, but for another.

Tan blinked and quickly drew on a shaping of earth and spirit. Amia let it wash over her without moving. With the shaping, he sensed a quiet stirring of life within her belly, something that he wouldn't have noticed had he not shaped his love, something that he never did. With the bond between them, there was usually no need.

A worried smile crept across her mouth, and she nodded. "Yes, Tan. You will soon be a father to more than the draasin."

Tan pulled her to him in a tight embrace, and they stood in the draasin cavern, with the two hatchlings and fire burning all around him, holding each other. At least in that moment, they found peace.

---

Broken of Fire, book 9 of the Cloud Warrior Saga:

A new threat to the elementals emerges that puts everyone Tan cares about in danger.

After the most recent battle, the Mistress of Souls is missing and Tan must find her before another attack. With Amia's pregnancy changing the connection between them, Tan fears involving her and must rely on new friends, including a strangely intelligent draasin hatchling for help. Worse, an old enemy has returned, one surprisingly welcomed by Theondar.

A darkness nearly destroys his draasin friend and reveals the true threat to the elementals. To save them, he needs to understand the secret of this darkness, one that leads to a surprising realization about the defeated Utu Tonah. Tan risks everything to stop it, but even after everything he's been through, he still might not be enough.

---

Book 1 in a brand new series set in the world of the Cloud Warrior Saga, The Endless War: Journey of Fire and Night

A warrior who cannot die. A water seeker who wants only to save her people.

Jasn, a warrior known as the Wrecker of Rens, seeks vengeance for the loss of his beloved to the deadly draasin during the Endless War, wanting nothing more than to sacrifice himself in the process. When an old friend offers a dangerous chance for him to finally succeed, the key to understanding what he finds requires him to abandon all that he believes.

Ciara, a water seeker of Rens living on the edge of the arid waste, longs for the strength to help her people. When the great storms don't come to save her people, she will risk everything for her village on a deadly plan that could finally bring them to safety.

As the Endless War continues, both have a part to play in finally stopping it, but Jasn must discover forgiveness and Ciara must find her inner strength if they are to succeed.

I'm excited to share with you book 1 of a new series, The Lost Prophecy: The Threat of Madness, available for preorder now!

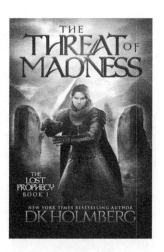

The arrival of the mysterious Magi, along with their near invincible guardians, signals a change. For Jakob, apprentice historian and son of a priest longing for adventure, it begins an opportunity.

When his home is attacked, Jakob ventures out with the his master, traveling alongside the Magi, beginning a journey that will take him far from home and everything he has ever known. As he travels, he gains surprising skill with the sword but begins to develop strange abilities, along with a growing fear that the madness which has claimed so many has come for him.

With a strange darkness rising in the north, and powers long thought lost beginning to return, the key to survival is discovering the answer to a lost prophecy. Only a few remain with the ability to find it, and they begin to suspect that Jakob has a pivotal role to play.

---

Want to read more in the Cloud Warrior Saga? Check out Prelude to Fire, Lacertin's story set prior to events in Chased by Fire.

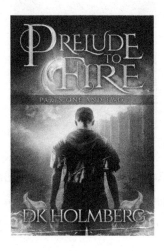

A warrior to a dying king discovers a destiny he never imagined.

**Part 1 - First Warrior**

Lacertin has served his king faithfully for decades, but has failed on his final mission for him. When he returns to the kingdoms, he discovers a dark secret to the king's illness, and the only person who can truly help him hides a secret of her own. Lacertin must decide how much he will sacrifice for the people he cares most about.

**Part 2 - Servant**

Trapped in Incendin and tormented while searching for answers, Lacertin is rescued by a mysterious priest of Issa. Released from his torture, the priest reveals secrets of Incendin that challenge everything Lacertin thought he knew, and gives him a chance to be something more than the warrior he had been… if only he's willing to believe in his calling to serve fire.

# ABOUT THE AUTHOR

DK Holmberg currently lives in rural Minnesota where the winter cold and the summer mosquitoes keep him inside and writing. He has two active children who inspire him to keep telling new stories.

Word-of-mouth is crucial for any author to succeed and how books are discovered. If you enjoyed the book, please consider leaving a review at Amazon, even if it's only a line or two; it would make all the difference and would be very much appreciated.

Subscribe to my newsletter to be the first to hear about give-aways and new releases.

*For more information:*
www.dkholmberg.com

ALSO BY D.K. HOLMBERG

*The Cloud Warrior Saga*

Chased by Fire

Bound by Fire

Changed by Fire

Fortress of Fire

Forged in Fire

Serpent of Fire

Servant of Fire

Born of Fire

Broken of Fire

Light of Fire

Cycle of Fire

*Others in the Cloud Warrior Series*

Prelude to Fire

Chasing the Wind

Drowned by Water

Deceived by Water

Salvaged by Water

Shadow Cross

*The Dark Ability*

The Dark Ability

The Heartstone Blade

The Tower of Venass

Blood of the Watcher

The Shadowsteel Forge

The Guild Secret

Rise of the Elder

*The Sighted Assassin*

The Painted Girl (novella)

The Binders Game

The Forgotten

Assassin's End

*The Lost Garden*

Keeper of the Forest

The Desolate Bond

Keeper of Light

*The Painter Mage*

Shifted Agony

Arcane Mark

Painter For Hire

Stolen Compass

Stone Dragon

Made in the USA
Monee, IL
02 September 2022

13032635R00184